Mummy's Boy

Mummy's Boy

J A Andrews

hera

First published in Great Britain in 2020 by Hera

Hera Books
28b Cricketfield Road
London, E5 8NS
United Kingdom

A CIP catalogue record for this book is available from the British Library.

Print ISBN 978 1 80032 162 5
Ebook ISBN 978 1 912973 42 2

Printed and bound in Great Britain by Clays Ltd, Elcograf S.p.A.

Dedicated to my mother, Susan Barry, and to my sister, Sarah Parker. Two great mothers in their own right.

Prologue

Patricia Mullner – Then

Wednesday, 11 September 1998

I held my beautiful baby in my hands as I shook with worry and fear. This lovely little boy had been born without any complications, and now I could take him home. Every inch of his small body was perfectly formed; this fresh new life needing to be nurtured, to be shaped by our love.

Labour had been a traumatic ten hours of intense stress. The pain, both emotionally and physically, for such a length of time had my heartbeat pounding like crazy. Every minute that passed felt like time was slowing down. The nerves and the anxiety were all too much of a strain for me. I was so worried about the first time I would meet my baby, but, in the end, it was all so much easier than I'd thought. The minute I held his head against my racing heartbeat, it was worth it. I'd go through it all again.

It was a shame that my handsome fiancé wasn't able to be here for the birth, but I had carefully planned the events of today. Despite all the planning, nothing could have prepared me for the rush of emotion when I saw my baby's face for the first time. I cried tears of joy, not only from seeing him, but because the stress, tension and intensity of the last ten hours of labour was over.

I was in a hurry to get home; I needed to rest as the strain of the last nine months had now come to a gorgeous end. I was still exhausted, but I needed to be in my own home. I needed my own surroundings; while my healthy baby boy could rest and feel safe at home with me – his mother.

My little boy was here; I couldn't believe it had finally happened.

I left the hospital with him tucked in with a blanket, carefully strapped into a car seat that I clutched with both of my hands. At just six pounds, two ounces, he was small and vulnerable. I needed to get him back safely in the warm so I could look after him: he was due a feed soon. I had my fears, but I knew that it was natural. He was barely two days old. I was thankful that he was sleeping while I rushed around to find a taxi. I had to get out of that hospital because I wanted to be in my own home and shut the world away.

I was shaking with excitement that my boy had finally arrived. Nine whole months of constant planning, adapting and preparing for this joyous moment had taken over our lives. This small bundle was here in the world. My little boy, who had turned us into a real family, was looking at me. All I had ever dreamed of was a family of my own. I promised him that I would love him and care for him my whole life.

My baby, my beautiful son.

I had never experienced such a rush of love as the moment when I first saw his little face looking up at mine. I felt complete. He was perfect in every way, but I wanted to get out of that hospital to be back home. I wanted to take care of him on my own without everyone looking at me or giving me their advice.

I knew what my little boy needed.

Andrew was mine, and no one would ever separate us.

One

Patricia Mullner – Now

Sunday, 9 September 2018

Every time I close my eyes, I can see his face.

I remember the look in his eyes – he was staring back at me as he closed the door behind him. Andrew had looked lost, or maybe it was my mind playing tricks on me? Every time I relive those last few seconds; I conjure up different emotions to assure myself that he did not appear depressed. His short mousey hair, the whisper of stubble on his chin that was barely a beard yet needed a shave; all five feet seven inches of him etched in my mind. Now gone for what feels like an eternity. One cruel moment that changed our lives forever.

I can picture every fine detail of his smile that distracted from the look he was giving me with his eyes; maybe I'm over-analysing him. I wish I could stop torturing myself with the mental images. At times I visualise him leaving the house with a happy smile, although other times I am sure he was giving me an evil look with a glaring stare. The seventeen years that he was part of our lives have been ruined due to that one day. I'm not even sure I would recognise him now if he passed me in the street, but I hope and pray that he remembers above all else that we love him. Thomas and I are his parents, and I would never forgive myself if he had left home because of me.

The last good memory I have of my son on his birthday was four years ago, when he turned sixteen. I watched him unwrap the gaming console he so desperately wanted. I never knew how to operate modern technology like he did because in my younger years we occupied ourselves by sneaking outside to get drunk on cider or hang around bus stops trying to flirt with the local boys.

I was always envious of the girls at school because I spent most of my time alone in my bedroom. I used to practise my makeup and dream about the day I would be happy with a boy of my own. Communicating back then could only be face to face even to initiate getting someone's phone number because social media didn't exist. Mobile phones didn't even have cameras attached, but we made our own fun in ways that kids would now deem old-fashioned. I wish I had been more outgoing.

I remember the hug Andrew gave me in appreciation for his console. I will never forget how happy he was. He wasn't one for showing much affection towards me, but I told myself that boys are like that; however, that hug was warm and loving. I was proud that I had made my son happy on his special day. I can close my eyes and relive the memory; the smile on his face lit the room while that look in his eyes cemented our bond. Although now I wonder whether that very console connected him online to someone who could have manipulated him.

I don't trust the internet.

Aside from checking my emails or looking up my medical symptoms on the internet, I have no other use for an online presence; social media confuses me. It amazes me now that so many people rely on their mobile phones. I have one, but I barely use it for anything other than calling Thomas when I need him. He's been my rock throughout this ordeal.

Andrew did show me how his gaming console worked, even though there are days I regret shouting at him for skiving off college to play online all day. We argued a lot, but he was a teenager. All teenage sons argue with their mothers, don't they? It was a typical adolescent insolence. My role as his mother is to provide for him, keep him safe and guide him in the right direction in life – even if he did disagree with me at times. I know he never liked to be disciplined, but if there is anything that I learnt from my mother it was to keep trying harder and harder to be good at what I wanted to be.

'You'll regret playing on that thing all day if you fail your coursework, Andrew,' I remember saying while he tried to have a conversation with me about the competit-iveness in online gaming.

'It's all about the kill streak, Mum, because it's a double-points day. Give me a break will you. College isn't all that important you know. I will still have to find a job somehow when it's all over.'

'Just remember those words when you end up working in charity shops like your mother,' I said. 'I only want what's best for you. I know how hard it is to study because I used to want to be a midwife. Putting in all that effort revising for exams and having no life while my friends were out partying. Well, what friends I had back then. Look at your father: he has to work all the hours under the sun in his taxi to pay our bills.'

I miss him; I love him. I hope he is safe. I would give anything to have him back here looking entranced by the war game he seemed addicted to playing with the volume on full blast. It's still in his bedroom, lying on the floor in the position he left it. Everything has been left untouched except for his bed, which is freshly made for when he comes home. I still believe that he will walk in one day as if he had never left. When he does, I will make him his favourite dinner – a nice chicken with roast potatoes. My Andrew loves his roast potatoes.

'Your potatoes are the best, Mum,' he used to tell me. 'Nothing is as good as your roast dinner. Dad tries his best, but I do prefer yours.'

I miss his lousy attitude too: the way he never did what the hell he was told. I understand he was almost an adult, a grown man in his own right, but he was our only child. As his mother, all I want is the best for him. Nothing could have ever prepared me for the feeling of loss and helplessness that day he walked out of the door and never came home. You hear about it happening up and down the country, but that's other people's children, not mine. The realisation that my son is missing can be too much to handle. My brain is continually working overtime, wondering what we've missed and looking for the links.

Sitting here, at the same kitchen table, as I face the back door I am reliving that day. I look at the door with a new birthday card in my hand just in case he should wander back home. The sun is glistening through the window with the light catching the floor to illuminate a space of warmth. It reminds me of our old dog, who used to sit in

8

those sunspots to sleep. I wish I could get some sleep, just one decent night.

You would think that on his birthday he might remember his family – today of all days make some form of contact with his father and me?

If he does not come home today, I will place the card in his room with all the others I have bought him over the last three years. Birthdays, Christmases, Easter; if I do not buy a card, I feel it is as though I am letting go of him. I don't want to let go of his memories. I want him to see that I still care even if he's not around. That I have included him as part of this family. There's nothing more I want than for him to walk through the door and say how sorry he is. Being left without any explanation is the most torturous feeling with my anxiety issues. I can't seem to forgive myself even though the anger towards him for what he has done lingers.

He is twenty years old now, I tell myself. He may even have children of his own. I could be a grandmother. I'll never forget holding him in my arms the day we walked out of the hospital together. That was the day that my life changed forever. I was a mother.

At times I daydream about looking after the grand-children or all of us being one big happy family at Christmas time. Missing potentially significant moments in his life, which could include him getting married, having children, is disturbing me. The not knowing anything is what hurts the most: the guilt I live with cuts deep.

There wasn't even a note. You hear that some children leave home, but at least they voice their reasons on a piece of paper on the kitchen table – or in their bedroom. I scoured Andrew's room top to bottom and found nothing. After the first few days I had turned the whole house upside-down in case I had missed something, and still not a sign, nor reasonable explanation for his sudden disappearance. I convinced myself that he might have been murdered; however, now I believe he is out there somewhere, living his own life. I have to remain hopeful because no body has ever been found.

His disappearance has put a strain on my marriage to Thomas. Some nights we sit watching television without saying a word to each other all night. I know he still loves me, yet I sense he blames me in some way. Thomas doesn't talk about Andrew anymore, which upsets me. The silence can be unnerving. I can't just forget about him, nor will I ever give up hope.

Thomas says that we need to move on with our lives. If Andrew can walk out and forget about his parents, then we too should be selfish. I wouldn't be able to forgive myself if he left because of something we had done or said. Thomas remains adamant that I should start letting go of Andrew. To live my own life now without the fixation on his whereabouts.

But I'm his mother!

The tears rolling down my cheeks taste salty as I wipe them away from the corner of my mouth. There are so many unanswered questions about why Andrew turned his back on me or why he never made contact. His disappearance shocked the whole village, who could not help enough. After the first few days, I rallied some support for putting up posters in shop windows, contacting his friends, walking through fields to see if he was hurt, injured, or worse – dead in a ditch somewhere.

Mary, from across the street, was by my side for most of the first few weeks after he vanished. I used to talk to her constantly about things Andrew did or said leading up to his disappearance in case there were any clues. It was good to hear someone else's opinion in case there was something I had missed, even if it was something small. Andrew never had any friends that he visited. He mostly enjoyed playing online games in his bedroom; it didn't make sense to any of us.

Did someone on the internet persuade him to leave home?

After the first few days, the media presence with the local press was continually hounding us for updates. While I appreciated their support, because Andrew was not a young child with any obvious signs of being kidnapped, it died off very quickly. To them he became just another teenage boy who had left home.

It's the little things that friends do to support you that make all the difference. From hanging out the washing, or cooking a hot meal, to just being there to listen as I cried into my cup of tea day after day. After the first few weeks, I started to get used to him not being around, telling myself he was just at college all day. I do wonder if he still thinks about us.

Does he even care anymore?

The phone did not stop ringing with potential sightings of Andrew at various places in Plymouth city centre in the first few days after his disappearance. Despite being hopeful that each phone call could be the answer to our prayers, none of them turned out to be him. It is as though he just ceased to be in existence.

There's no way my Andrew would kill himself. He is not the type, not that I suppose you can pinpoint a kind of suicidal person, but I know my son. If Andrew had killed himself, he would have left me a note. He wouldn't have had to leave home to do that, and there would have been a body found by now.

'He's out there somewhere,' they all tell me. 'He'll come back home to his mother when he's good and ready.'

I should start to move on with my life, if I listen to the advice given by my colleagues in the charity shop. Even the few women who I converse with at charity fundraising events I can tell are sick of me chattering on and on about my son, but it's okay for them who haven't suffered the anxiety of such a loss.

Nothing can distract my attention away from the fact that my son is missing, but what makes it even worse is that my memory of that day is blurred. Being overcome with grief could be clouding my recollection of events. I remember his birthday; I remember that we argued. The two events replay in my mind over and over like a video before halting to a stop as if the movie has come to an end. I cannot seem to rewind or fast forward. Some days I stare at the wall knowing that it was my fault. I blame myself constantly because perhaps he needed me when I was too interested in my own life. As a mother, did I fail him?

The thought of my Andrew being out there has given me hideous nightmares. If he has mental health issues, then is he making wise decisions for himself? It has crossed my mind that he may be homeless with limited access to money. I hate to think of my son sitting on street corners begging the public for money, or worse, to fund a drug habit. What if he has hit rock bottom with no one to turn to? Not knowing anything about his life will drive me insane. We all believe he is out there somewhere. I'll find him; I know I can if I build up the mental energy to get out there again and gather up some support in locating my son.

'I love you, Andrew,' I whisper to myself at night. 'I pray for your safe return home.'

Two

Patricia Mullner – Now

Sunday, 9 September 2018

The oven alarm sounds a repetitive streak of beeping noises that make me jump out of my skin. One of the downsides to having anxiety problems is that the most random of noises or situations can trigger an instantaneous fear that sweeps through you. I have to sit down and catch my breath again. I have stopped shaking and am better composed thanks to a few painkillers to shift the headaches.

I am not thinking straight today, with it being Andrew's birthday. My head is an utter mess, filled with so many unanswered questions. I keep thinking about the last thing he said to me as well as his behaviour leading up to his disappearance. The more I try to concentrate, the more the line is blurred between what I actually remember and what my mind is trying to convince me. The torment is becoming a burden on my sanity.

I don't remember him doing anything out of character.

I hope this cake I am baking to remember Andrew turns out to be as delicious as the recipe book pictures imply, not that I have followed it all in the exact order.

Sometimes I like to mix up the recipes by adding a few of my own ingredients to try and improve it, but this time I thought I'd make it a cake to remember.

I convince myself that Andrew will just walk through the door. I fantasise about the moment.

'I'm sorry, Mum. Sorry, Dad – I had to go and sort my life out, but now I'm back,' I say out loud, while I think about the possibilities. 'We'll talk about it later; it wasn't your fault, Mum.'

The oven is a perfect 180 degrees; the butter, caster sugar, eggs and lemon zest well blended to form the mixture, but I'll see if it's ready. I've run out of vanilla essence. It might not make all that difference to the taste; I haven't got sprinkles either for the top. I am disappointed with myself for not getting everything I needed to make this cake, but my mind is in overdrive today.

'Fuck it,' I whisper. 'Fuck the lot of it, and Thomas is no fucking use to me lately.'

Thomas will eat anything that is put in front of him, so I am not bothered if it doesn't look quite as it should. I suggested that we should have a celebration dinner since our boy will be twenty years old today. With the cake almost ready I can start to think about cracking on with the roast and peeling the potatoes. I peer into the oven and can see it has risen to a perfect peak.

'I hope you're hungry, Thomas?'

Oh, no damn reply again. Playing deaf to suit.

'I said, I hope you're hungry?'

I can hear him agree from the living room, but I might have another sneaky drink to help my nerves. Vodka with a drop of this lemon zest tastes better than I imagined. It's like flat lemonade but gives it an excellent kick at the back of my throat.

Andrew loved my homemade cakes. Especially the ones with chocolate or lemon frosting that he used to help me bake to raise money for the old folk at the nursing home down the road. He has grown up with my homemade cooking his whole life, which is why he turned out to be a chubby little thing as a child. I know he was being bullied at school for his weight when he was younger, although he would never admit to it. I had a few words with the mothers at the gates in my time too, the bitches. I know kids can be cruel at times, but I blame the parents.

Do people blame me for Andrew's disappearance?

I've burnt the cake, I realise as I open the oven door. I have been daydreaming too and forgotten that every minute in the oven counts on this damn cake. The singed scent of overdone cake mixture lingers in the air. I thought I'd be third time lucky this year. No matter how hard I try, nothing will ever go well for me on this day. Andrew should be here; we should be sitting down together to eat dinner as a family. The misery at the loss of my family is starting to take its toll on me again.

Where is he? Where is my boy?

I need a drink to calm myself; otherwise, I'll end up losing the plot and have a binge session on all the bottles stashed in the cupboards. Thomas hates it when I drink because he knows my mood can change at any given moment. The odd vodka and lemonade now and again aren't too bad for me, but I did go through a stage of drinking heavily a few years back. I know I am going to have to get myself a drink in a minute. I want today to be over.

Every day I blame myself for making him walk out on his family. You would think that as a grown man now, potentially with a family of his own, he would know how hard it is to have your child just vanish.

This cake looks ruined.

Maybe the oven has given up on me too, just like my son and my husband. He's been no real support to me during the last three years, acting as if Andrew no longer exists. I am working myself up to having another drink; I can feel it. A vodka would be lovely right now with some diet cola. I seem to have gone through all the new bottles I bought recently. If I ask Thomas for some more, he will start to suspect I am back on the bottle hard. I can do this; I can cut down. I will start to cut back next week – possibly next month. I've lost my son, and no one seems to give a shit, maybe it's because there hasn't been any closure.

'Did you hear that, Thomas? You've been no real support to me since Andrew left. I can't just fucking forget him. Why don't you even acknowledge that he was part of our family? Andrew is our son.'

Again, Thomas fails to respond because he is sitting in the living room with his eyes fixed on the weekend football showing on the television. I reluctantly admit there are moments when he talks to me. I zone out, lost in my own thoughts. He could be dealing with Andrew's disappearance in his own way, yet the silence at times can be unnerving.

Thomas and I are not as close as we used to be, nor do we regularly make love anymore; it's barely a twenty-minute session every few months. With all the alcohol and the constant draining thoughts in my mind, I'm not feeling very sexual most days. I try my best for Thomas if the truth be told. When he's on top of me, I look up at the ceiling, hoping for an early finish.

How can I think of anything other than the whereabouts of my boy? I am going to need another drink after this one.

'You've never been any support to me, Thomas. I love you. I'd do anything for you and what makes it all worse is that you sit in this house every day watching me suffer with this pain I feel.'

'There's nothing I can do or say that will make him walk through that door, Trish. Why can't you just accept that he doesn't want us? I miss him too, but I can't stop living my own life because of it, and nor should you.'

The cake is an utter mess. I've thrown it on the kitchen side in disgust. And I'm annoyed at Thomas's response. He always has an answer for everything; which annoys me because he means well but upsets me at the same time. I am struggling to deal with my own emotions right now. Outside the house, I plaster on the face that everyone wants to see. I volunteer in the charity shop, smiling that fake smile the customers want to be greeted with as they walk through the door. Inside, a little part of me dies each day as my mind drifts into the depths of despair. *Is he still in Plymouth? Is he alive? Why can't I remember much about that day?*

As time goes on, my memories of Andrew are slowly becoming distorted. There are times I think about past birthdays and family events but fail to recollect the specific day. When he fell off his bike, *was it his tenth or twelfth birthday?* When he jumped up and down at the circus, *was Andrew eight or six?*

The last three years of hell have tortured me, and I just want this day to be over with. I constantly think back to what Andrew was doing that day, what he said the night before, but it is all a blur. I can only focus on the loss.

I'll never forget when he had his first proper girlfriend. He was fifteen, and she was a horrible selfish bitch. Acting as if she knew my son better than I did. Katrina, she was called. She preferred Trina for short, although at times I deliberately called her Kat. She hated me, but I pretended to like her for my son because I knew they wouldn't last. I was proved right when they split up after only a few months of being together. Kat was no good for him, as both me and Thomas had decided. However, he might have just been agreeing with me since I often caught them laughing in the hallway.

Were they laughing about me?

The scent of lemon is starting to come through now that the cake is cooling down. It doesn't actually look that bad once I chip away at the burnt sides. If I cover the whole thing in icing, it will disguise the dark brown top. Thomas will eat it, and this year I even have a candle to put on the top that I'll blow out myself. My only wish will be for Andrew's return, or at the very least some communication to make us aware that he is alive and well.

That alcohol is now calling me; I've tried to resist having more, but I do really need it. I can feel my saliva building with excitement at the thought of another sip. Taking the glass from the cupboard and looking around in the lower cabinets, I can see a couple of half-opened bottles of rum, gin and vodka. I do not even care what they are – I want them. I might just pour them all into one large cocktail glass. The vodka is the fullest of the bottles. I'll have a little drink of that with some lemonade just before dinner. The one bottle cannot hurt, surely?

'Here's to you, Andrew,' I whisper into the air. 'Happy birthday, my beautiful son.'

I look at the kitchen door again to remind myself that he walked out of there without a care in the world. Looking at the cake and thinking of the dinner, I'm already exhausted, but it helps to take my mind off the anguish I feel. Some days I have emotions that scare me, but I refuse to talk about them or have them unearthed. I'm frightened that if I let them out, there will be no going back.

'Thomas, I'm going to be busy in this kitchen now. I'll shut the door, so I'm not distracted by the television.'

I hear another grunt of acknowledgement as I close the kitchen door. I want that vodka so bad; it might even stop my hands from shaking. I'm definitely twitchy today, but that's to be expected. It's been a long three years since Andrew's disappearance; however, I find that out of all the days of the year it's this one day – the anniversary of that moment – that I can't ever forget.

I miss you, Andrew. Please, my dear son, come home.

Three

Sunday, 9 September 2018

When Andrew disappeared, it was not just my son I lost, but my wife too.

That day changed everything in our lives, and our marriage has never been the same since. Despite the bright sunny day today, there will always be a dark cloud looming over us. The sudden loss of contact hit Trish hard, which is to be expected. I try to get on with daily life, but there has been a chasm cut right through our relationship. I think our marriage is on the verge of being consumed by a black hole.

Every year Trish continues to bake a cake as if he will walk in at any minute. With the same routines at the same time for the last three years, I know she'll burn the damn fucking thing and place it in the centre of the table. Neither Andrew nor I even liked her baking. She does have a passion for making spectacular cakes for the charity stalls. They would look stunning, but she was not renowned for her taste buds – she often mixed different ingredients to create her own flavours. I'll never forget the poppyseed and tofu concoction she attempted a few weeks back just because Sandra down the road was vegetarian. She tries too hard to please other people. But I like how it keeps her occupied, and I should encourage her more.

I drift off most evenings after work in front of the television daydreaming about how life before Andrew's disappearance seemed perfect. We were one of the families in the street that others would like to talk about. If we bought a new television or oven, you can be sure it would get talked about around the road. If we had deliveries of parcels, the neighbours would be hanging out their windows trying to break their necks to see what we bought next. Then every few years when we traded in our family car for a new model – others would try to keep up. We were that kind of family.

Now, we are the most talked-about family in the street for entirely different reasons. I know that people struggle to talk to us about it; I can see it in their eyes when I make random chit-chat. The neighbours watching us while no doubt restraining themselves from asking us that all-important question.

'Have you heard anything from Andrew yet?'

I snap back sharply that there's no news. I am sick of being asked now; I'm tired of the talking behind our backs. The looks, the stares, the conspiracy theories that have spread around this village can drag us both down. Nobody wants to be seen as being nosey, yet everyone wants to know our business all the same. Village life is sometimes about gossip. It is unavoidable in a little place like Elmton.

'How are you coping without him; I can't imagine being in your shoes?'

Just a few lines the locals seem to throw in our direction. We've always kept ourselves private. Neither of us minds the odd gossip here and there, but we've still tried hard not to attract the attention of others if we can help it. Our business is our business, and that is just how I like it.

If I could have my time back again, I'd never have chosen to live here. Trish wanted to live in a rural setting with the option of having a town close by. Because of that, Elmton was the perfect location. Quiet enough to keep yourself to yourself and a safe distance from the hustle and bustle of life in central Plymouth. There's not much here: a few shops, a park and only the one road right through it. I call it a drive-thru village. Blink and you miss it if you're passing through.

As a self-employed taxicab driver, I can work my own hours up to a point, but if I want to earn some decent money, I have to put the long hours in over the weekends. Last night was busy; one of the busiest in months. All the students are back in Plymouth now; it is a brand-new academic year and with that comes the money that flows through the local bars down the Barbican. They never tip though, but that's not British culture. I look at them wondering if Andrew would have enjoyed university if he hadn't opted for college instead. I often think about what he would look like now too, especially to see if the chubbiness in his face had turned more masculine. I wonder if it was because I teased him about his weight, maybe he left the house with body issues?

Andrew was never the brightest child at school in comparison to his peers, so it was no surprise he opted for a college business diploma instead of a university course.

Of course, his mother and I had high hopes for him, but I am more of a realist. I knew Andrew wouldn't have amounted to anything as a grown man. He was lazy and regularly played computer games. Not driven enough to think about turning a passion into a career, he was happy to just sit in his room all day and let life pass him by.

Andrew was never self-driven or interested in the world like his father. I felt an emotional disconnection from my son, which I blame myself for. I was ignorant when it came to his upbringing. I can't count how many times I offered to take him fishing, or for a walk around the village to mend that bond between us, but he was never interested. I admit, come his teens, I gave up bothering to ask. Trish did all the hard work of parenting. I was happy to watch her shape him into the teenager that ended up walking out on us.

I have a great relationship with my father; although there is a bigger age gap between us than there is between myself and Andrew – my father used to take me fishing, swimming, walking across Dartmoor, and we had a bond that I hadn't managed to nurture with my own son. As his father I can only blame myself; I reflect a great deal since he has left. I think about all those 'what if' moments, but the past can't be changed.

Trish used to spoil Andrew rotten. I think this contributed to Andrew being lazy. He always knew that she would allow him to get away with murder, but I came from a family that worked on a farm. I was taught that hard work puts meals on the table, whereas Andrew always just expected it. As father and son, we are so different to each other, but I appreciate it's a different world for kids now. Everything to entertain children nowadays supports them staying indoors. I was always active, come rain or shine, and couldn't wait to see my friends after school. Andrew, on the other hand, was so reclusive. Everything he did revolved around isolating himself.

I blame myself for working such long hours. I should have been more encouraging as a father.

A seven-year-old Andrew was the only child that walked the egg-and-spoon race and quit half-way. We argued about him being lazy even when he was younger, but I wanted him to have the drive to succeed. I pushed enough when he was older to make him understand that you cannot grow into a man with responsibilities by sitting in your bedroom. Those computer games weren't teaching him how to get out into the world and earn a decent living. I could have been more than a taxi driver, but I made that choice when Andrew was born. I am a family man with the values that my parents taught me, that family come first and foremost, and having a wife and child gave me all the success I needed. I wanted Andrew to be more academically driven.

Maybe I pushed too hard?

The house is so quiet without Andrew, and Trish is fast losing her mind. Her drinking, the arguments we have now – we're giving up, aren't we?

Andrew disappointed me many times. There are times I regret shouting at him; other times, I tried to get the best from him. I really hope he is out there living a great life.

Did I go too far? Does Trish blame me for his disappearance?

I know she is back on the bottle again because at night I come home to find her sipping yet another glass of vodka.

Shaking uncontrollably on the sofa, she blames herself as we both mourn our son. It's all the 'what if's that are bringing us down. With what we are going through, such a heavy train of worrying thoughts every day, how can we live a healthy life?

What do other people know about him?

It is a constant worry where you're on edge most days. I try not to lose my mind and carry on with daily life, yet Trish is more inward – she struggles more emotionally. I wonder if her most significant problem is not that Andrew disappeared, but her fear that he rejected her, if he deliberately planned to leave. I struggle to understand how a lazy kid with no real drive or ambition can make that decision to just simply vanish. He had no friends that I know of who could support him or hide him.

After Andrew vanished, I teamed up with his college lecturers and we put leaflets through doors in the local area. A small handful of his classmates offered to help and put posters up at his college. Together with Trish, we also contacted all of the public transport services, but no one confirmed any sightings. Although it is possible that Andrew could have been murdered, I always assure Trish that Andrew wanted to leave because, mentally, I know that by clinging on to the hope that he is alive, she will get through this. I want her to accept it was his choice. I hate seeing her this way.

Where the hell did he go and what the fuck was he thinking?

Trish now clings to the hope of finding him or that his return is imminent. I don't think she will see him any time soon, but I can't stop thinking about the past; our history, our lives together as a family. I also think about all the times I walked him to school as well as the times I would drive him to college if he missed the bus.

Andrew never understood the sacrifices we made for him, nor was he really ever grateful for everything we provided. I love him, but it was his decision to leave – not ours. His decision is final in my opinion, and both Trish and I have to accept once and for all that our son didn't want us.

Have I failed him?

I am beginning to doubt if I still love my wife like I used to. I don't know her since Andrew left us, because she has become too obsessed with the belief that he is on his way home. We never spend much quality time together since Andrew left, and the whole situation has ripped us apart. It is as though we are now two strangers living in the same house. Although I work nights, I tried to make sure we had dinner together at least once a week, but it was to no avail.

Trish and I have the same routines day in and day out. Without Andrew, the house is quieter, yet I can see how she feels she has no purpose. She doesn't know what to do with herself, and it is crippling her mind. She's a great mother. All she ever wanted was to become the mother that she never really had herself. Her mother was something of an emotionless witch who despised everyone and anyone that got near her daughter.

When Trish comes in with the cake, I will, of course, tell her how lovely it is and I'll eat all of it so as not to waste any. I hate wasting food, and she has spent so much time and effort despite the burnt bits. If she starts to sway on her feet, I'll know she's opened the vodka in the cupboard. I know she isn't aware that I know how much she has been drinking lately. I choose to withhold my opinions because the build-up to this day, Andrew's birthday, has been hard for us both.

Selfishly, Trish cannot accept that I am also dealing with the loss of my son, my only child.

Probably caused by the worry, doubt and guilt, Trish's memory loss is a minor issue that could grow into a severe cause for concern. There have been many other instances of her forgetfulness, but it's now starting to escalate outside of the house. I had to rush home from working mid-week because she had gone out shopping and realised that she had forgotten her house keys. The first I knew of her overlooking her keys was a phone call last week from our neighbour Joe.

'Something's up with Trish, mate.'

I thought in that instant she had been rushed to the hospital or something far worse – she'd killed herself.

'What has happened, what the fuck has happened?' I remember shrieking down the phone. 'Tell me everything is okay. She hasn't done anything stupid, mate – has she?'

'She's having a panic attack, mate. Looking like she is having a mental breakdown in the village shop.'

It took a little over twenty minutes for me to make my way back to Elmton from the city centre. Joe, fortunately, was in the village store at the same time and was able to witness the fear on her face.

When I got her home, she told me that as she went to the till to pay for the groceries, the realisation that the house keys were not in her pockets struck her. She dropped the shopping all over the floor, placed her hands over her head and tried to run out of the shop while unable to catch her breath. Of course, the village gossips were talking about it for days on end. All she wanted to do was run home to check if the keys were still in the door or scurry around the bushes on the trail back home to see if she dropped them somewhere close by.

Knowing I was at work and wouldn't be back home for a few hours triggered a minor anxiety attack. Trish had a few when Andrew first disappeared, but this was entirely out of the blue. Thankfully it hasn't happened since and we have had a spare cut that the neighbour kindly keeps for us in an emergency.

'It's more for my benefit, Joe,' I remember stating at the time, 'in the event of an emergency.'

I need peace of mind. I'm starting to worry about her again as her behaviour is all over the place. Erratic is just one word I could use to describe her emotions, as they swerve between tears of despair, then move towards anger and hatred. Every day appears to be a new day of emotional turmoil.

Trish doesn't really see it from my point of view. However, I wonder at times, *is she hiding something from me? What does she know that I don't?*

Has Trish known all along what happened that day?

I am scared to confront her because I am convinced that she is on the brink of a breakdown.

Four

Andrew and Patricia Mullner – Then

Sunday, 9 September 2001

I couldn't believe how quickly the last three years had flown by. It barely felt like five minutes since I'd brought Andrew home from the hospital. That little bundle of joy who made our family complete was continuously changing at that young age.

Where had all that time gone?

'Happy third birthday, Andrew,' I said; he never took any notice of me while he was mastering the art of climbing all over the sofa. 'My little man, you are three today, are you going to open your presents from Mummy and Daddy?'

Andrew ran around the living room floor in circles, his speech was coming along nicely, but it should have done since he had become the only person I spoke to all day.

Some days I regretted encouraging Thomas to become a taxi driver. The pay was great as it supported all of us, but I rarely saw him that often as the night shifts took their toll on him. When he was home during the day, he just slept most of the time while I did all the hard work looking after Andrew. I hated him for not being around more, but I had my precious son to myself. It helped me to strengthen that bond with Andrew.

I knew Thomas struggled to bond with Andrew and blamed himself for not being there during the birth. It wasn't helped by him working all those long hours at night, then sleeping during the day. He was missing out on so much vital development time with Andrew. But we needed the money.

'You'll spend more time with him as he grows up,' I assured him. 'He will love you as his daddy. You said a little boy was all that you wanted to carry on your family name. You knew it would make your dad proud. You'll get your turn.'

I wished Andrew would stop running around the carpet and pay more attention to the presents I had spent all morning wrapping.

Thomas and I had both written some lovely comments in Andrew's birthday card too, not that he could read it, but we kept all his sentimental things in a keepsake box for when he was older. I thought he would probably be embarrassed about it, but he'd understand how important it was when he grew up and had children of his own. I hadn't realised that time was so precious until I had Andrew.

I couldn't imagine myself as a grandmother. I would be some evil old witch that no one wanted to bother with. Left in an old-people's home to rot. I didn't really want that.

'Mummy,' Andrew had said in a cute voice. 'Running, Mummy.'

'I know you are, my boy,' I replied. I looked at his face and saw that he was growing more handsome each day, as his facial features became more prominent. I felt so lucky to have him. 'Mummy can see you playing, my little man. Let's open your presents together, shall we?'

Andrew didn't even acknowledge the pile of presents on the sofa, but instead was continuing to have fun running around the circle patterns on the carpet. His birthday the year before, he had loved pulling at the wrapping paper and playing with the empty boxes, but I'm sure on this birthday he found some enjoyment from the toys inside. We had bought him a new train set that made realistic sounds, and a set of battery-operated drums so he could make some noises to entertain himself.

And he probably pissed off the neighbours.

I had tried to look after Andrew and continue my midwife training, but when depression took hold of me after Andrew's birth, I couldn't connect with him. All I'd ever wanted was a family, a child of my own, yet here it all was in front of me, and I still wasn't happy. I reassured Thomas that it was not postnatal depression because I loved Andrew, I knew that I loved him, but I couldn't describe it other than that I had a sense of loss about it. Something was missing.

'Maybe because all the attention is not focused on you being pregnant anymore,' Thomas had suggested. Of course, I went mad at him for suggesting I needed such attention from other people. I hate attention; it's not like he doesn't know that. I would love nothing more than to be one of those people who walks around unnoticed.

'Don't be so bloody foolish,' I'd replied, 'you know how much I hate being fussed over.'

That period of my life has passed now. I spent the first year never leaving the house if I could help it. I just wanted to stay indoors and be safe with Andrew. Every time I walked the streets, even if it was only to go to the local shop, I felt everyone was staring at me. *They doubt my abilities as a mother*, I used to think. The paranoia was terrible. Motherhood was all new to me, and almost every mother in the village who came and looked at my baby would try telling me how to do something. Whether it was the way I dressed him, the teething issues, how to make his milk correctly; I couldn't get their interfering ways off my mind.

'Andrew, look over here. Come to Mummy.' I called him over as I held the first present in my hands. I can remember him directing his attention to the wrapping paper as I rustled it to make some noise. 'What have I got for you, Mummy's little man?'

'Mummy,' he replied, walking now in my direction. 'Is it mine?'

'That's right,' I responded with a warming smile. 'These are all for you. Why don't you come to Mummy and sit over here with me? Let's see what you have got for your birthday?'

Together we sat on the floor and unwrapped the presents together. He had some new clothes, the train set, the drums, a handful of small picture books, but I wrapped my arms around him to give him the biggest hug. That feeling of happiness overcame me, it brought a tear to my eye.

'I love you so much.'

Andrew didn't acknowledge it with words but he leaned up to give me a kiss on the cheek. He squinted his little eyes and returned my smile with laughter of his own. Now that I understood this mother and son bond, I had a purpose in my life.

'Come and give Mummy another hug?' I asked, but Andrew ran off, wanting me to chase him from one end of the room to the other. 'I'm coming to get you, come to Mummy?'

The presents were scattered all over the living room floor. For a few minutes, I played with Andrew, but I was unable to stop him from running around the carpet. I wanted to get it changed or cover the large circles that he loved to run around with a rug. I was concerned that he would fall over and hurt himself. Andrew seemed to bruise really hard.

Thomas had come home from work about six months beforehand and noticed some bruises on the side of Andrew's face, one on his back and two on his arms.

Andrew had fallen down the stairs. I'd only turned away for two minutes while I rushed up the stairs to use the toilet. I explained that to Thomas, but he made me feel as though I was a bad mother. The last thing I wanted to hear was that I wasn't good enough; I couldn't take another blow to my self-worth.

'We can't take him outside,' I'd said. 'What will people think of us with a baby covered in bruises.'

Thankfully Andrew didn't have a broken arm; otherwise Thomas said we would have had to take him to the hospital. I remember panicking and shaking with worry. I couldn't take him to the hospital; I begged Thomas not to go. Too many people rushing around and too many bad memories.

'I did complete some of my midwife training,' I reassured him. 'We don't need to go to the hospital. If his arm was broken, I'd know how to fix it. I do know how to fix a broken arm. We would only need to find a sling.'

I was so mentally detached from Plymouth Hospital and all my training. I knew I needed a different direction with work, and maybe when Andrew was older, and at school full-time, I could think about doing something else. I liked the idea of doing something for charity because that's what good people do. I wanted to give something back to the community with a sense of purpose. It would really show this village how nice a person I could be. A caring, loving mother who could use her spare time to do something great.

I'd struggled to make friends in the village. Coming from a busy urban environment in central Plymouth to this small village on the outskirts was a culture shock, but it made me feel disguised in my own little corner of the world. I had tried to make friendly chit-chat with the neighbours, often at times I joined the woman across the road for a natter about the news and weather. I looked at them and felt their indifference towards me because I'm not sure they had ever met anyone like me before. Maybe I was just being paranoid because I never felt like I fitted in here. I've never really had a feeling of belonging anywhere. I would rather not have any friends than waste my time on fake conversations.

I said to Thomas that I had given up on the neighbours. We'd just keep ourselves to ourselves and get on with our own lives. When we first moved out of Plymouth, I felt that everyone wanted to know my business and judge me here. It was intense and stressful because I thought village culture was about keeping yourself private. Most of the neighbours wanted to know who we were, where we came from, what we did. I hated that, but nobody really bothered with us anymore, so Elmton suited me perfectly for the privacy I craved.

'We have to fit in here,' he'd reminded me. 'It's better to make friends than enemies.'

Thomas was the more talkative one out of us both – he could chat for hours on end about all kinds of random crap. I knew he must resent me at times for him leaving university to support us as a family. It was his choice to do so, but I really loved how supportive he had been to me since we had had a child in our lives.

Having Andrew completed me. I knew what direction my life was heading in. I got the depression in the beginning because I felt a little out of control and living together with a baby was new to both of us. It was thanks to Thomas I had my stability, my sanity and my beautiful family.

I didn't have anyone else to support me. I have never felt that loved in my whole life.

Andrew had taken hold of the small drums and was inspecting them with his tiny hands. He was unsure what to do with them so he walked towards me, shaking them up and down.

'No, they don't work like that,' I said, taking them off him. 'This is how you do it.'

I placed the drums flat down on the floor and banged my hand on the left drum, then patted the right one with less force. Andrew was stood in front of me, watching with awe as he witnessed my hands make a sound that he had never heard before. I had gauged his interest with something he loved. He was smiling at me, and the sound of his laughter was music to my ears. I had made my little boy happy on his birthday. I had a feeling of warmth rush through my body as he watched me play the drums for him.

'Look at me, Andrew,' I said. 'Copy Mummy.'

Andrew turned around to abandon me. He went back to run around the carpet again. He had disowned me in a moment when I thought we were connected by his learning. I was growing upset; I couldn't shout at him because he was only three years old, and he had succeeded in making me feel like a useless mother.

I'm trying to do my best for you. Working so hard.

I picked up the drums and threw them against the wall. Andrew stopped running around the floor, jumped and stood still as I had startled him. It was such a loud bang that I could guarantee the neighbours heard the thud against the wall. The plastic broke into many pieces, some shards would have been dangerous for Andrew to stand on.

'Now look what you've gone and made Mummy do,' I said in a firm voice. 'I thought you loved Mummy.'

I'm not convinced he even liked me, let alone loved me.

I sacrificed a lot for you, Andrew.

Five

Staring at my own shadow dancing on the wall as the candlelight flickers is mesmerising. These guilty feelings that eat away at me make me think that I deserve to be punished. My eyes are focusing on the flickers of light, but in my head all I can hear is my mother's words coming back to haunt me.

'You're evil, Patricia. You are damaged.'

My mother would have beaten me if I'd ever told her the secrets that I kept from her, despite my father knowing what he did to me. The secrets I keep from my family now are far bigger than I can cope with. All my life I have felt like a disappointment, but now I've done something this terrible. Maybe I deserve to feel this way.

Maybe I am evil?

The living room is quiet as I sit in silence watching the glimmer of light from the candle I lit in memory of my son. Andrew did not come home today after all. I am disappointed and upset, but deep down, I never really expected him to walk back through the door. But I refuse to let go of the hope that one day it could happen. The only way that he exists to me now is in my memories.

Thomas retired to bed about an hour ago. I've been on the vodka ever since because the pressure of the thoughts in my head is driving me insane.

He's dead, isn't he? The police never found the body?

My worst fears have never been confirmed, but I always wonder if he's decomposing face-down in a ditch somewhere. I often think that he might have met someone who murdered him, hid the body, or even if he had ended up drowning by accident in a river. However, I push to the forefront of my mind that while there's no sign of him, there is still hope that he is out there somewhere living a life. I wonder if I had given him more freedom and cared a bit less then he might still be here with us today.

People around me think I am going insane; I can see the look in their eyes when they talk to me. I can see them all stare at me as I go about my routines in the village. Maybe I should move away to start a new life, but then Andrew would never know where we are. So long as I live and breathe in this house, he will always know where his home is. If we moved, then I would still be worrying about him coming back, and finding we were gone.

Forgive me if I wasn't there for you more, Andrew.

A pang of ravaging guilt consumes me as I tread deeper down this road of not knowing what happened. It is evident to me that no one understands what I am going through, because for as long as I have lived in Elmton, no other mother's son has vanished without a trace. All I ever wanted to be was a decent mother with a child who knew how much he was loved, wanted, and the freedom to make his own choices. I am concerned that Andrew had built up an inner fear of something, or a hatred towards his father and me.

Something happened to make him run away from us both? Why couldn't he talk to me about it?

My own mother was very strict in comparison to the way I took the lead in Andrew's upbringing. There were times as a child when I wasn't even allowed to speak. As a young girl, aged about six or seven at most, I had to ask – if not beg – for permission to leave the dinner table. If I wasn't home from school on time, then I remember many times when my father had thrown my dinner in the bin. I was never severely beaten as a child, but my mother gave me the odd punch to the ribs if I didn't do as I was told. I had become accustomed to the occasional bruising, and in some instances, I developed a resistance to the jabs to the chest. My pain threshold developed over a few years that consolidated with my mother hitting me harder as I grew older. I learnt to forgive her.

No one ever knew about my home life because I thought it was normal; there was never any need to talk about something you don't consider irregular activity when it is your parents. My naivety in primary school had me thinking every child's home life was similar to my own.

Didn't all fathers whip their children with belts for answering their mother back?

Growing up, I soon learnt to understand that the way I was treated by my own parents was abusive. Other children at school talked about going to the beach, being taken to the funfair. Conversations in the classroom as I grew up were not about being punished. I realised I was alone, so I decided to keep my secrets to myself.

I felt that for whatever reason, they resented me. My mother always used to talk about the career I had ruined when she'd got pregnant with me, while my father blamed me for my mother's temper. She would always tell him of my behaviour as soon as he returned home from his job delivering coal. We had a coal fire in our house instead of central heating and I'm sure we were healthier for it. I never got as many colds or minor illnesses as I do now. My mother hated modern things like central heating, we were barely even allowed to watch television.

Having made my father angry because I dared to disobey my mother, I was often punished. You learn to switch off from it in the end because it's a pain you get used to, like mind over matter. You know what is coming, so it is easy to zone out into a world of your own.

I'm still convinced that my parents loved me despite not being able to show me any affection. My father did so more as I approached adolescence, he told me once or twice that he loved me. I grew to forgive him for his behaviour because I blamed my mother for everything. I'm sure my mother was even jealous of the attention that my father showed me during those years.

Unfortunately, both of my parents died in a car accident a few months after I met Thomas. I eventually discovered that my father had been drink driving. Although it hadn't ever been confirmed, I had a gut instinct my mother drove him to constant drinking to switch off from her abuse, and they no doubt argued in the car over something trivial that upset her. I believe he took his eye off the road and unfortunately hit the truck. They would have died almost instantly. I sometimes had nightmares thinking about their crushed bodies in the confines of that twisted metal shell of a car. I was informed by the police that their bodies were so severely damaged that identification might be distressing. I didn't identify the bodies because I had suffered enough trauma.

There might have been issues with the brakes that day?

I felt mixed emotions of utter sadness, yet relief that my torturous childhood had come to an end. Life got better after time, but it's a cold existence when you feel as though you're a burden on someone else. I met Thomas at the right time: he taught me that not everyone was the same. I trust him. I love him.

At school, the bullying became worse when I got older, as a teenager I became more isolated, but I was hardened by my father's traits, although weakened by my vulnerable mental state. Physically the abuse had stopped, but mentally, the cracks started to deepen, which affected my behaviour.

Dealing with the loss of my parents, combined with the reality of my abuse, made me feel like I was worthless. Those feelings, the sense of worthlessness, are beginning to return. Most of my adult life I have been able to control the emotion, but tonight I feel like I only have a few readily available options – do I take the knife, do I swallow the tablets, or do I walk out of here into oncoming traffic?

Would I be a loss to anyone if I chose to end my life right now?

All I did for Andrew was show him care and love. How could he be so cruel to us both? He never once had it as hard as I had growing up.

'I don't think I can take any more.'

No one answers me, no one even asks how I am anymore. I've turned into a shell of the person I once was, and I can't see an end to the misery of my existence. I wish I could stop crying because it changes absolutely nothing. The pain and hurt are festering within me and I want to scream until every last breath is sucked out of my lungs. It would be easier if I was dead too.

I wish these tears would dry away.

I've learnt to conceal my feelings over the last few years by burying the guilt in my heart. That smiling, happy face I show the world outside evolves into a solemn expression when I isolate myself indoors.

'I don't think I can do this anymore. Is anyone listening to me?'

Maybe if I shout loud enough, someone will take notice.

Thomas has rolled over in the bed because I can hear the metal springs bounce and creak as he turns over. If he comes back down the stairs to check on me, we'll only end up arguing again. I don't want to keep hurting him, but I'm starting to feel like a burden.

The emptiness is so powerful that nothing can improve my mental state. Every teardrop that slithers down my face is a reminder of the despair in my soul. I want to die.

Suicide is such a selfish act in my opinion, but all the 'what if's have taken their toll on my tired mind, my darkened confused eyes and the memories that slowly fade. Lingering in the back of my thoughts is the hope that life will eventually return to normal. Normal seems like a historical reminiscence now; if I ever really knew what normal was to begin with. Death may be an easy way out of this world, and I might one day take it.

Staring at the knife and the tablets, I know I have two choices if I'm going to go through with this. I wonder what method causes less pain?

If I slit my wrists, the pain will be excruciating. From my trainee midwife days, I am more than aware of the painful process of bleeding out. If I make a quick deep stab in the right area, I could hit an artery. I'd be out in seconds; blood would spray and splatter across the room as I slipped away into unconsciousness before my own body tried to save me. I know that I would lie weak and in fear that my adrenaline levels would rise with the speeding of my heart. With almost no chance of surviving because of the drop in my oxygen levels, death would be imminent.

I contemplate taking my life: the torment, torture, grief and guilt would all be over. My failing kidneys would fight as my temperature dropped; yet slipping away from this world seems all too easy. The tablets could just make me sick, with the damaging effects taking days. Organ failure and hospitalisation for weeks – I would rather a quick way out.

Sometimes, all I want is peace.

Six

They are blissfully unaware of my presence as I watch their house from the wooded area within the sports field. From behind the housing estate my view is a clear shot of the back garden and all its exposed accesses, and my planned route comes together in my mind.

I can see Patricia's wooden arch at the entrance to the washing line area, where I have seen her once before. From this spot in the overgrowth, I can just see her kitchen window – if I squint.

Currently, the weather is hazy, but no one can see me from behind the trees. The echoing squawks from the crows are the only sound. I observe them with envy since their darkness conceals them while their wings provide a fast escape from the monotony of surveillance. Crows sit in the shade and watch; I too hide in the shadows waiting for my moment. My moment will come soon, and much like the crows it will be from the darkness, and they won't see me for dust when I'm done. This morning mist provides the perfect scene for murder, but I do not intend to kill – not today.

I have binoculars for when I am desperate, but Patricia seems to have the same regular routines from my analysis. I hate her. When I look at her living and breathing, I can barely breathe myself. Angry to the point of feeling the adrenaline rush to my kidneys, I could run at her with an axe.

This woman destroyed me!

I am waiting for Thomas to leave in his taxi, he should be gone in about an hour. From past viewing sessions, he seems to be away from the property for around eight hours during the day, but he can randomly come back at lunchtimes. If I get closer, I shall avoid the lunch-hour break, just in case he returns. I'd hate to alarm them. I'm not ready to face them both with my surprise today.

Patricia has ruined my life and left me without a future. Each day I live in fear for my sanity; she should pay for what she has done to me. She gave me her word and I trusted her with my secrets.

It's cold outside, even though the sun is shimmering through the trees, giving the appearance of a summer's day. The wind is slowly picking up pace, delivering with the air a scent of damp from the overgrown bushes. As I move along slowly to hide from the view of oncoming dog walkers, the crunch of small branches and grit sounds around me.

I love to watch. I love to hate.

I am getting a sense of satisfaction from the fact that I can see Patricia, but that she cannot see me. My need to watch her fuels my anger. Sometimes I need the anger to drive my thoughts towards revenge, but I want her suffering to be slow and painful. There is no greater pleasure when you hate someone than watching them, scrutinising their every move. That bitch will pay for what she has done, and I cannot wait to see the look on her shrivelling face when I confront her.

But confronting her would end this moment. I enjoy the watching; I appreciate the loathing and I am hooked on knowing everything that she does: the places that she visits and the people that she sees. I need to observe her, I need to watch this despicable woman because I can't get her out of my head. I don't even think that she is aware of the full extent of the damage she has done.

Would she even give a shit?

If I walked up to her, she wouldn't recognise me or even know who I was. I get some fulfilment from that, because when I am able to let go of all this pent-up frustration and deal with her face to face, she'll be the equivalent of a gazelle to a leopard. I'll be fast, furious and she will not be able to see me coming for her until it is too late. By then there will be no escape as I've hunted her into my territory to devour her. When I am ready to reveal myself, I want her to suffer.

I need to watch her pain despite the turmoil she caused me. I trusted her, I believed her, but I couldn't have been more wrong. I have no idea why Thomas is attracted to that beast, but if he ends up as collateral damage, then so be it.

Edging along the pathway to hide behind the trees, the crackle from the branches gave away my location to the oncoming dog walkers. I slowly tiptoe to the most massive trunk I can find before crouching down to tie my shoelace to conceal my presence from their view. I clutch the bag with a gift for Patricia; I need to deliver it to her door without being seen. One witness could ruin everything. I cannot afford to be seen.

It was Andrew's birthday yesterday, which is why I should have placed this gift on her doorstep last night. I was here, I saw her.

Patricia appeared suicidal from the bottle of alcohol beside her and the turmoil on her face. I clocked the sharp knife that she was staring at while, at one point in the evening, she slowly slid it across her wrist, but it appeared to be a trial run. I did not want her to die – my plan would have been ruined. Her suffering cannot end this easily. I intended to knock on the window or shout. But I placed a hand across my mouth as she once more swigged the vodka with the kitchen knife so readily available to harm herself. My anger was rife.

The darkness, the excitement, the misery of her misfortunes almost made me help her finish the job.

She cannot end it this way; that is my choice to make. Her suffering is mine.

Managing to stifle my heavy breathing, I watched as she sat there toying with the idea. She pivoted the knife, which glistened in the candlelight. Its sharp edge made me fantasise about holding it myself and thrusting it with all my force into her heart. I would stare at her face when the colour drained from her cheeks. I'd give a smile as I acknowledged and owned that I had killed her. For the life that she ruined, for the life that she selfishly destroyed – mine.

Why should I end up imprisoned for that cunt?

I have tried to walk away and to live a normal, ordinary life. I cannot forgive her. This despicable woman has walked this earth without so much as giving a fuck for the hurt that she caused. I don't want her to just end her life in the blink of an eye because that would be yet another selfish act.

How can she leave her husband to suffer another loss?

The world cannot revolve around Patricia Mullner any longer. Why can't all those around her see through that woman's mind games?

I bet that she is lapping up the sympathy from her neighbours over Andrew's disappearance. I have stayed in the distance, following her at random times – sometimes going months without needing to see her, but now I can see that three years of anguish is ruining her. Watching her play with that knife was all too tempting. As much as I want to see her die, I don't want her to have that choice. It's my choice. If I had placed this gift for her on her doorstep, it could have sent her over the edge.

I came here today to make sure she was still alive, still able to receive this token that should send her spiralling, but not enough to trigger more suicidal thoughts. This little gift of mine should ignite her curiosity. It is what she will choose to do with it that will make it all the more important. I have faith that she will want to remain alive to see this through.

Now is my perfect moment. I can see that Patricia is nowhere near the kitchen window. Her neighbours have gone out – or appear to still be in bed with all the curtains shut. Thomas is at work in his taxi, and there are no more dog walkers in sight. If I run fast enough to the edge of the field, I should not be seen. The problem with little villages like Elmton is that everyone seems to know everyone. As I am an outsider, my face will become etched on the memory of anyone who sees me.

I make my move closer to her back garden while my eyes scan for anyone nearby. I have my hood up, but the latex gloves could draw attention if spotted, so I place one hand in my pocket, while the other is hidden by the bag that carries the gift. Shaking a little with nerves, I'm excited anticipating her finding this. My legs are trembling, and I am tense, hoping that the mist will screen me from anyone watching as I approach Patricia's garden. With a short yet silent flick of the back gate, I am inside.

I only have seconds. My heart is pounding in my chest as I walk down the pathway, through the arch and I take out the gift from the bag and place it on the doorstep. I knock on the door as loudly as I can. Two swift bangs, and then I run. The damp from the grass is clinging to my jeans although I am certain that not a trace nor thread from me will be discovered.

My breathing is uncontrolled. I run back to the field and then lower myself so that I am no taller than the nearby bushes. As I run closer to the woodland, I am once again in the safety of the crows. They are my only witness as they watch from the tallest point of the treetops. I am sure they recognise me from the other times I have stood here over the last couple of years. I made it, with no watchers, no dog walkers and no one anywhere in sight. The first clue was a success, and I sit down to catch my breath.

Any minute now Patricia will get the surprise of her life, but my work here is not done. I need to hide or destroy my footwear – a cheap pair of slip-on shoes that I will bury in the woods. I swap my shoes, dig a small hole with my hands and place the latex gloves and the carrier bag inside. I cover the hole with grit, mud and fallen leaves. My hood is down and my exit is clear. I will walk through the woods in the opposite direction from Patricia's house – it's approximately a one-mile walk to the nearest road. I daren't catch a bus; I daren't call a taxi. I'll arrive at Plymouth after another two-mile walk. It's all been worth it.

I cannot keep what I know to myself any longer. I have tried to put this pain to the back of my mind, decided to forgive and forget. Now I will seek my revenge.

I hope you like my gift, Patricia. Andrew wore this gold chain when he left you that day. Do you remember that, Patricia?

How well do you actually know him?

Seven

Patricia Mullner – Now

Monday, 10 September 2018

'What time did you finally come upstairs to bed, love?' Thomas yawned at me over breakfast this morning. 'I didn't hear you come up last night, but I was probably out for the count.'

'I went up really late because I wanted some time alone – you know, so I could think about our missing son, if you haven't forgotten about him already?'

You could have cut the atmosphere with a knife as I got up from the kitchen table to moan once more about the dishes being left for me to do, yet again. My mood isn't at its best today, but what would he honestly expect? I feel alone with my own thoughts, which have me trapped inside a bubble of constant loss.

I hate these cloudy miserable grey sky days, they make me feel more depressed. A sunny day gives me the option to leave the house – even if I choose not to do so. When it's raining, I feel further trapped in the house, which entices me to drink more, and my fears are released in the arguments I create with Thomas. Although it is my little safe haven, there is nothing worse than being stuck indoors with limited choices.

The cake from yesterday is still perched on the table, uneaten. The birthday card I inscribed with a message about how proud I am to be able to call Andrew my son is left unopened. I'll put it in his room later, with all the others from previous years. At least when he returns, he can see we still care enough to consider him and think about his birthdays. Small things that might make a world of difference later on. Whatever caused him to walk out, I still want him to know we love him – regardless of what he may think. Even not knowing what he is thinking is driving me crazy.

'Andrew never came home in the end, did he?' I asked Thomas, 'not a sign of him anywhere was there?'

Thomas had a look in his eye that I recognised. I can tell that he sometimes doesn't know whether to say something that would please me, or potentially offend me.

I already knew the answer, but I wanted to put him on the spot. I need to talk about Andrew. I just wish we were back to being the family unit we once were. I want to be like all the other mums who feed, care for and love their child.

'No, love,' Thomas responded before looking back at the local paper. 'He didn't come home. Maybe, he might show his face next year as it'll be his twenty-first birthday then. Our son will be a grown man. Hard to believe it, really. Isn't it?'

I watched Thomas eat his breakfast without a care in the world. I know he still thinks that I should see a therapist, or at the very least talk to a doctor again about my issues.

Why doesn't he speak to me about how he is feeling? What good does it do to talk to complete strangers who haven't lost their son – how can they begin to know how I feel?

I was not able to return to work fully when Andrew left: the worry and the grief destroy you. *Time is a great healer*, people have told me, which is right in some respects, but the worrying just shifts to the back of your mind a little bit more – it never really goes away. That's what causes all the torment and mental suffering when something just continuously grips your thoughts. It keeps me awake at night when I try to fall asleep; it shifts my concentration span whether I am out shopping, working, volunteering or just daydreaming on a bus. One day, I wonder what it would be like to never have to worry anymore about Andrew.

Will the questions stop torturing me so I can sleep at night?

I can't fit everything into one mind, something has to give way.

I also asked Thomas if he remembered when I first told him that I was pregnant. 'Yeah, of course, I do remember, love,' he replied. 'That's when I knew you were the woman that I wanted to spend the rest of my life with.'

Thomas was over the moon when I first announced that we were to have a little man in our lives. For the first few weeks after I told him I was pregnant, all he talked about was his hope for a little baby boy. I knew I had made his dreams come true because I had never seen him that happy. He had been ecstatic, whereas I had spent nine months worrying, panicking and trying to ensure everything I had planned around the pregnancy fitted perfectly into place.

I smile, knowing that I made the right choices in life. When I look at Thomas, who is now a heavy-set middle-aged taxi driver, so far gone from the days of being a slender administration assistant and university student, I couldn't love him any more than I do already. He is my world, my rock and my saviour, who helped me escape the torment from my evil mother, who disapproved of everything he did for me.

I remember January 1998 like it was yesterday; my mind doesn't seem to play tricks on me when it's historical moments that shaped the woman I am today. Thomas and I hadn't been dating for long before I announced that I was pregnant. The first few dates had been in local cafes on Plymouth Hoe before we moved on to bars and restaurants a couple of months later. There couldn't have been a man better made for me. Thomas was a hard-working, ambitious, protector type of guy who wanted me to be happy. I knew he was falling for me, but I couldn't fully trust others not to take advantage. When I knew he was the man I wanted, I put myself on a plate for him. I needed him.

Thomas and I were not serious to start with, as our relationship was only just beginning to blossom back then, and I knew that he had been dating other women without telling me. There had been times I followed him to work without him noticing me. Other times I would wait for hours on end to see if he really was staying in all night to study, or if he was lying to me.

My mother used to tell me when I was growing up that no man could ever love me because I was the ugly duckling of the family. When someone says something to you enough times, you end up believing it. When Thomas finally asked me out on a date, I thought it was a joke.

How could someone like him, like someone like me?

I used to think that maybe Thomas wasn't attracted to me, that he was playing games. My mother made me feel worthless, and I hope with all my heart that Andrew never felt that way about himself. Or, worse still – that he blamed me just as I blamed my mother.

As I became more involved romantically with Thomas, when I knew he was beyond boyfriend material and that one day I could marry this man, I admit I became possessive. He was mine, and no girl in the world was going to take from me the only real love I was beginning to feel. I was alive in a world where I was always treated like everyone's second-best. I was never physically violent with the women I saw him speak to, but I was persuasive enough to let them know he was my man.

I'll never forget the look on Jessica Black's face when I told her I'd seen her practically shoving her breasts in his face. I'd watched them both from behind the trees as they went on what appeared to be a romantic walk. I had followed Thomas for most of that day to remind myself that I could trust him. In my head, I was geared up to allow him to kiss her as we'd not been dating long. He never did, thankfully, but I bumped into her on the way home – we were practically neighbours, we lived two streets apart. It took courage to stand in front of her, someone I considered far more beautiful than myself and tell her that Thomas was mine. All mine.

She was a fucking evil looking bastard, I hated her.

'Get your dirty fucking hands off my man,' I told her, up close as I could get. For one of the rare moments in my life, I felt like I had become my mother, talking to me in the same way as when she caught me stealing food from the cupboards. 'Thomas is my boyfriend and…'

I remember pausing for a moment, as in the space of a few seconds the idea of it became real.

'I'm having his baby.'

For the first time, not only did I *really* know that I loved Thomas, but I connected with the pregnancy.

I'm having his baby.

That look on Jessica's face was priceless. In that short, sharp moment of vindictiveness, she slapped her cold hand across the side of my face. A ring on her finger caught the corner of my eye as she swiped to the left. It sure as hell hurt, but the satisfaction of upsetting her was more significant than the pain of my bleeding cheek. I turned and walked away without showing an ounce of remorse or pain. My mother had hit me many times, and harder than the bitch-slap I had just received.

'Fucking bitch,' I heard her say as I smugly rolled my eyes. I was ready for a fight, but I had already won that battle.

Throughout my childhood, I thought I was the one with the problems.

My mother used to hand visitors cakes that she had baked herself. I would hand them out very carefully on a plate so as not to drop a single crumb. Otherwise, I'd get a gentle punch later in the evening. I was forced to watch everyone eat the most beautiful slices of sponge that I was never allowed to touch myself.

'You'll make too much mess,' she used to say. 'You get too dirty and ruin everything. You don't need any muffins, you are fat enough already, sweetheart.'

I knew I'd never have been capable of bringing my baby up the same way my mother had, insulting me my whole life. I knew I would love my baby and treat him with absolute love and respect. I also know that Thomas will always care for me, still love me when I'm old. I made the right choice.

When Thomas dropped out of university all those years ago to find a full-time job to support his son and me, I felt honoured. I knew I had found the man of my dreams; a truly supportive fiancé who I wanted to spend the rest of my life with. He had saved me from some dark times, and – although I had suspected him of returning to his old womanising ways – I knew that by having a son, a family, a new life to support, he was all mine.

I have never let Thomas know about the times I saw him chatting to other women when he thought I wasn't watching, nor have I ever mentioned the lipstick marks I once saw on his shirt. These were all before we were truly serious with each other, and during the pregnancy, he had treated me like a queen. I know I am all he could want. I had given him a new baby son. Together we were the perfect couple.

I love you, Andrew, I miss you.

If it were not for my mother and father dying in a car crash, Thomas and I wouldn't have gotten so close. He was there for me to console me and save me from myself. I was alone until he and Andrew became my whole purpose in life. Without them, I am nothing.

I am worthless.

Eight

Thomas Mullner – Now

Monday, 10 September 2018

Driving around the city centre of Plymouth in my taxi is often the only form of escape I have from the misery of my wife's pain. Looking at the hustle and bustle of the shoppers as they run through this heavy rain, I know I'll have a decent income today. I could not be without a car in this weather. We've had such beautiful sunshine over the last few days, but finally a bit of rain to encourage people to use taxis in Plymouth town centre rather than a cheap bus.

I don't know how they do it? You wouldn't find me waiting for a bus either. They barely even turn up at the best of times.

As I sit here waiting for a fare, my mind wanders back to the haunting episodes I've had to endure of Trish with her intense moments of grief. The sleepless nights she doesn't realise I am aware of, and the zombie-like state she gets herself in when she has downed a litre of vodka. I'm not sure how much more I can cope with.

Trish is going through hell; I admit that I should be there for her more – but she needs to move on with her life. Andrew has been missing for a few years now, and the police have all but given up hope of finding him in Plymouth. At an age where he had no credit card, debts or other forms of traceable identification, he could have started a new life anywhere under any name he chose. I know too well that there are cash-in-hand jobs out there for people with no identification. With my farming background, there were many times my parents would take on workers for a few weeks here and there. They were all paid in cash, no trace of it through the accounting records.

Will anyone ever know what happened to him?

Without a body ever being found or any trace of him in the locality, we have to assume he is a missing person who doesn't want to be found. Andrew didn't even so much as leave a note to explain why he left home. Without answers, I can only assume that he rejected us as his parents.

We never did eat that cake for Andrew's birthday. I tasted what I could of the burnt edges, and the rest of it went into the bin. I said to Trish that no charity stall could sell that piece of rock. She means well, but I want her to slow down because she can barely keep up with the racing of thoughts in her mind – it's no wonder she suffers from memory loss. I think the memory issues happen when she is at her most anxious. Some days I have seen her sitting indoors with all the curtains closed and a pair of sunglasses on. I blame the anxiety and depression that has fixed itself in her daily life.

'Andrew is probably living in a shared house working for some cash-in-hand job.' I remind Trish of my thoughts now and again. 'I bet he's living it up somewhere not knowing how to make contact. It's been that long; he might not know where to start. Andrew might have regrets about walking out on us, but we have to accept that this was the choice he made. He was the one who decided to leave us.'

Andrew was being bullied at school. I remember a conversation he brought up with Trish which made me wonder if this continued into college. We both saw the bruises on his arms, but Trish assured me she had dealt with it. The school had kept a close eye on the group of kids who constantly teased him about his weight.

'They're just jealous of you,' Trish used to tell him, 'other kids aren't as fortunate to have computers, decent food. Learn to ignore them and they'll go away.'

Maybe he was being bullied again?

I remind myself plenty of times that Andrew would be a grown man now. That boy who walked out of the door as he was approaching adulthood made his decision. I accepted it. My heart is torn between the grief of losing my son and wondering what he would be up to now; I miss him.

Trish doesn't think about how I feel.

Trish was late to bed last night, but I could hear her downstairs, sobbing faintly. For a good nine months of the year, she can manage reasonably well on a day-to-day basis, but the build-up to Andrew's birthday and the weeks that follow create a downhill trend in her state of mind. I tread on eggshells as I don't dare upset her or say the wrong thing that leads to an argument. If I even hint that he might not come back it sets off another mood swing, another argument, another night of bawling her eyes out. The only constant in her life right now is a bottle of vodka or rum. The following day will be the headache tablets to shift the hangover.

Our marriage is heading for destruction if Trish and I don't pull it all back together and sort our problems out. Trish is desperate for answers, while I am mentally remaining strong, which makes me appear insensitive at times to her trauma.

In the first few months, the anger took hold of her as she smashed up furniture, threw cutlery in my face and often found herself wandering the streets at night with a lost expression. I demanded that Trish seek some professional help, but she refused outright to speak to a counsellor. The more I suggested it, the more she put up a fight and argued. For days she would be unable to sleep until her body physically wore itself down to a state of trance. I can often see her eyelids droop as she fights the tiredness. After forty-eight hours awake, she would sleep only because her mind forced it upon her. I still have to go to work every day, she promised me things would get better.

When a year had passed since Andrew had vanished without a trace, we received notification that the search for him had wound down. The media were no longer interested either, but I think that is partly down to Andrew being almost an adult. It was assumed that he was an unhappy teenager who had just left home. Unfortunately, in media terms, as time moves on he becomes less and less significant, but to his mother and I, the despair deepened.

With no body found after the first six months, nor any evidence of his whereabouts, the sergeant in charge of our case told us that possibly our son just didn't want to be found. On some advice given to us after his eighteenth birthday, we wrote a letter to our local benefits agency to ask if Andrew had made any claim for unemployment benefits, but due to the data protection restrictions under legislation, they were not allowed to inform his parents anything about the information on their systems. All they had to do was a national insurance trace, but that data belongs to Andrew. In legal terms, it wasn't the benefits department's right to share it, nor our right to know it. Our son had reached eighteen and had all the same legal rights as any other adult now. This wasn't concrete proof of him being alive, but it gave us hope as we concluded it was a tactfully worded letter to inform us that they knew more than they were letting on, but it was none of our business where he was living.

Trish felt that this response was hopeful, but I had told her in no uncertain terms that they wouldn't tell us anything – even if he wasn't claiming – due to breaching the data protection act. The law and fairness are two entirely different things. Sadly, the letter we wrote and the response we received were pointless.

Every couple of weeks, Trish will remember and acknowledge that he was my son too and ask me how I am feeling. This comes after the many insults that I do not talk about our son, that I have forgotten our son – and that I could never have really loved our son. Nothing I say or do can console her, but if the two of us reacted the same, we would have lost it altogether. Our home would be ridden in debt. Rather than be thankful for the strong character that I am, Trish turns against me, but I know she later regrets the tension she causes.

Admittedly, I sometimes wonder if it was because I wasn't around much when Andrew was a baby that I feel like I never really bonded with him. When he was a few months old, I looked at him, thinking, *this is my son, this bundle of arms and legs is my boy*, but I had never felt a deep-down connection because I tried too hard to force it. When we were out shopping, I would look at the way other dads smiled at their children, noticing the glint in their eyes as they expressed sincere love and care. I would often look at Andrew and feel nothing. I would keep these feelings to myself of course, yet my smiles and proud-father public displays of affection were not genuine. I struggled to bond with him as he grew older too and I blame that for the lack of father–son relationship in our lives. I was always working all the hours under the sun to provide food on the table.

There were times I blamed him and his mother for not allowing me to live my life. When I was in my twenties, other friends of mine were living the dream, getting decent careers and seemingly becoming highflyers. I, on the other hand, dropped out of university to find a steady job to support my girlfriend and our newborn son. I had to be a man, but the love didn't come until after the first year, when Andrew became ill. It was either measles or mumps, I'm not really sure because his mother refused outright to take him to hospital. Trish didn't want him exposed to more germs there. She had started her training as a midwife, so she knew best, or so she told me. A little medicine soon brought his fever down. Together we nursed him through our fears and concerns for our son. It was this fear that assured me I loved him because I nearly lost him.

During the illness, with Andrew's burning temperature and constant bouts of sickness and clear signs of distress –

I stayed home to look after him. I placed cold flannels over his head, I fed him, I ignored the screams of discomfort and fever. After a week, he finally showed signs of improvement, and I remember how I felt about losing him at that time. Hoping he wouldn't die. I've never been much for religion, but even I got a bit scared during that week – afraid enough to pray for his recovery.

We both feared the worst when Andrew was ill, but without that period of care, I might never have loved him – or maybe I just needed that kick up the arse to actually feel it inside of me. I wasn't used to dealing with children, I only learnt then how to be a father.

Well, a father that cared anyway.

It's a shame that as he grew up, we never really got on well. I often put it down to a clash of personalities, but I am sorry for everything I didn't do for him. I have a son that only seemed to live in his bedroom. I cannot explain the reasons why he never made any friends, nor can I defend myself against the jibes I made at him for being lazy. I hope he knew that I only wanted what was best for him and to try to push him in the right direction.

I miss you, Andrew. I'm sorry for everything.

Nine

Tuesday, 20 December 2005

I really didn't want us to have a dog because of the extra responsibility. Thomas had convinced me it would be good for Andrew, but I think it was a distraction from not being successful in our attempts to give him a little brother or sister. We tried so hard, counting down the days until I was most likely to conceive with an ovulation calculator, yet every month my period had come like clockwork. It had been so frustrating for both us. I felt another failure in my life.

'We have to just let nature take its course,' Thomas said a few months earlier. 'Maybe one day it will just happen out of the blue. If it's not meant, then we should stop beating ourselves up over it.'

I felt so guilty, it hurt. Not being able to give Andrew a sibling because I was constantly stressed with the motherhood of one child. I thought that Thomas wanted more than I was able to give him. I was unsure if I really could go through with all the pressure again; all that worry and concern. It would mean going to hospital and all those reminders of my past. I didn't think that Thomas understood what was going on in my head.

There were times I convinced myself that I was pregnant; I was sure I felt it. I recognised the signs from when I was pregnant the first time around. Andrew was seven years old then, and he should have had a brother or sister to play with. Neither of us liked that he was an only child. All those times I was kidding myself I had finally conceived. Those missed periods were merely days late. I was worried Thomas might walk out on us.

I did stop getting my hopes up after two years of us continually trying. I agreed with Thomas that whatever would be would be, and would happen in time if it happened at all. I accepted I would get pregnant when nature decided.

I couldn't help but feel saddened by the whole pregnancy situation, and I knew Thomas wasn't able to understand my guilt, but, as a woman, not being able to carry a child when you so desperately wanted one hurt. The disappointment cut so deep it affected my mental state on many levels. I had to let go; nature would decide for me if it didn't find me guilty of my past transgressions. Thomas never understood my grief.

Maybe I had caused some internal damage to myself. Who knows?

I got angry with myself to the point of wishing I could have turned back the clock and changed so many decisions that I made in my life. I had regrets, but every day I lived with them. I put my worst fears to the back of mind, and I went about my day like the niggling didn't exist. When those niggles came back, I was haunted by them, but we all have a past, don't we?

I used to look at Andrew and see all the love he had for me as his mother. It was all worth it – I finally had that bond with my son. A mother's love, which I had craved.

It was just a shame about the bloody dog situation.

'All of Andrew's friends have dogs. Why can't we get one for him?' Thomas had asked me at the beginning of the year. 'I grew up with pets. Didn't you? It could help with Andrew's development.'

'I grew up with disappointment and a constant feeling of loneliness,' I replied. 'My mother was something of a different breed, if we are going to talk about dogs.'

He knew she was vile towards me at times, but sometimes I forgot that she was even dead. It was as though a massive piece of my past had died with her, but the mental scars still surfaced at times to remind me that I am my mother's daughter.

And so Andrew and that damn dog we bought earlier in the year were running around the front room. Andrew was excited for Christmas, and although he was seven, we weren't going to tell him the truth about Father Christmas until he was a bit older. We wanted to enjoy the magic for at least a few more years with him. The excitement he felt was magical. Christmas was for making memories. Memories I never got to make as a child myself.

'Are you skipping indoors again?' I shouted from the kitchen, peeling the potatoes for the dinner I was going to cook when Thomas came home. 'I've told you, Andrew, to take that rope outside, and while you're at it why don't you take Max out with you, he must need a wee by now?'

Andrew called the dog to follow him outside, I felt the chill of the cold winter air blast inside as the back door opened. It was the coldest winter we had had in a long while.

'Make sure you do your coat right up to your neck,' I shouted at Andrew. 'I don't want you catching a cold – and put your gloves on as well. You'll catch your death out there in this weather.'

At least he would occupy himself and the dog, leaving me to prepare dinner in peace. I wished Andrew's school hadn't introduced him to skipping. He skipped with that rope every day for weeks. It was just a phase, but he wanted to prove a point to his teacher that he could skip faster and better than anyone else. He got his competitive streak from me, but I recognised Thomas's stubborn attitude in him. I closed the back door, and I am sure they both played for an hour or more in the garden to burn off their energy. He was so adorable and excited to unwrap his Christmas presents.

Christmas for me as a child was a time of dread because of the arguments in our house. My mother would end up drunk and blame me for all the wrong decisions she had ever made in her life. I don't think she ever really wanted to have children, because I felt, growing up, that she resented me rather than loved me. I am so fortunate to have found what I have with Thomas; he changed my life forever. He turned my life around. I knew he was the man for me, the minute I set eyes on him – I wanted him.

He is MY man. No more regrets.

I glanced out of the window to watch Andrew skipping on the pathway. The dog was jumping up and down in time with the rope. Content that he was safe, I continued to peel the rest of the vegetables for our stew. I'm not big-headed about my cooking, but I know how to make a great stew, and it's so simple. Thomas loved it, so I always made sure I had two massive pans on the go. I got a great sense of enjoyment from cooking, watching my family eat the food that I had cooked from scratch for them. It was my way of giving back the happiness that they brought to me. It made me feel needed too.

When they cleared every last bit on their plates it gave me a feeling of achievement. Because Thomas was out all day driving his taxi, I appreciated everything he gave to us. All that lost time with his son, everything that he had given up – this was my way of paying him back. I worked part-time in a local charity shop in the village. It paid a small wage, but nowhere near what Thomas was bringing into the home. He allowed me to keep all of it as spending money for clothes and bits and bobs for Andrew, but I had been buying a lot of presents for Christmas from a range of catalogues on buy-now-pay-later, so most of my money went towards clearing those debts. Thomas was never aware how much my catalogue debts were: he was never home to get the reminder letters.

I wanted them both to have great Christmases.

Christmas for me growing up was anything but a time of excitement. I'd get excited as a child about the build up to Christmas without really knowing why. I think it was picking up on the excitement of the other children at my school, or the advertisements on the television. While other children would get board games, dolls, skipping ropes; all I ever received year in, year out would be toiletries and clothes. I'd never get anything that was fun or entertaining. Sometimes I was sure that the clothes were second hand.

I wanted Christmas with my own family to be perfect. I wanted Andrew to remember it as a magical time with gifts he would remember and a massive family dinner. I used to cook a feast for us all. My memories of Christmas dinner were always sat in silence in an atmosphere of my parents arguing with each other. I daren't speak to my mother because of all the tension she created, all angry and resentful towards my father. He would start drinking first thing in the morning and by the afternoon he would be abusive. I used to eat my dinner, then sit alone in my bedroom. My mother used to shout at me that I needed the toiletries because I was such a dirty, smelly little girl.

I believed her for so long.

The sound of Andrew's screaming was so loud I dropped the peeling knife to the floor in an instant. I ran to the back door. Anxious and shaking with worry I opened it to run towards him. The bitter cold air tingled against my face as I saw him running towards me, holding out his hand. Blood was dripping to the ground. I was shaking uncontrollably with fear.

How could I make this better?

I bent down and realised the dog had nipped at his hand. It was a small incision that should be washed and covered with a plaster.

Thank god I had a well-stocked first aid kit.

'Have you been tormenting that dog again?' I asked Andrew. 'I've told you before, haven't I, that he is not a toy. Next time it might be a whole lot worse, and you could need stitches. You would hate it if you couldn't carry on skipping now, wouldn't you?'

The thought of the dog biting him angered me. It could have been so much worse.

What if it bit his hand deeper, or even his face next time?

'I was only playing with him,' Andrew assured me. 'He just jumped up and snapped at my arm, he caught my hand. It really hurts, Mum.'

'Looking at it, you need to wash it and put a plaster on,' I replied. 'You go and get yourself inside, and we'll leave Max out in the garden as punishment. Show him that when he does bad things, he is to be separated from us. That'll teach the little beggar.'

'That's bad, Max,' I snapped at the dog, who was sat by the washing line, shaking. 'You're such a naughty dog. Bad, bad dog.'

'Bad dog,' Andrew responded, joining in, holding his hand out. 'Stay there and sit.'

We both walked inside and closed the back door, leaving Max to sit outside. With all that fur on him he couldn't have been that cold. If it were raining, I'd have brought him indoors, but he needed to be taught a lesson. Biting was very bad. I couldn't wait until I could tell Thomas. I knew something like this was bound to happen sooner or later.

Fucking annoying dog.

Andrew was sitting in the living room watching the children's cartoons on television when I put on the stew. The vegetables were boiling away nicely as I stared into a daydream watching them cook. I had done the dishes, put away the pots and pans I didn't need to use after all. Everything was organised in my head.

'Andrew?' I asked. 'Are you all right to check on the dog while I carry on with the housework upstairs?'

'Sure, Mummy,' he replied while I grabbed a cloth from the cupboard under the kitchen sink. 'I'll do it in a minute.'

'It's okay, I'll do it myself,' I muttered under my breath. 'You just sit and watch your programme, when I've been slaving away in that kitchen all afternoon.'

I thought I heard the back door open, but I could have been mistaken. The vegetables were simmering away noisily on the stove.

Having given the upstairs a freshen up with a couple of cloths, I decided that I would vacuum the next day because I had too much to do that night. I knew there was a good drama I wanted to watch when Andrew was in bed if I could get a look-in with the new television. We had just upgraded to a widescreen, and it was like a mini cinema screen for me to enjoy. I liked the escapism.

Thomas was due back soon, and the vegetables were simmering away beautifully with the stock. Dinner was almost ready. I took a moment to glance out of the window, and I could still see the dog lying down by the washing line. I heard the sound of the engine as Thomas's car pulled up at the front of the house. I was distracted, but eager to tell him that the dog he wanted so badly had bitten Andrew's hand.

He should know exactly what a bad dog he is now.

Thomas walked through the front door; I instantly noticed the mud on his boots before remembering I hadn't vacuumed. I had almost snapped at him for no reason again. He had argued with me that week about my temper, I was trying to think before I spoke.

'Why don't you go and look at your son's hand?' I asked him. 'Go and see what that dog has done. I told you it would happen, didn't I?'

'I've just come through the bloody front door; don't I even get a minute to unwind,' Thomas snapped at me. 'What has the fucking dog done now?'

He walked into the living room, and I heard him having a conversation with Andrew about the dog biting his hand. I knew we shouldn't have got that dog. I thought that Thomas would think I was taking out my anger for not having another child on Max, but if I had have gotten pregnant, would the baby have been safe around Max? I'd only have to turn my back for a second, and he could savage the life out a small child.

Thomas walked into the kitchen as I turned off the stove. Dinner was ready.

'Where is Max?' he asked. 'He usually greets me when I walk through the door. He's not in the living room.'

'He's outside, I had to show him how naughty he has been by leaving him out there while I made dinner.'

The disappointment on his face could not have been any clearer.

'Trish, it's fucking freezing outside.'

Thomas opened the back door and called Max, who didn't come running inside with excitement that Thomas was home, like he usually would. Thomas went outside to investigate.

Fucking close the door behind you, I remember thinking. You're letting the cold air inside.

I closed the back door behind him and started to serve up dinner in large white bowls. I opened the cupboard above the microwave to pull out a loaf of bread that would have been great for dipping in the juices from my homemade stew.

Thomas walked in without Max. He was crying.

'What's happened?' I asked. 'Thomas, what's wrong?'

He closed the kitchen door behind him.

'I don't want Andrew to see or hear this,' he responded, holding his chest as his breathing started to deepen. The tears streamed down his face. 'He's dead. He's outside by the washing line with a skipping rope around his neck. Trish, he's gone.'

I stopped still at this moment. My jaw dropped, but I made an effort to console my husband. He was so upset, the most upset I had seen him in years.

'Andrew was out there earlier with the skipping rope,' I replied, rubbing his shoulder. 'He must have got caught up in it in some kind of freak accident. I know you're upset, but we need to think about Andrew. We need to move Max, so Andrew doesn't find him.'

Thomas, unable to speak rubbed his eyes with his sleeve and nodded his head in agreement.

'We'll just tell him that Max ran away in the woods at the back of the garden,' I replied, thinking on my feet. 'He doesn't need to know about the skipping rope. This cannot ruin our Christmas; he's too excited.'

I threw my arms around Thomas as he cried softly on my shoulder. I rubbed his back as he released his grief. I struggled to find some compassion because I had never connected with the dog in the first place. My priority was towards Andrew and making sure he had the best Christmas. It's all about making memories at that time of the year.

That dog was nothing more than a nuisance.

Ten

The knock on the back door is so loud it makes me jump out of my skin. I am on the edge of my nerves as it is lately, but at least this afternoon I enjoyed some peace and silence, which encouraged me to rest my thoughts. Loud noises like this one send shockwaves through me, though. The tension in my body, combined with the knot in my stomach, creates a sense of dread as I walk to the back door. It's not easy to explain this feeling to anyone, but the way my body reacts to the slightest noises at times is like the sound has been enhanced ten-fold.

Goosebumps prickle across my arms as I begin to dread the disappointment before I even know for sure that it is not Andrew. I don't expect to see his face waiting at the door; surely, he would have tried to walk in, just as he walked out. However, I hold a little piece of hope in my heart that he knows I'm still here for him.

My last memory of Andrew is him walking out of that door – it haunts me enough every day that I could do without reminders. As I edge myself with anticipation to the kitchen, I cannot see the shadow of any person standing behind the glass. Outside it's misty, but there's still enough visibility to etch an impression of the caller. *Who is it? I wonder. Why the back door?*

Opening the door to reveal the quietness of the world, except for the crows calling in the distance, I stand there motionless. My breath fades into condensation that rises from my mouth as my jaw drops. The realisation of what I'm looking at sends blood rushing to my head. Spinning faster and faster, my consciousness edges into a state of confusion. It can't be. It absolutely can't be. *Is this Andrew's neck chain? The chain I gave him for his fifteenth birthday because it had initially* been a gift from my father for my eighteenth birthday.

Why, what, how, who?

'Andrew,' I call out, but there's no response. The neighbours must surely think I am deranged, but for that split second, I expect to see him.

'Andrew, are you there?'

My heart is pounding as I struggle to breathe, but short intermittent bursts that lead to gasps allow me to survive. All I can sense is shock as my eyes flood with water into sad tears. He isn't there; he will not walk back through the door.

What do I do next?

I pick up the chain and examine every inch of its curves. The gold glistens in my hand as the reflection from the sun starts to break through the clouds, but there seems to be no trace of anyone. Shaking profusely, I take the chain inside and place it on the kitchen table. It's definitely the same one; I haven't seen it in years. I know with all my heart that it is his chain because it was once my own. Each slightly damaged dent of the rugged gold curbs still haunts me with the memories it holds. Memories I have never really told anyone. I forgot until now.

This chain has opened the floodgates to what I had shifted to the back of my mind for many years. Needing to sit down, I clutch the chain in my hand, and I can't help but stare at it. My eyes are squinting to examine all the minute scratches, but it has to be the same one that was whipped against my back as a punishment. My mother was evil. Right now, I am trying to stop myself from having a drink. It's been a stressful few days, and I don't need things to get any worse.

Giving this gift to my son was a way of handing on something of value that joined us together in family history. With all the bad memories of the beatings and the jealousy my mother raged with when my father gave me this chain; I wanted to pass it on to Andrew as a token of my affection. I thought he might remember me and how much I love him when he wore it. I knew that Andrew would cherish it. Having come from a loving family, Andrew wore it with pride. For the first time, I was able to look at it with happiness, knowing that the pain I suffered because of it had turned into a memory I cherished.

The chain being left for me to notice it on the back doorstep is a mind game in itself. Did someone who knew Andrew find it – return it? Did Andrew drop it back because he knew it had sentimental value to me? What the fuck is going on here?

I really should call Thomas, but he's at work. When I've messaged him at work before he said that work is his only escape from the woes of this family. I don't want to trouble him with this. I need to work out why it was left here and who could have been responsible. I am tempted to call the police, but they will think I am stupid or not believe me because of the times I went crazy before. My memory is a blur at times too, so that doesn't help me much when I try to recollect. Sometimes everything just melds itself into one long period of craziness, loneliness and loss.

Then it hits me – someone knows something. For it to be left on the back doorstep is a homage to the very last step Andrew took from this house. The knock on the door was to alert my attention. I should call the police, but I can't bring myself to go through that mental stress again. They never believed me two years ago when I was sure I had seen Andrew in the shopping mall in town. I caught a glimpse of a young man I was convinced was him. He was wearing the same colour blue hoody that Andrew wore when he left, with his hair similarly swept to the side. He was about the same height and build and I thought it was clearly him, although the young man ran away from me as I bolted towards him.

'Andrew – it's me, your mother,' I screamed as I ran forward, pushing past those who got in my way. Like dominoes, they fell to the ground. In my head, I was hurtling towards my son, who I had not seen for over a year at that time. The excitement was uncontrollable as I believed he would turn to run towards me.

The young man, whoever he was, headed into a coffee shop and by the time I caught up to get inside, he was gone. I walked past their customers like a wild animal as I was screaming for my son. I can't forget the look on some people's faces. I knew they thought I was mad.

'I saw him, I definitely saw him,' I yelled. 'Andrew, I know you're in here.'

Andrew never came, and I was comforted yet hurried out of the store by a young female assistant who assured me no one of that description had come inside. I thought she was lying and ran towards the toilets despite her best attempts to walk me to the door again. I knocked on the door, all the while screaming his name. I turned to see a shop full of faces gawping at me. The look in their eyes was haunting, with signs of concern that was either for their safety or my own. Andrew never appeared, and two policemen came to question me a few minutes later.

Having explained the situation again to the officers, who knew my story after I gave them my full name, I saw the wry smile on one of their faces. It was twenty minutes before I was able to go home; I'd been sitting on a granite bench surrounded by a flurry of advertisements and a horde of shoppers. The police reassured me they would analyse CCTV footage and if it was conclusive then they would contact me immediately. A couple of days later an officer knocked on my front door to inform me they were unable to see close-up footage of the man I believed to be Andrew and that the angles weren't decent enough to be able to tell if he had gone into the coffee shop or not.

I know what I saw; it was real to me. The way he walked, the way he ran, and even the way he was dressed. I know my own son, or at least I think I did until he vanished. I ended that night by finishing a bottle of cheap vodka to blur out the sadness. Andrew felt like he was in touching distance. If only I had run quicker, if I had just reacted sooner, I might have been close, and been sure it was definitely him. I still believe it was him, but Thomas thinks that the police would have known if it was. There was another row about my feelings that night.

I cannot remember much after that day, but I visited the shopping centre on the same day of the week, at the same time, in case Andrew had made regular visits to the mall. I never bothered to tell Thomas; he would have thought I was losing it altogether back then. Now, though, it is as though he doesn't care as much. I see him tell me things I think he says for the benefit of keeping me in high spirits. Talking of which, I know I must cut back on the drinking, but it has become a personal thing that keeps me connected to Andrew.

Me, my vodka or rum and the memories soon come flooding back. Little things I think I have forgotten come back to the forefront when I am tipsy or flat-out drunk. It is as though the alcohol is awakening something from the back of my brain to help me remember when we were happy as a complete family unit.

I take another look outside just to make sure that no one is nearby. Whoever put that chain on my doorstep might come back again.

Maybe they can't face me? Perhaps it's a sign?

I don't see anyone as I walk up and down the length of the garden. I have peered over the fence to see an empty field with nothing but the sound of the wind blowing through the trees in the distance, leaves rustling as autumn fast approaches.

I still have the chain in my hand. The bad memories are in one corner of my mind – my mother beat me for not being decent enough to have received such a gift from my father. Yet in the other corner, I have the look on my son's face as I handed him something that I treasured from my father, which he could look after for the rest of his life. A chain that linked us together from one generation to another. Despite my father beating me at times, this chain was the only real gift he ever gave me. I take it symbolically that it was a gift as a way of apology. That deep down he loved me really.

After I pour myself a vodka to calm my nerves, I need to decide whether I should call Thomas or the police. My head is telling me to call the police, who might be out here like a shot, but I'm not sure what use they would be. They could take prints from the chain, but I have had my hands all over it. My heart is telling me to call Thomas and let him know that, somehow, Andrew's chain has landed back in my hands.

Holding the phone to my ear, I can feel the tears in my eyes. I sip from the glass before placing it on the table.

'Thomas – it's me. Call me back when you get this message. A necklace, it's Andrew's necklace. I can't. I just… erm… can't believe it. I don't know what, or how, I just know it appeared. There was a knock. I think there was a knock. Call me. Please call me back soon. Someone knows. I am *telling* you that someone knows.'

There, I've done it.

Taking deep breaths, I sit and stare at the chain for the fiftieth time. Sipping the vodka some more I decide to just let it take me into its world. I sip and pour another glass before the pain starts to fade. I have a couple of painkillers to shift the niggling tingle across my forehead.

Am I one step closer to finding Andrew?

Eleven

Thomas Mullner – Now

Monday, 10 September 2018

Trish is too agitated on the phone. So agitated that something must have happened to her. It seems as though she can hardly breathe. This sets me off into a panic, but there is little I can do when I am driving.

What might be a vodka-induced bout of nerves could also be another anxiety attack. It is hard for me to tell the difference anymore as the fine line between sober and hysterical can sometimes be blurred. All I keep hearing is 'necklace'. Something about an old necklace has rattled her. Far too many times now over the last few years, I have dropped what I am doing to run back home.

Someone knows, she tells me.

My life now seems to be a constant state of ensuring my wife is mentally stable enough for me to leave the house. The last three years has revolved around her so much that I am beginning to feel forgotten about. Little things such as, how are you feeling today? Are you okay? I am not sure that she even cares anymore about what is going on inside my head, but for the sake of keeping the peace, I soldier on with my thoughts.

Every year Trish is convinced that someone, some-where knows something, but no one has ever come forward. The fear and the worry have taken their toll on her mental state over the past few years and I fear it is ruining our marriage. I don't know what to do, and nothing I say can make the circumstances any better.

How do you help someone who doesn't seem to be able to help themselves?

Sometimes she doesn't respond to my text messages, which grates on me. Not only have I lost a son, but my wife is fading from me faster than I could ever imagine. I love her, yet I am not sure if I am still in love with her. I believe that my life without her would be worry-free, and a fresh new start seems like bliss – yet I convince myself at other times I cannot let go of the woman I once knew.

Trish used to be more loving, kinder with words too, and a beautiful smiling woman who just got on with everyday life. Before she got pregnant, we used to have so much fun. I would take her on dates. But then during the pregnancy with Andrew, she used to get jealous if I ever talked to women. She would convince herself that I was about to leave her – I blamed the hormones. That was the period when the arguments first started in our lives.

I miss the times when we felt normal because every-where that I seem to travel now in this village, I am only that father who had a son who vanished. It's like all eyes are on me when I am out and about. I never really wanted to live in Elmton, this was Trish's choice of locality. There's very little to do here other than a handful of local shops, a village pub, parks and long area of woodland behind our house. Plymouth city centre is around five miles away, so thankfully because I drive, we have the option to go into town if we want to do something different, not that we ever really take advantage of it.

I'm not originally from Plymouth, but I had cousins I used to visit in the city centre on my mother's side of the family. My father was a fruit farmer in Somerset before he retired. I tried to convince Trish that we should stay closer to my family if she wanted a fresh start, but she wanted to settle down in this village because Plymouth is all she knows. I never really understood why leaving Plymouth was not an option when she was pregnant, especially since she had complained about wanting to move away. My mother and father were going to pay for our wedding, but we took the money and used it as a house deposit. I still wish at times that we had moved elsewhere.

When I think back about getting married, I sometimes wonder if I rushed into it too soon. I was too swept away with the idea of building my own family and doing Trish proud. I knew she wanted commitment from me, but if she hadn't had been pregnant, I might have waited a few more years.

On our actual wedding day though, I knew I had made the right decision. It might have all been done on the cheap in a dingy little registry office, but when the woman I loved walked down that aisle holding on to her bump – I felt responsible. I had grown up in that moment, I had become a man. With a wife and child to support, I couldn't have been prouder.

All those years ago, when Trish and I first met, I would have done anything for her. You name it, I'd have done it. The broken woman she is today is dragging us both downhill so fast that I am not sure she'll ever recover. She needs to get a grip on the situation and accept that he is gone. I don't believe she was this down on herself when her parents died in a car accident. I knew they treated her like shit, and naturally she was upset and went through the grieving process, but I stood by her and said I'd be there for her through anything. Marriage is not just about love, but a commitment to each other.

I wish she would consider my feelings more.

There are days I feel numb. So numb that I know I am walking through the day almost carefree, but everything around me is moving at a much faster pace. I am holding it together so that I do not allow the heavy thoughts of recent years to stop me from living altogether. I think that if it wasn't for Trish needing constant reassurance and support from me, I too would have cracked under the strain and become a shadow of my former self.

Thankfully work does keep me occupied and I can make my own hours. Although I keep my feelings hidden, as I try to keep my mind focused on work to carry on with my day, but there are times when the emotions crack. Occasionally I want to have a new start with or without her. I know she will never allow us to sell the house and move on because it is the last location Andrew knew of our whereabouts. It's his family home, but something needs to change. Trish and I are so far apart now we might as well be on different planets. I know I am going to have to tell her how I feel if she doesn't improve soon.

I had better rush back after this fare.

Looking in the rear-view mirror, I admire a regular fare, an attractive woman called Rachael. She would look like a movie star if she wasn't so rough around the edges, but she looks great. I always see her wearing short dresses with her blonde hair tied up on her head, while her sunglasses are on no matter what the weather. I have noticed those breasts of hers, I think they're possibly implants, but I try not to stare too hard. I don't want to come across as rude.

I have picked Rachael up a handful of times over the last few months, and we have both spoken quite openly about our lives, because that's how you pass the time in cabs. It's just the little things that include her holiday plans, her work, my shopping trips out, how I met my wife, random television chit-chat – you know the sort of programmes that allow us to hate reality contestants, but she seems so friendly. Friendly enough to get to know better if I dare to ask.

I haven't spotted a wedding ring on Rachael's finger, and she seems to take an interest in me whenever we meet like this. She is always asking me questions, but her voice is so soft I sometimes struggle to hear her. I'm confident she is single, and she's never mentioned any kids of her own even though I end up talking about Andrew every single time we meet. I don't know her well enough to become good friends – not yet.

Trish would hate me being friends with her.

I have never cheated on my wife, but the idea of the escapism attracts me to it. I am not convinced I have the courage; and I love Patricia too much. Before we were married, I had the odd fling here or there on drunken nights out with university friends, but nothing memorable. She is hurting enough already. I just wish for an escape some days. I am not happy at home, in my marriage, and I see how everyone else around me is simply living their lives. I miss those days of normality.

Rachael sometimes relies on my cab service on a Monday after work. She says the buses don't run very regularly on the other side of Plymouth, which I can believe – the traffic is terrible out that way near the hospital. And she requests me by name so I must be doing something right. I don't mind because those five- to ten-minute conversations help me forget for a short while that I am Thomas Mullner, the guy who had that son who vanished. The guy whose face was in all of the local papers asking for help in finding my lost son. The very guy whose wife is beginning to lose herself in vodka-induced rages. The man who felt like life had dealt him a cruel hand; the man who once had a happy family.

I must remember to stay strong.

Being a taxi driver is not just about sitting in a vehicle and transporting passengers from one location to another. It requires a lot of systematic thinking and good timing, but unfortunately it wasn't the answer to a wealthy, comfortable life like I once thought it would be. I get a sense of freedom from my work – although I still have plenty of rules to follow even though I haven't a manager on my back.

I haven't always been a people person, but the job kicks you into shape pretty sharply. I enjoy being self-employed, but I begrudge paying the weekly fees to the company for the use of their fare calculating equipment. Without them, I'd have less work. Without work, I'd go insane or maybe Trish and I would both end up doing something else like killing each other.

I am worried about that phone call; however, I can't get near her until I've dropped Rachael back home. She's done a night shift at the hospital – like Trish used to when she was training to be a midwife. It never really worked out, she left due to work-related stress. I can't really remember the full story now since it's been twenty years, but she was being bullied by her colleagues, or there was a fallout with her management.

Thinking about Trish's training days at the hospital, I never got to meet her colleagues all those years ago. Friends to her were just acquaintances or people she had no choice but to talk to out of politeness. She said her colleagues bullied her in training for not learning the requirements of the role as quickly as the others. I couldn't believe at first that people could be so cruel to her. By the end of it, she was coming home in tears practically every night, which drove me to hell and back. I always supported her, even back then. I told her she should quit and do something else. It was hard for her, but after Andrew was born, she finally gave it up to concentrate on becoming a full-time mother. A lot of policies have changed since then, I imagine. You wouldn't get away with harassment in the workplace in this day and age.

Maybe that's why Andrew struggled to make friends; he took after his mother?

It was only in the late nineties, when she was at home all day with Andrew, that I realised she was as depressed as she has been the last few years. The post-natal depression was self-diagnosed but kept hidden from the doctors because she always protested against taking medication – she wouldn't even swallow a painkiller for a headache. Now she would take a pill for anything; we have hundreds of them piling up in the cupboards.

The internet provided a wealth of information for her. Trish sought comfort from chat rooms and forums to unload her anxiety issues about being a parent. Neither of us is great with technology, but we had a computer and taught ourselves how to use an internet browser.

All I had to do when Andrew was younger was go to work and back, take care of the household bills and repeat the process each day. I enjoyed those routines because I felt like I was contributing to the family I could call my own. We struggled a bit for money in those times, with the house expenses and a newborn child, but we got by enough to afford the odd takeaway as a treat every couple of weeks.

I am meant to be her rock.

In times of hardship, anger, pain and distress, Trish always said I was her rock. She'd be lost without me.

I should be home in less than half an hour now. Rachael is sitting in the back seat, staring out of the window as the drops of rain trickle down the windows with the wind. It's wrong that I admire her short skirt and blouse that fits tightly against her breasts. My mind wanders, but I need a break from the constant worry. I've lost Andrew already – I cannot lose my wife.

My life needs to change, we both need to change. I need to convince Trish we both have to move on with our lives. It's the only way we can get through this dark patch and begin to rebuild our sanity. We need to move to a new house too. Maybe it is time to rebuild our lives again from scratch. I have all of these great ideas, but the hard-hitting reality is that Trish doesn't want to do anything other than sit in the house every day waiting for Andrew to come home.

Twelve

Thomas must be home. Either that or the phantom door knocker has returned with some more of Andrew's belongings. Thomas isn't going to be happy to see me drunk like this. No doubt we'll have another row when he's taken his shoes off.

The door is unlocking and I can hear him faffing about with his bag and jacket, which makes that crinkle sound like static when you move around in it.

'Thomas, is that you?'

I know full well it must be since he is the only one aside from myself who has a key. He hasn't spoken a word yet, but he's gone through to the kitchen.

The vodka has been demolished except for a few shots at the bottom, and I can hardly blame anyone except myself. I've gone past that point where the burn of alcohol makes you shake your face with every neat sip. It slips down smoothly – this time without adding lemonade. My legs are like jelly and I can hardly stand up. I tried earlier, but somehow my feet shuffle along the carpet with my legs a few seconds behind them. My head is pounding, and my tears have dried to salty dust on the top of my lip. I have taken a couple of painkillers to shift the headache, but it will not budge.

This beautiful necklace. I almost forgot how this chain linked us both together.

'Thomas, come through to the living room. What are you doing?'

I hear the clunk of the kitchen cupboards; he is likely looking for something to snack on. He hasn't even shown his face in here yet. You would think I'd be his first priority when he knows I am struggling with today's events. Someone knows where my Andrew is. They must know – how did they obtain the necklace?

Andrew would have walked right in with it.

The kitchen taps – he's washing his hands.

'Thomas, for fuck's sake get in here. I need you!'

Here he is at last.

'Someone knows where our son is. Look, look at this – his necklace. It just appeared on the doorstep. I think there was some kind of knock at the door. I rushed, well, ran to the door, but nobody was around. It's all a bit of a blur now. Thomas, why are you looking at me like that? Someone knows – look, *someone* knows something.'

'Because you're drunk. Because I've barely been at work half a day and already I have you shouting down the phone at me. You're making me think you're in danger – or worse – drinking yourself to fucking death.'

I look at Thomas in a state of confusion.

'What is wrong with you, woman? I don't know how much more I can take of this. You are always thinking that someone knows something or other. Are you sure that's even his necklace? Maybe it was one of your own that you accidentally dropped? Look at you. You're pissed, aren't you?'

I can't believe he is shouting at me.

'I heard a knock, and then I saw this necklace on the doorstep. It was all a bit quick, I think. I can't quite remember. No one was there when I opened the door, but Andrew's necklace was. The necklace I gave him for his birthday. The necklace that was my father's. The fucking necklace my mother punched me over is fucking here! You know my history with this necklace. Look at it. Just look at my hands. They're shaking. Shaking because no one understands me. I thought it was Andrew.'

Hold on, did he really just ask what is wrong with me?

'How dare you ask me what is wrong. You know what is wrong – you know our son is missing. You know our boy is out there somewhere, and we have no idea where the hell he is. He could be dead for all we know.'

'Your drinking is becoming a burden on our marriage. Trish – I still love you. I know you've had hard times, but it's been three years. Three years since he left us. We can't stop living our lives; it's becoming unhealthy. I am trying to work and be strong for the both of us, but your drinking needs to stop. It's as if I don't even know you anymore. I'm sorry that you just can't help yourself. You need to move on and try to get back to a normal routine. Find a job at least. Something to get you out of this house. It's turned into a fucking prison.'

How dare he turn this all around on me? I always knew he never really cared enough about me. Inside I want to scream, but I am shaking with fear of losing my mind. I'm too drunk, I know, but I can feel the rage burning inside me.

'How can I find a fucking job in this state? You expect me to just forget about him – he vanished. Just vanished. I can't remember everything and it's driving me up the wall. I am fast forgetting other things too. I can't stop thinking about our son. Why. Thomas, why?'

He's staring at me – this moment's pause is at least allowing me to try to calm down.

'We've been through this before, and you already know how I feel. I will always love and miss Andrew, but I accept he has gone. I know you have taken it the hardest, but when he walked out – you were the last person to see him. You can't remember anything else of that day other than that?'

'Nothing – everything about that period of time has all merged into one. It has stopped me from focusing on anything else. My mind sticks to that last moment when he left. The last time I saw his face. I was just sat at the table, and I let him go. I let him go and I feel like it's all my fault.'

'I think you've had enough vodka for today. This shit really doesn't help you, and it triggers an aggressive streak in you I don't like. That same kind of aggression you had when you were younger. Do you remember when you struggled to cope when we first had Andrew? It's that kind of aggression, and it scares me, love.'

'Get rid of it for me then – please. I agree it's not helping today, but there have been times I can drift off drunk with happy thoughts. Memories of his childhood come back to me and…'

'You need to get some rest. Let me take another look at the necklace. Maybe we should call the police and let them analyse it. If his DNA is on it, we'll know for sure if it's Andrew's or not won't we?'

I can't go through this again. I can't have that stress and strain. The questioning for hours is not going to bring him back.

'No – I can't go through the ordeal of the police coming round here. They already think I'm crazy. You think I'm crazy too, by the look on your face. They'll be all over the place and asking me all kinds of questions which still won't bring Andrew back.'

'But they might see something on a camera somewhere. Maybe the police will find whoever left it, if you're absolutely sure you didn't find it somewhere – like Andrew's bedroom, for instance, since you sit in it all day sometimes?'

'I don't fucking know why I bother sometimes. I have told you that it was left after someone knocked on the door. I might have a terrible memory, but I haven't lost my fucking marbles completely. I don't want the police involved just yet. Maybe whoever sent this will come back with something else. I am convinced that someone knows where he is. Maybe it's even Andrew. Please, I am begging you – do not get the police involved.'

Why is he smirking at me?

'I bet you anything that you can't even stand up right now. In all seriousness, Trish, and I am not joking when I say this: if you don't get a grip, you will become more unstable. Do you think if Andrew came back that he would want to come home to see you looking like a drunken mess?'

'Fuck off, you inconsiderate, cold-hearted bastard.'

He'll get full-pelt rage in a minute if he doesn't just fuck off back to work. He knows full well that I drink to spare me my depressed thoughts around this time of year.

'Why don't you fuck off yourself, you self-absorbed, selfish mare.'

He slams the door behind him, which makes me jump out of my skin. I've been on the edge of my nerves for days. No consideration, that man – just a useless bastard at times who doesn't consider that I relive the horror of my loss. Our loss, our son. Andrew.

Someone knows something.

'Thomas – get back here you selfish fucking bastard.'

'What?'

I can hear the thudding of his footsteps coupled with the rustle of a carrier bag. *He's up to something out there – he's coming back.*

'I don't know how much more of you I can take right now, to be honest. I have spent hours indoors worrying about you and treading on eggshells when I'm in the house. When I'm out and about in my taxi, I spend hours worrying about your safety because I never know how much booze you're necking back. It's not healthy – this endless pit of misery you've sunken into. The booze is not helping you; it has to stop.'

'The drink gets me through it. I was all right today until that knock on the door. You're making me angry, and I just don't want to go back to *that* place again.'

'I'll just fuck off back to work, and we'll talk later. Sit in your pit with your vodkas. Just think about what you're doing. Your memory is all to shit, Trish. I need you to be sure about the necklace because I think we should call the police.'

'I SAID NO POLICE!'

How many times do I have to tell him I can't have the police involved in this? I need to know who delivered this necklace to me. Someone knows something about Andrew.

Thirteen

Thomas Mullner – Now

Tuesday, 11 September 2018

I've calmed down since the argument I had yesterday afternoon with Trish, who must be bordering on the realms of alcoholism. Don't ask me why Trish continually refuses to go to the police with the necklace; her behaviour at the moment isn't rational. I am sick and tired of feeling as though I am treading on eggshells. This is why I snapped yesterday and went all guns blazing, my tension levels reached boiling point. Sometimes, it is easier to let her have her way because of the grief I will get later on, or even a hard hit in the face.

Her drinking has increased to almost a litre of vodka a day this past week, but her mind and her memory loss are what convinces me the necklace was probably found in some old drawer. I am convinced she doesn't know that I am aware of the volumes she had been consuming all these years. I have tried to suggest some professional help, yet she just tenses at this idea and refuses to go back to the doctor for support.

She promised me she would stop drinking or at least try to give it up.

The stress is intense enough for her to wade through the day without realising her actions. At the moment, my concern is for her own safety. Our relationship is crumbling, but I love her enough to try to make it work again. I meant every single one of my vows. I have always said that, and I refuse to be a failure.

She'll pull herself out of this misery eventually, surely?

Trish has been moving bits and bobs about continually over the last few months. In one breath trying to move forward and in the other unable to let go. Simple things like a pair of Andrew's socks or an old chocolate wrapper under his bed. Little memories chain her to the past. Refusing to accept he has gone is hurting us both – although I am beginning to wonder what more there was to that day leading up to his disappearance. As this week goes on, I am starting to have my doubts. At times, things don't make much sense. It's like I am alive in my own nightmare, unable to wake up to a better reality. I hate myself for thinking that Andrew might have had the right idea walking away from us both. I am Trish's husband, and I have to try and fix our marriage.

Is she hiding something from me; or is the strain she's putting on our marriage causing these doubts?

She slept like a baby last night. For the first time in over a week, she didn't wake me in the night talking in her sleep. There are times I turn over and ignore her, but something she said has stuck in my mind. I keep hearing those few words over and over like a radio in my head that refuses to stop.

'I'm sorry, Andrew. I didn't mean to hurt you.'

I heard her say it quietly under her breath. I thought I had dreamt it or imagined it, but no – I absolutely know what she said. It was as clear as anything. Softly spoken with sincerity. I'll question her about it later. I'm not in the mood for another argument because I'll just snap and leave the house. There is a prominent link to the necklace and her conscience. She seems to be afraid of something too; that concerns me. I hate all the not knowing. I hate not having answers, but I despise myself mostly for not being there when it mattered. I wonder if I had been a better husband in the past, would it have changed our circumstances today?

What's done is done.

That hangover she'll be nursing will have put her in a foul mood this morning. I was able to take a walk to the village shop to buy a few things to see us both through another couple of days. I can't get her to go into a supermarket anymore. The anxiety she experiences sends her dizzy; the crowds of people heading around in different directions make her want to scream. Trish tells me it's like a beast trying to escape from within her. The people anger her. I hear how different things anger her more and more lately. I'm not sure what doesn't anger her nowadays. She has always had a temper on her, but I find that she's unpredictable. I daren't even speak some nights. Actually, we do not talk at all much anymore.

The necklace has intrigued me. I do remember it and have definitely seen Andrew wearing it, but I have no idea how it got there. Surely Andrew wouldn't have come back home to leave a necklace on the doorstep? In fact, when I think about it, I know that she kept some jewellery that belonged to her parents after their deaths. I am sure that Trish might have had other similar necklaces over the years. Maybe it fell out of her pocket? Her memory is not like it used to be. I blame it on the stress and anxiety she is suffering.

She hasn't mentioned the beatings from her evil mother in a while until today. That bitch hated me; I'm sure she wanted me dead. If she hadn't died herself, I know she would have always been in the background criticising everything Trish and I did in our lives. If there ever was a woman who was as cold as ice with not an emotional bone in her body, it was her.

I have more memories of Andrew locked in his room on his computer games or continuously on the internet looking at new games releases than I do of anything else. He had an interest in wanting to create websites once, and other times he wanted to sell timeshares abroad. I had even helped him look at courses, but he was not motivated enough. He was lazy, and I blamed his behaviours on the gaming because I am convinced that he was up most nights into the early hours playing all kinds of war games. His mood changed after he played them – he would be timid one day, but angry on other days. You wouldn't dare speak to him as he would snap your head off in a gaming-induced rage.

'It's not good for you,' I used to tell him. 'You should focus on your college studies more. Or get out there and have some fun, make some friends.'

I realise now that he is no longer around that I was always telling him off for unnecessary things. I never went to school plays; I hardly ever went to parents' evenings at school. He annoyed me, there's no denying that, but life without him is not how I could ever have imagined. What he did makes me angry, but I cannot tell Trish that. She will just have another go at me if I tell her anything that isn't all about positivity and love around him. He played me for a fool.

Maybe he hated me for coming down on him hard some days?

That necklace has also reminded me of a time we took a caravan holiday to Wales. It's just come back to me. We went away for the weekend to a small family-friendly park in the summer. This was only a few weeks short of Andrew's sixteenth birthday. He never really wanted to come with us, but Trish was adamant we were all going to have some quality family time. Suggesting we should all go for long walks, have a picnic in the forest, browse the local shops – she was convinced spending more time together would bring us closer together as a family. There was an incident with the necklace. He'd hurt himself quite severely to my knowledge, but I didn't think much of it at the time because it was a freak accident due to Andrew's carelessness. I was worried, but thought he'd be more careful in future.

Thinking back, the marks around his neck looked sore. I came back from going to the on-site supermarket, and Andrew was standing there in the living room in tears. It wasn't often I saw him cry, but Trish had her arms wrapped around him as any caring mother would have. Andrew had bent down to swill his mouth with some water after cleaning his teeth in the bathroom, and the necklace had been caught up in the curved taps as he stood up. I remember him sobbing his eyes out as he described to me how it nearly choked him. The fear in his eyes is starting to flood back to me. That poor lad was petrified that day.

'Just learn to be more careful in future,' I remember Trish yelling at him, fraught with fear. 'Think about what you're doing.'

She rarely shouted at him in front of me. I was always the bad cop. He would still run to his mother after I had yelled when he was a young lad, knowing that she would cave in to his demands. Never mind that it undermined my authority, Trish could never resist his cute little face, she'd tell me.

After he told me that he'd nearly hanged himself with the necklace, he stayed in his room for most of the night. That was nothing new and I was used to not seeing much of him. Andrew liked his own company. I am wondering if he tried to kill himself that day.

Did Trish find him? Did she shout at him, does she know more than she let on?

Something just doesn't seem quite right because this was about a year or so before he left. Trish must know more than she's telling me. Possibly more than she has informed the police. Maybe I'm just foolish. She loves him; we both love him. Trish is in pieces right now.

I need to stop doubting her: it's not healthy.

My life has changed since Andrew's disappearance, but I think Trish has changed more. She's lost herself, but a mother's love is ultimately a sacrifice you see as a gift. She once said to me that she'd kill for him and even die for him. There have been times over the years I certainly believed that. Her temper is something that fires up when you least expect it. When she turns, that temper turns her for the worse.

She is starting to scare me, but I need to make her see sense.

I need to convince her to seek medical help.

Fourteen

Andrew and Patricia Mullner – Then

Saturday, 23 August 2014

We hardly ever went away as a family, but that summer bank holiday weekend, Thomas surprised Andrew and me with a weekend break to Wales. My constant complaining that we never spent any quality time together had encouraged him to book a caravan trip for all of us about five miles west of Swansea. I knew it was meant to be a surprise, but I had to applaud my manipulation skills. I'd planted the seeds in his mind, and I'd watched them grow. When he sat us down in the living room and said to pack our bags, I threw my arms around him.

'We all need this time together,' I said. 'We aren't communicating well as a family. Something's changed. This break will do us good.'

Andrew stood up and stormed up the stairs back to his bedroom. He was spending nearly all of his time in his room except for when his dinner was ready. Thomas suggested we took him to see a doctor. I couldn't have that.

'Certainly not,' I responded forcefully. 'We aren't taking him anywhere. It's his age: he's almost sixteen, everyone has a bad attitude at this age. Don't you remember being a teenager?'

Andrew seemed to have lost contact with his friends, and I worried that he had no interests.

'What happened between him and Katrina?' Thomas asked. My eyes rolled as I was sick of hearing that bitch's name in my house. 'I haven't seen her in a while. Are they still together?'

'That evil bitch is out of his life now,' I replied, my annoyance at a peak. 'She was trying to come between my son and me. He is far too young for a serious girlfriend like her; it could lead to all sorts. She's a tramp. Trust me, she is no good for our son.'

'Trish, come on, they're only kids.' Thomas always just brushed everything off without seeing the bigger picture.

'What if she wants his baby? What if she takes him away from us? What damage can she cause to our family?' I asked, staring him in the eyes. 'That manipulating little bitch hates me. I had a word with her, and he hasn't seen her since. I can take care of my Andrew. I told her, he doesn't need you.'

'He needs to do something with his life,' Thomas had said in worry. 'I'm scared he can't make his own choices. I know he isn't doing well at school, but at this age, he should be thinking about what to do as a career.'

'Our little getaway will do us all some good,' I replied, calming down. 'We'll have a great time, and maybe we will feel refreshed, and I'll have a proper talk with him when we are back.'

Later on, in the evening, Andrew had asked if he could stay at home alone while his father and I went for the weekend instead.

'Certainly not. Don't be so rude to your father,' I said. 'Look at the effort he went to to make sure this was a surprise, and you've already heard me say we need to do more together as a family. Try to be respectful, Andrew.'

I regretted shouting at him as he walked up the stairs disobeying my request to sit down at the table and hear me out.

'Trish, it's not healthy. All that time he spends up there. I feel useless because I am at work all the time to pay for this fucking house,' Thomas said. 'You don't tell me anything he does or doesn't do. I don't want our son to turn out like us; I want better for him.'

We argued for over two hours that night. I thought that Thomas was starting to resent leaving university to find a job that paid the bills and allowed us to live as an average family. I don't associate success with wealth. I had my husband; I had my son. I had everything I had always wanted. Money certainly doesn't buy me happiness, but without Thomas, I am nothing. Without Andrew – it would have all been for nothing.

The drive up to Swansea from Plymouth had taken us five hours, after stopping for a thirty-minute break and a little detour when we got lost down some winding lanes. The scenic rolling green hills as the sunrays streamed down from the clouds were mesmerising. Devon is spectacular in parts, but Wales was breathtaking. Everything around me looked like it could have been from a different planet. I was struggling to understand the strong local accents. Welsh people must have thought I was stupid with my constant vague expression. I muddled through it.

Andrew hadn't spoken to me for most of that day. For the whole drive, I don't think we even heard him talk to us. He just sat in the back seat with his earphones in, playing on some random game on his mobile phone. I spotted that he was wearing the necklace I'd given him. I had a few moments' thought for my father who gave me that very chain.

I don't half miss you, Dad. I still forgive you.

I knew that Andrew would be challenging for the whole weekend, but for the sake of my sanity, I tried to ignore his behaviour. I wouldn't ever have dared to speak to my mother in the manner that he spoke to me at times; she would have given me a hard slap, or worse depending on her mood swings.

We arrived at the holiday park earlier than the late afternoon check-in time on our booking confirmation: we'd set off from Plymouth earlier than we'd planned, to allow for traffic problems and getting lost, but we still arrived early. The young man on reception was doing his best to ensure we noticed his excellent customer service skills, but that talk doesn't wash with me. I knew he wouldn't care about what I thought or felt personally – and why should he have to. He was paid to stand there all day handing out keys and welcome packs to guests.

Who would enjoy that job?

'Have you ever been to our brand of holiday parks before?' he asked while I judged that he could barely even shave yet. 'If not, then I would like to take this opportunity to welcome you. Here is your key, and your location is marked on this map. Have a great stay.'

Thomas and I cringed. We laughed about it for a few minutes as we walked to our caravan. Andrew walked behind us holding his travel case, expressionless with his earphones still plugged firmly in both ears. He could have at least made more of an effort. I wanted this weekend to be filled with memories. Great memories to cherish as a family together.

When we walked through the caravan doors, we couldn't believe our eyes. Even Andrew raised an eyebrow, so I knew it must have been good. This was nothing short of luxury. I walked around the caravan from room to room, feeling that warmth inside me because I felt instantly at home. It was modern, but cosy. Every room had plush interiors and there was even a fully fitted modern kitchen. I imagined the three of us all sat around the fire watching television after lovely days out or playing board games; something I never got to do as a child that I wanted to experience with Andrew. I wanted this to be a trip that brought us closer together. I wanted us to do more as a family, we needed this break away. I needed an escape from Plymouth.

Thomas walked around the caravan for a few minutes, checking that all the drawers were empty. I was more shocked to see that all of the beds had been made up for us before we arrived. That saved us a job I was dreading that evening. The kitchen was tiny and just off the lounge area, but adequate for making small meals. I could imagine getting stressed out cooking with limited space, and the refrigerator didn't seem big enough to hold a substantial amount. It's just for the weekend, I reminded myself. It's my only complaint.

'While you both settle in and unpack your cases, I'll head off to find the shop. We need to get some milk and a few other bits.' Thomas asked, 'Anybody want anything? I'll only be a few minutes.'

Andrew shook his head while I paused for a moment's thought.

'Don't forget to get some washing-up liquid and some cleaning products, oh and toothpaste,' I replied, thinking on the spot. I was unusually disorganised that day. 'I think I forgot to pack ours.'

'Trust you to think of all the domestic things,' Thomas had joked. 'You'll probably complain I haven't bought anything good enough anyway.'

We laughed as he then left the caravan. Andrew finally took out his earplugs. It was a perfect opportunity for me to try to win Andrew round to the idea of joining his father and me on long country walks, we could visit some sights – and even take turns cooking the dinner. I took one look at his face and knew he didn't want any part of it. It saddened me, my own son looking so dismissive when I wanted this to be a break away when we could share some quality time together.

'Andrew, what is your problem?' I asked. 'Can you at least try to make an effort. If not for me, for your father?'

'Nobody cares,' Andrew replied. 'Dad is always going on at me to do more. You're always telling me what to do. I am sick of it, Mum. I miss Katrina. I really like her a lot. She doesn't talk to me anymore.'

'Don't make me tell you again, because I have told you already. You're better off without her. She won't be back, so you'd better get fucking used to not seeing her. I mean it, Andrew.'

'What did you do to her?' he yelled at me. 'What have you done to her?'

'Nothing,' I snapped back. 'Just leave it at that, do you hear me? Don't make me angry. You're not to go near her.'

'I know you must have had words with Katrina, Mum. I know it was you who scared her away.'

The adrenaline pumped its way through my body as anger gripped hold of me.

How dare he bring this up now.

'I told that manipulating bitch of yours not to show her face around our way again. You should be putting all your efforts into your learning. You don't need a girlfriend until you're older. I just want what's best for you. You don't need that tramp.'

When Andrew first told me about his girlfriend, I knew I should have been happy for him. He never had many friends, and I pretended to be over the moon. I knew I had to play that game to get to meet her. I needed his confidence and trust in me.

'Bring her round,' I had said. 'I'll cook you both a nice roast dinner. I know how much you love my roast spuds.'

The moment I first clapped eyes on the bitch, I knew what she was after. They met in the playground; she too had been bullied. That girl was not using my son as a way out of her miserable life. I played the part of a loving mother in front of them both. I watched her eyes and the way she flirted with my son in front of my face. I could see myself in her. I recognised the darkness behind that smile, and she was not going to take my son away from me. Over my dead body.

I hated her.

I don't know how I didn't choke on my dinner when she gave him a kiss on the cheek. It was the first time that she'd met me and I thought that kind of interaction in front of me was disrespectful. It told me everything I needed to know about that tramp. I warned her away.

After the meal, I took her to one side, out of Andrew's earshot.

'I know your game, you fucking hussy,' I told her, and watched as the expression on her face turned to instant fear. She knew I meant it. 'You're not getting your claws into *my* son. Stay away from him after today; call it off. Otherwise I will make your life hell. He will hate you by the time I am finished with you.'

Thankfully I never saw Katrina again, and she had stayed away from Andrew.

Andrew's face had gone red with anger when I told him that in the caravan. I recognised the frustration and the disappointment, but he had to learn. He needed to respect his mother because I knew what was best for him. Katrina was not a suitable girlfriend for him in my opinion. She stayed away, which proved my point. I knew what she was after.

Andrew and Katrina split up about three weeks before this short break away. I knew he could tell I had had a word with her, but I didn't think he would dare challenge me. We had short brief spats leading up to this moment, but that's why I wanted this time away to bring us closer together again. I wanted Andrew to see sense, not to hate me for thinking about his wellbeing. I'm his mother, I know what's best for him – even if he can't see it himself.

'Your dad will be back soon,' I told him. 'Stop whatever game you're playing with me and put an end to it. We will all get along this weekend and have a great time. Do it. I mean it.'

I noticed Andrew's heavy breathing, but he had got me annoyed. I knew that I needed to calm down before Thomas returned, and he was due back any minute. It was so intense. I couldn't believe that my son was disrespecting me.

How dare he.

I was trying to control my breathing, but Andrew had put me mentally back in that place. That place where I started to hear my own mother's voice shouting back at me. My eyes welled up with the anger and upset; I was shaking with rage and fear of what I might do next. I heard my mother's voice ringing in my own ears. My temper had taken a turn for the worst. It was out of my control.

Evil, evil. Such an evil little girl. Nothing you do is good enough.

Andrew walked closer to me. I could see he was worried but brave enough to challenge me at this moment. I noticed he too was shaking, which triggered another flashback to when I was a child. I remember standing and shaking with fear as I answered back my own mother. She beat me so hard. I had to learn my lesson.

'If you've hurt her, I will never forgive you. I hate you. I absolutely hate you for interfering in my life. If I want to go out with Katrina, that's my choice to make. Not yours.'

Andrew's words hurt me, but I needed to keep him under my tight control. I could not have our secrets exposed. I raised my hand and slapped his face, short and sharp with a speed that I knew would have hurt him. Andrew came towards me with gritted teeth and raised his hand to me for the first time. I didn't give him a chance to come any closer as instinctively I grabbed the necklace around his neck and pulled him so that we were face to face. The anger was unleashed, but all the time, I was trying to remember that this was my son. I was struggling to contain my emotions while I wrapped my hands around the necklace tightly. I could hear him struggle to breathe, but I didn't stop.

'Do not ever mention that cheap tart's name in front of me again. Is that understood?'

Andrew was coughing while I gripped hold of him tightly. My face in his as I tried to speak through my tightened jaw. I was raging. Furious at his behaviour towards me.

'Your father will be back soon, and I want this to be a happy family weekend. Do as I say, have you got that? Have I made myself clear?'

Andrew started crying and lowered his eyes towards the floor, nodding fast. From the corner of my eye, I could see Thomas walking closer from the window, holding the bags of shopping. The caravan door opened, and I wrapped my arms around Andrew to comfort him. I had to act fast. I didn't want Thomas to suspect I had been so vicious towards our son.

'What's happened?' Thomas asked, looking confused. 'Andrew, is everything all right? Trish, what's wrong with him?'

'He frightened himself. He went to the bathroom to clean his teeth and got his necklace caught around the taps,' I replied, thinking on my feet once more, holding Andrew's head as close to my chest as I could with force. 'He'll live. He's just in a bit of shock from the force as he tried to stand up. It pulled really tight around his neck.'

Thomas walked through to the kitchen and unpacked the shopping into the fridge.

'But,' he asked, 'I didn't think we had any toothpaste. That's why you wanted me to pick some up at the shop. Are you sure he's okay?'

I let Andrew go from my grip; his eyes were red and puffy from the tears, and the marks were clearly visible around his neck. Feelings of guilt crept into my mind, but I had to get this situation under control. I was nervous, but confident that Andrew wouldn't disobey me again.

'You're fine now, aren't you, Andrew?' I asked calmly. 'Just a little scare, wasn't it?'

Andrew walked past Thomas crying, describing the bathroom scenario just as I had explained. I'm glad that boy knew what was good for him at the time.

'My mouth just felt like it needed a clean,' Andrew explained, looking fearful, but wiping his eyes dry. 'Now that you have the toothpaste, I'll try again.'

'Just learn to be more careful in future,' I yelled, fraught with fear that he could expose my anger. 'Think about what you're doing.'

Andrew disappeared into the bathroom, likely to compose himself. I knew that he would spend the whole evening in his bedroom attached to his phone to occupy himself. I was disappointed that he didn't even want to be there with us in the first place.

'Thank you for this short break away,' I said as I cuddled up to Thomas. He smiled at me. 'I love you.'

'I love you too,' he replied. 'We will have a great time this weekend. I want it to be a weekend to remember.'

I took another deep breath to calm myself, hopeful that Andrew had got the message. But I was worried about him exposing me.

It was all his fault though. He asked for it.

Fifteen

There are no photographs of Andrew when he was a toddler anywhere. I have looked almost everywhere, except for the loft because I can never undo the latch correctly, so I use Thomas for that. I shall ask him to take a peek up there later. Heaven knows what he will find among the Christmas decorations. There should be many toys that I bought for Andrew when he was a baby, others when he was a young boy. Seeing all that will break my heart if it is even possible that it can be broken any more.

I was never one for photographs. Who needs pictures anyway? Most just sit in unsightly frames hanging on the wall like dead trophies. My mother used to hate them too. She used to tell me they are small stills in time that freak her out. Now that I am older and wiser, I understand what she meant. You can look at an old photo and reminisce about the events within it. Relive the memory of that day but also the misery of it too. And that misery could haunt you forever.

'Dead trophies,' Mother would hiss at me, usually after a beating. 'No point crying over that boyfriend of yours.

You'll be looking at the photo reminding yourself of the upset. It'll play with your mind, young girl. Stop being a little pitiful fucking bitch.'

Despite the pain that my own mother caused me growing up, I can't deny that she was right. If I had some pictures of Andrew here with me right now, I would sit and soak them with my tears. To look at his face again, remember how he was. The times when he needed me as his mother; all those times he would shout at me – and I'd calm him down. Letting him know that he would be safe. I failed as a parent. The failure of being a bad mother only adds to my depression. If I had any photos, I would torture myself.

Thomas could be right: I should start to move on. My mother is right, photos do only add to the misery of disappointment. How dare she still be controlling my thoughts after all these years?

When I had my photograph taken in one of the photo booths in Plymouth bus station as a teenager it was with my first boyfriend. I barely remember his name now, could be Jack or Jacob. I think he might have been Jacob but preferred being called Jack.

Fucking memory of mine.

I took the photo home to show my mother. At first, she smiled and called me into the kitchen. She said we looked a lovely couple. That brief moment of acceptance that I had managed to find a boy at last filled me with joy – this is all way before Thomas. I was only a young girl, probably fourteen at most. Jack used to write little love notes in school and get his mates to pass them to me in class. It was all childish things, like how good my hair looked and how much he liked me at the time. He bought me some small chocolate bars on Valentine's Day and asked me to be his girlfriend. I couldn't believe it at first. This young man with a face full of spots was someone you could tell would grow to be very handsome. I didn't know why he wanted me.

Was it a bet, a dare? Could I really believe it?

Jack wanted a girlfriend, and he chose me. It was a moment of happiness that made my heart flutter with anticipation. The first hope I'd had that my life was about to change. Puberty was a brutal time in my life, when I couldn't have thought that I was any more worthless.

I was nervous about telling my mother and father about Jake. Mostly fearful of my mother, who had firm opinions. I kept him a secret for a few weeks because I didn't want to share my happiness. He was my little secret – but I started to take care of myself better. I wanted cleaner clothes and I would shower every day. My mother knew something was going on, so I had no choice other than to confess.

'First love,' she said. 'You'll never forget him. He looks a sweet young boy.'

I was stunned by her reaction. I even took a sigh of relief because not only was my secret boyfriend exposed, but my mother seemed to be accepting of him. She looked pleased and I started to think that maybe she was happy for me. I didn't realise the psychological trap she set up, luring me into a false sense of hope that our relationship was starting to improve.

She looked carefully at the picture and noticed he had put his arm around me. We were both smiling with happiness. I liked him a lot back then. He was the first boy to really show any interest and I was such a shy girl. I couldn't understand why anyone would bother to talk to me. In my world, I was just that girl Trish who would rather talk to the stray cats in my lunch hour than mix with the in-crowd, all showing off their designer clothing. I was just that girl Trish who used to get sworn at for wearing the same clothes a couple of days in a row. That girl Trish who could never find a boyfriend – until that time when Jack couldn't care less that his mates warned him about me, my family and my smelly, holey jumpers.

'You look like a fucking prostitute.' I can almost hear those words coming back to haunt me. 'You look like a slag that's caught the cock of the week. Look at you practically throwing yourself at him. Have you no self-respect, girl?'

Her reaction came out of nowhere, which felt like another blow to my confidence. She had tricked me at first to get me to open up, spill all my thoughts and feelings while turning on me shortly after. I should have known better.

My mother disapproved the moment she saw his arm around me. I was only wearing my long school skirt with my creased blouse tucked in. I was just fourteen, we had only just kissed and done nothing else of any sexual nature. Naturally, I was curious about sex as my sexuality developed, but at fourteen it was just about hanging out together. Sharing albums and sitting out until the evening sunset, when you know it is time to go home for dinner. I wasn't an adult, so I have no clue why my mother always spoke of me as if everything I did back then had an ulterior motive only to spite her.

'You filthy fucking slag. Go to your room, you little bitch, before I tell your father you've been shagging all the local schoolboys. He wouldn't want to have raised such a dirty slag like you for a daughter. Do you want to upset your father?'

I ran to my room in tears. I had no idea why she was that way, but I accepted her for who she was. She hadn't had to come to terms with me having a boyfriend before; allowing me to have an interest in someone outside of the world she created for me. That life where she thought I would never escape. Later down the line, I realised that her behaviour was because she had noticed my blouse was undone slightly. She told my father I was a hussy who was desperate for a boyfriend.

Eventually, Jack was scared away by my family's issues, but I cherished the memory that he had been the first boy to show me any interest. I cried over that photo we took for days and nights on end. My mother came into my room and caught me, so she destroyed it. She ripped it into tiny little shreds before tossing all the pieces aside on the bedside cabinet.

I screamed at her to stop. She slapped my face, which hurt like hell, but I knew better than to react. I allowed her to bully me; I was helpless. There are years of torment ingrained in my upbringing. It was a world that I thought was normal; I was convinced that everyone else lived their lives as I did – so I never spoke out because I thought it was the same for everyone. School life was just turning up, listening, reading and getting on with it. I never asked about the home life of my school friends, well what few friends I had. Only the fucked-up kids with issues played with me, I didn't realise until I was much older than I was an outcast. I never wanted this life for Andrew. I vowed never to treat him like my mother treated me, and when I strangled him with that necklace it gave me flashbacks. It was a rage I couldn't control, but I could see my mother in me. The last thing I ever wanted was to become her.

'Get over him,' my mother said. 'You'll realise as you grow up that no man will really want you. You need to toughen up, girl. Expect to be disappointed, and you'll have no upset in later life. Nobody will want you.'

She was right in a way. No one really wanted me. That's why Thomas is special. Our relationship is different because he was the first to understand the difficulties I had with her. He is my saviour. The family we created together helped us escape the ghosts of our past. I love him so much because he has stuck by me through some troubling times.

My father used to turn a blind eye to her. He believed her lies that I was a child with problems who presented my mother with nothing but hard work every day to keep me in check. He worked full time in the local tyre factory and was away most evenings. My mother kept her dark side hidden from his view, and most nights I was in bed when he worked and at school during the day when he slept. Occasionally he would have weekends off to spend quality time with us all – but my mother was on her best behaviour; you could have mistaken her for a saint.

I'm calming down more now the days are moving on from the anniversary of his disappearance. Arguing with Thomas yesterday afternoon was a release; I was just letting off steam. He fails to grasp that someone out there knows what has happened. He doesn't believe me – he'll have to if it happens again. I definitely heard a knock at the door despite his doubts. It's worrying that someone could be watching us. Every now and then I think to myself, maybe it was me. Maybe I misplaced it and dropped the necklace earlier on in the day only to find it later. I remember the knock so vividly because I hate answering the door. I froze with fear, so I know what I heard.

Is my mind playing tricks on me again?

I might be going slightly insane with the memory loss, but my muddled thoughts are little crashing waves through an ocean of torment. My mind races on, and with someone out there having knowledge of where Andrew is or what has happened – it unsettles me. Every now and again I convince myself that I can hear a knock at the door. I run down to check, open it and look around only to find the same garden fence. The grass overgrown and the stone steps to the washing line looking like a safe haven from the birth of a jungle. No one is ever there. The wind whistles to me before I slowly shut the door, reminding myself that I am paranoid.

A good vodka would go down nicely right now. I'm really trying so hard not to hit the bottle. I am in control of it, so I'm not an alcoholic. I just drink more at this time of year. My emotions are all up in the air – it's to be expected.

The more I am bringing back memories of my childhood, the more I want to forget. This is why I stand by my joke that memory loss has its advantages at times. If I could rewrite history, I would forget my mother ever existed. I blame her for the way that I am; my life could have been so different. I might have known what normal was if only she had told the truth sooner. She hated me and never admitted it.

My mother made me believe that I was a problematic child in a perfectly normal family, but she made me this way. Inherited fears, personality traits that send a shiver down my spine when I realise I am just like her at times. My temper flares up, and I take it out on Thomas, but he knows how difficult it was for me. He stood up to her many times when she tried to warn him away, but her illusions of a problematic teenager were hitting deaf ears. Thomas loved me, he wanted me, he had me, and I gave him my all. He was my escape.

I really should check the loft for some old photos. There must be some around here of us all together?

All I ever dreamed of was being the head of my own family; Andrew has broken that link. He's destroyed everything.

Sixteen

Thomas Mullner — Now

Tuesday, 11 September 2018

At least the vodka bottle is not out on display like a trophy for the ugly mess it is turning Trish into this week. I would not be able to pinpoint precisely when the drinking problem started, although the beginnings were evident years ago, even before Andrew disappeared. Now I am beginning to remember when the vodka bottle made an appearance at Andrew's birthday parties.

'He's just six years old, Trish,' I remember saying. 'All those kids don't want to smell that shit on your breath.'

'It doesn't leave a smell,' she would sharply reply. 'I'll just have a few mints to cover it up.'

Trish's childhood issues from having an abusive mother are the cause for her need for vodka at times of stress and worry. I don't know how to help her, other than constantly ask that she seek some professional help. If I take away all the bottles, she'll go mad at me and scream every night. Alternatively, I can let her drink her vodka and she'll pass out on the sofa or drag herself to bed in an emotional mess. Either way, it's awful. For me it can be mentally draining at times because I've gone from a father and a husband to her carer in just three years.

Thinking back to when Andrew was about four, I remember her nerves kicking in when she used to convince herself that he had come to some harm. Checking on him every few minutes as he played in his bedroom, due to a fear that he wasn't safe, became normal behaviour until he was about seven and started to make friends of his own.

'There's nothing to worry about,' I used to yell at her. 'He's only four, he can't get up to that much mischief with a box of toy cars and a handful of teddy bears.'

At least by the time he was around ten or eleven everything around us was a constant. We all had the same routines, the same friends, and everyone thought they knew us so well. I didn't want people to see that I had never bonded with my son. I tried so hard at times, overly hard, to compensate for the emptiness and sadness that made me feel like I had failed as a father. I loved him, but the bond wasn't there, which led me to think other people might be able to see that. Andrew wouldn't have known because I was rarely at home, which was the root of the problem to be honest.

I should have been there more.

Trish never wanted her family or extended family to have anything to do with us. She washed her hands of all them after her parents' death. Her mother was a bitch who was both cold-hearted and vindictive. Having so little family around Andrew might have isolated him more. I thought he would make friends at school, and eventually come out of his shell, but at one point Trish even suggested taking him out of school completely. We had a few arguments about it, but she accepted he needed his education and instead taught him to ignore the bullies.

Looking back, I think she spoilt him at home with his consoles and food because it made up for the torment he had at school.

We did it all wrong.

By the time Andrew was older, he was accustomed to being in his room all of the time. Trish knew his whereabouts at all times, she was virtually psychic with his behaviour as she grasped his every mood, his every trait, and could read him like a book. Being out of the house at work all of the time, I had no influence on his life. No wonder I felt so disconnected from my son. It explained why he never listened to me on my days off. Some days I would work a full week for months. As a cab driver, every day at home is lost income. With Trish not at work full time we needed the money.

Andrew, I knew, felt safe in his room. No one could bully him in his own space. He loved drawing and painting as a child and that later developed into mostly playing computer games. He must have had every games console under the sun up in that bedroom, but at least we knew where he was and what he was doing.

When Andrew started school at the age of four this was another difficult time in Trish's life. That moment when she had to let him go and find friends of his own. I know that she found this period a nuisance. There were school meetings, other parents inviting us round to their houses for coffee, his school friends having parties, school plays, the playdates at someone else's home. All of these otherwise ordinary incidents were such a tense time for her. She didn't want Andrew revealing her past in case she was tarnished with the same brush. We always taught him that if anyone mentioned his grandparents, just tell them they died in a car crash – no one should ask any more questions.

'He hasn't mentioned anything to anyone,' I reassured her so many times. 'Andrew knows what to tell people if they ask.'

It was around this time she used to reach for the vodka bottle stashed away at the back of the cupboard.

'It means having to communicate with all sorts,' she used to rant. 'People will want to get to know us. I don't want to talk about my past with anyone.'

'I'll just have a shot,' she also used to tell me. 'It'll relieve the worry and get rid of these heart palpitations.'

I believed her at the time. I thought it was just the one shot she used to have until I once checked around the door and saw her necking back the bottle. A couple of times I ignored it or laughed it off. I chose to be ignorant towards her addiction since at this period of our lives she was never as aggressive as she can become now. I didn't think it would impact our lives as much as it has.

'Everyone poking their noses in will stop when he's a bit older,' I used to tell her. 'Kids make friends and it's natural that people have to integrate. We need to get to know them more – otherwise, we'll just look like outcasts in this village. Do you get my drift?'

We have had a few friends over the years. Neighbours who knocked doors with parcels, those random faces you see at the same shops on similar days that you end up speaking to.

I have my own regrets.

I should have spent more time with Andrew as a child. I have so many regrets that as a father I might have failed him, ultimately leading to him never returning home. It hurts that he could never come and speak to me about his worries or fears. I can talk to my parents about anything, and I have never had that relationship with my own son. I can only blame myself for that.

The vile aftertaste of vodka turns my stomach. I don't know how Trish can drink so much of it, but she's used to it. I think her body has developed a taste for it. My theory is that over time she must be craving more. Years ago, I used to buy her one bottle a week in the days that she couldn't leave the house. It soon crept up to two or three, but I lose count now. I've given up, but I need her to speak to someone. I can't take control of all the household bills, the mortgage, work and be her therapist.

I need her to see sense.

My duty as her husband is to keep Trish happy. That's all I ever wanted from the moment I first met her: to give her security and a safety net away from that mother of hers. I meant those vows when we got married. I gave up the potential to have a career to support Trish and my child. I've given us a home, a better life, we've never had to go hungry – and I don't want it to have all been for nothing. We have to work on our marriage, it has to have been worth it. She's been my life for the last twenty years. What would I do without her?

I am concerned for Trish's safety lately because her anxiety issues are spiralling out of control. Each year she gets worse, so I hate to imagine what she'll be like on Andrew's next birthday. We have to accept that if he is alive and living his own life, we are likely to have grand-children that we might never meet. I don't understand how he could be so cruel as to deny us being a part of his life.

Was I that bad a father?

Trish outright refuses to speak to a doctor, so I am the only person in the world I feel can help her. Her mother has a lot to answer for. Trish says that they will get her to bring up her past and make her talk about her life. She really doesn't want that. I understand how difficult that might be for her, even though I've not had to suffer in the same way. My parents worked me hard on the farm, and although at the time I hated it in all the bad weather – it actually taught me that family matters, that by working hard you achieve things. We wouldn't have had a roof over our heads otherwise.

The three years since Andrew's disappearance have been difficult for us both, yet I had confidence we could both move on and live out our lives. I understand her point of view when she says that her purpose has gone; she had that need to be a mother, to love Andrew and give him a life that she never had.

This has to have been the worst year for Trish's anxiety and depression. The drinking is out of control, her anger issues are starting to build more – and I know what is coming. I fear what happens next, but I can't make Andrew return. This, I believe, is what is driving her slowly insane; all that stuff about the necklace. I think in reality that she most likely found it and dropped it by the back door because she was so drunk that day. I've seen her barely able to walk at times and dropping anything in her hands. Andrew wouldn't return to the back door only to drop off his necklace. It doesn't make any sense.

She's becoming more and more forgetful.

I know that soon the past may catch up with us. Andrew left for a reason, and neither of us saw it coming.

A part of me hopes that Andrew never returns. Not because I don't miss him, as I do *really* miss him. However, I fear it will give Trish a breakdown. A breakdown so hard that she'll never be able to recover from it. All she ever wanted to be in life was a good mother. To have a son who would love her and be proud of her. She gave Andrew everything he could wish for. I worked myself at times to sheer exhaustion to enable my family to have decent food on the table, decent clothes on their backs.

Since Andrew decided to leave us there have been days when I selfishly hope he never returns. If I ever told Trish how I really felt, she'd leave me too. At the moment I am her strength. I need her to have a reason to get out of bed in the mornings. I keep her motivated, and she knows that I love her. Sometimes I wonder whether, if we went our separate ways, this would lead to a better way of life; are we just prolonging the inevitable if we can't live together as a family anymore?

It's normal to think like that, right? It's natural to wonder about all the 'what if's and the maybe's?

Our sex life is practically non-existent, but there's been the odd quick session together here and there. I know that she needs to be mentally relaxed or that she's just doing it to keep me happy. I miss our lack of intimacy and closeness that we had, but I'm glad to settle for a cuddle or even a few hours chatting without feeling cautious nowadays.

I miss you, son, but I don't want you to destroy our future.

For the sake of Trish's health, I know that we need to move out of this area; maybe even out of town altogether. We need a fresh new start, that's for sure. I want my wife back.

I still need to confront her with how I feel.

Seventeen

The Watcher – Then

Monday, 16 July 2018

It was a risk that I had to take, one I was willing to take a chance on. I had thought about it for a long time because it was easier to get closer to Thomas than it was Patricia. Thomas drove a taxi, all I had to do was work out a way to get inside it without revealing my true identity.

I had bought the blonde wig from an online market-place; it was second-hand, but made with real hair. It was exactly the look I was going for. To complete my disguise I bought some hairgrips from the discount store not far from where I live, and I've had a pair of those cheap sunglasses for years. All I had to practise was the art of disguising my own voice.

I spent countless hours in front of the mirror for weeks in the build-up to the big day, and it reminded me of my high school days, when the teachers would try to get the class to disguise our Plymothian accents in basic elocution lessons. I had a teacher called Rachael; I thought that name would suit me, plus it was an easy one to remember. She hated me in my teens. I made no secret about how I felt about school either.

Rachael was a bitch too.

'Good morning,' I practised, trying to sound softly spoken and polite. 'How are you this morning. City centre, please.'

Something was missing. I still looked too much like me, sounded too much like me, only with a blonde wig on. I needed a distraction from my facial features, so I applied a decent amount of make-up. The glasses worked, but the make-up was a little over the top at first. I hated make-up; I could never be bothered to perfect it because I didn't find myself all that attractive. Despite what people saw on the outside, I knew what scars I had on the inside. I knew how damaged I had become in the hands of other people. People who had destroyed my life.

People I can never forgive.

I don't know how some women can put all the effort in. I knew that Thomas wouldn't be aware of who I was, or where I came from, but at some point, I knew he would eventually find out who I really was. I wasn't ready to give the game away. Not this day. I tried to keep my look as far away from my real identity because I was already spying on their house as my natural self.

Today was the day that I planned to get as close to him as I could. To see his face up close, hear his voice and ask him some questions about his home life. The very idea of it excited me because I could fantasise about all the information that I might find out about him and Patricia. I wasn't sure at first if I could pull it off, but I had to find the courage within me to keep going. Driven by my anger, with a lack of understanding where Andrew is, I managed it.

When I kept thinking about actually meeting Thomas in person, I wondered if I would be overcome with hatred and rage. I was expecting my anxiety to kick in and have me fiddling with my hair or swearing at him. Although I had always watched from a distance, I wasn't sure I could keep myself composed.

I needed answers.

I knew I also needed bigger-looking breasts to distract the attention away from my face. After a quick trip into town, I had bought a much larger bra and stuffed it with socks and tissues until the bust area was firm and stable. After I slipped on the dress, clipped on the wig, tied it up at the back to appear more realistic with strands covering the side of my face, I then popped on the sunglasses to complete the look.

Rachael was born.

I had a practice run-through in the afternoon at first with Thomas's taxi firm ensuring I had a driver that wasn't him. I was nervous, but it was easier than I thought slipping into a character when no one knew anything about me anyway. I had the driver pick me up from the street behind where I lived and take me into town. My new appearance received a lot of attention, but I still wasn't confident enough. The hardest part, as I had imagined, was keeping my voice under control. I had to get this right.

Then came the reality.

It was Monday evening and I was ready, confident and raring to get this done. I called the firm on my mobile and asked for Thomas by name. He always worked Mondays driving around town like clockwork. I had noticed from all the watching of his whereabouts I had done previously.

This was the only way I could think to speak to him without exposing my true identity. I had taken a bus to the hospital because it reminded me of why I am doing this in the first place.

My hatred for Patricia.

I waited outside the main entrance, a familiar place for me over the years, but I watched as Thomas's taxi cab pulled into the side of the road. I was trembling, not only from anger when I saw his face, but nerves were getting the better of me. For the first time, I was going to meet this man face to face with the intention of having a conversation. I had to compose myself.

At least in the back of a cab, there was some distance between us. If I wanted to remain silent, I knew that could be an option too. If I had brought a hammer, I would have probably smashed the back of his skull open.

'Are you Rachael?' Thomas asked as I opened the back door and stepped inside. 'And, you're going back into town, is that right?'

'Yes, that's correct,' I answered, not looking him in the eye although my large, dark sunglasses concealed my eyes. 'Just by the mall in town would be great, thank you.'

I didn't really have the money to waste on buses and taxis to town and back, but this had to be done. I kept my voice as soft as possible to hide my accent.

I needed answers.

I felt overwhelmed at first in the back of his cab. I remained silent, watching the view from the window. I knew it would be about a ten-minute ride, so I had carefully planned my questions in the morning. By the time my attention was focused on the back of his head and everything that I *really* wanted to get off my chest, I had forgotten most of them.

The more I kept watching him, the more I wanted to blurt out the truth. I was beginning to feel my rage brewing and I had to remind myself to stop talking to myself out loud. I wanted to reveal everything to him, right then in the back of the taxi. I could feel my hands twitching and trying to grab my own hair, but I managed to keep it all together. I kept counting to five in my head and remembered why I was doing this in the first place. I couldn't fuck it all up.

This was for Andrew.

I waited until we hit the traffic queues after the hospital, which would give Thomas some time to speak. I forced a smile on my face and tried to sound a bit ditzy.

'Having a good day?' I asked, to spark up some conversation between us. I already caught him looking at my breasts in the mirror – my plan was working. 'Have you been busy?'

Don't look at my face.

'Yeah, not bad, love,' Thomas replied. 'What about you?'

I started talking about my fictional job in the hospital. I was meant to say I was visiting a family member, but at the last-minute, I thought he would start asking me too many questions about my family. That's the last thing I wanted or needed. So the words just slipped out of my mouth: I told Thomas that I was a receptionist. I couldn't think of any other job where I would be wearing such clothing.

After five minutes, away from the traffic near the hospital and going in the direction of Plymouth city centre, I dropped the question I had been dying to ask from the second I stepped inside the cab. There was no other way than to just go for it.

'Do you have any children?' I asked. Thomas turned around to face me at this point. 'The schools break up soon for the summer holidays, don't they?'

I saw his reaction to the question, and it was a look of dread. I could tell that of all the questions, this was the one he didn't want to answer.

How was he going to explain himself?

'Just the one, love,' he replied, then he looked like he was concentrating on the traffic. 'I've got a son, but he doesn't live at home with us at the minute.'

'Has he moved out?' I responded, emphasising that he'd stated it was something temporary. 'Is he at university?'

Thomas stayed silent for longer than I expected, his focus still on the traffic. As a taxi driver, I assumed he would be used to these random questions. I was confident by this point that he had no idea I was wearing a disguise.

'No, he ran away from home. It was a few years ago,' Thomas said. He sounded upset and he looked really sad. 'It's coming up to almost three years since his mother and I saw him—'

'Here will do,' I interrupted. I knew it was rude, but I had to get out of the taxi immediately. I couldn't hold it back. I couldn't fight it any longer. 'Thank you, driver.'

I paid the fare, took a deep breath and waited until he was out of sight. The adrenaline kicked in and I felt a pain in my kidneys. I was raging. If only I had brought that hammer after all. Thomas must have known that something was up, something had annoyed me, but he wouldn't have known the cause. Not then.

Since his mother and I saw him.

It was a tense moment between us, but he had no idea who I was. I got out of the taxi, and when he drove away, I sat on the wall, took off my wig and started pulling at my real hair. It's a reaction to stress, I couldn't stop myself. It's just the way I react. I needed to punch something or someone.

Since his mother and I...

I couldn't stop repeating the words over and over in my head. Each time I could feel my blood pressure rising with the anger. It's a good job it was summertime and warm outside because I took off my heels and walked the rest of the way home barefoot to calm myself down. I didn't plan for those types of reactions in front of him.

It was a good first attempt at getting some answers, but I knew that I needed to control my reactions if I wanted this plan to work. I had to think of better excuses to see him, I had to think of better questions about Andrew for next time. I considered that maybe if I showed him enough attention, he might even start to fancy me as Rachael. That would distract him further from who I really am.

I'm still watching you both.

Eighteen

Patricia Mullner – Now

Wednesday, 12 September 2018

I noticed that Thomas was not his usual self this morning. By that, I mean he wasn't making his morning quips or ramblings about the news events of the day. Today he was quiet and got out of bed in silence. I normally receive at least a kiss on the cheek followed by a 'I'm going to get up now,' as a warning that the bed will go cold as he pulls back the covers. His silence was a sign of disapproval that I might have gone too far with my argumentative outbursts. I am trying to keep my behaviour under control. I know that sometimes I take it too far after a drink or two, but I am drowning in mixed emotions. He is fully aware of that and I get annoyed by his lack of consideration.

With how negative he has been recently, I am surprised he still has the energy to come home at night. At least with his taxi job he gets out from under my feet. I can tell he has a lot on his mind too. I can read my boys so well. I know when either of them has issues that are unresolved.

I asked Thomas to look inside the loft last night to see if there are any old photographs of Andrew up there, but he couldn't find any. All I have now are distant memories

– and even then, they're starting to fade. I'm struggling to remember what's what as time goes on.

Did Andrew say he was meeting friends before he left? Was he more quiet than usual?

The longer that Andrew is not with us, the more I dream about the memories I have left of him. I try to relive them in my head. I can only describe it as like playing back a movie over and over on repeat. I can see myself running towards him as he comes out of the school gates, talking away about the subjects he learnt that day. I remember the times when he wanted to go away on school trips, and the disappointment on his face when I always refused. I wanted to keep him safe; I felt secure knowing that he was in his room at home.

'It's because I love you,' I reassured him. 'You don't get on with any of the other kids, and these kinds of trips are dangerous. Anyone could snatch you when you're not looking. Teachers don't look after you like parents. You're not their own flesh and blood.'

Each time I relive the memory something minor changes until eventually, I doubt myself. I wonder if I had added in parts of other days so that all that I remember is one big blur – his whole life with us from the beginning to *that* day, just all rolled into one.

In all of my memories Andrew is happy; he knew how much I loved him and wanted to keep him safe. I get reassurance from them that I was a great mum to him. I know that wherever he may be now, he can't say I was a bad mother. I gave him everything he wanted; I nurtured him to be such a good, polite boy. I taught him respect, love and he should at least know that I was a mother that wanted him. Unlike the piece of shit mine was.

She hated me. I hated her.

My mother reminded me so many times that when she was pregnant she wished that she had aborted me. I was the scapegoat for my own mother's failures, and I was damned if I would ever treat Andrew that way. He knows exactly how much I love him and would forgive him if he came back home. I'd give anything to know that he was safe; even if it was just a short letter in the post.

Thomas came across as sincere and thoughtful for the first time in a long while last night. We discussed the day I brought Andrew home from the hospital. It is not like I could ever forget this, as this was the day I had everything I could ever want – a son. I placed a hand on my heart as I filled my thoughts with warm memories we had together as a young family. Andrew's first steps, the time he learnt how to ride a bike. I miss cooking for him. I liked to take care of him. When he left, a part of me left with him.

'A lot has happened in those twenty years,' I said while staring at Thomas.

Thomas threw one of those frowns at me. The sort that lets me know that he means business. Not just any old business, but serious business.

'Seriously, we need to rebuild our lives again. I think we should pack our bags and move to Somerset, like we should have done years ago. I can be a taxi driver anywhere in this country,' Thomas said, while I was holding back the tears. 'It's time, Trish. It's time to let go – and we knew that one day we would have to let him go. Whatever Andrew is doing out there now, he's a grown man, love.'

The knot in my stomach gave me an uncomfortable pain. The adrenaline hit me as the anger raged its way through my body. For someone who was meant to be his father, I couldn't believe he could say such a vile statement. I never wanted to move to Somerset just so he could be near his family. They don't need Thomas as much as I need him. His parents are retired and spend their days on holiday abroad. I don't need them and their lives in my face. His mother barely even calls me; they couldn't care less about Andrew either – except, in the past, for the odd cheque at birthdays or Christmases to pretend they care. They never knew him.

'Let go of my son.' I'd raised my voice. 'You're determined to have me forget him. How do you think it makes me feel as a mother, to be abandoned by her only child?'

I'm a failure.

He rolled over and went to sleep after about twenty minutes. Not another word was spoken between us. In that split second, I admit I could have strangled him for his insensitive comments. I watched him breathing, and the idea of suffocating him in his sleep was tempting. What hurts the most is that he knows how hard it is, living without Andrew in my life. I can't simply forget him and move on. I'm surprised he can be so dismissive.

The vodka is still in the cupboard. Maybe I should only have the one?

It may be hard for me to give up hope that Andrew is coming back home, but Thomas is so hell-bent on moving on that I am starting to wonder if he knows something about Andrew he isn't telling me. Maybe I am paranoid now or just hoping for answers, but I knew they never saw eye to eye.

Did he scare Andrew away?

As I lie on the bed listening to Thomas's gentle snores, he remains defenceless in his dream state. I can't help but stare at him as I wonder if he knows something that he isn't telling me. He has always been so certain that Andrew walked out and nothing else happened to him. I don't like his insistence that we need a new start either. The problem is that our son left us, that's what happened.

Does he want to leave me, a divorce?

It makes me question the commitment he has to our marriage. I never doubted it until now. Knowing how he reacts to situations allows me to think through my course of actions to manipulate him. He fights back at times with his opinions, and I let him get it off his chest when he needs to vent his frustrations at me. But deep down, I know he could never leave me. He's all I have left.

I talk to him when he is asleep – I tell him that I am thankful for him as my husband. I thank him for protecting me from my mother, and I thank him for all that he has done for our family. I often reminisce about the early days of our relationship, and I try to remember a time in our lives before we had Andrew. That feeling of emptiness can still bring chills to my spine. Before I had my own family, nobody wanted me. Nobody loved me.

Unknown to Thomas, he was my escape from my old life in many ways. Those manipulation skills came in to play even all the way back then. He was putty in my hands. I knew he was an easy-going guy, not unintelligent, but because he wasn't from my area, I knew he wasn't tainted with the rumours that went around my street. I know our family was known as *the freaks*. I didn't think he would avoid me, unlike everyone else I met. Thomas didn't judge me. I instantly loved him for that.

I first met Thomas by accident. I saw him go past my house a couple of times one summer, walking a dog. He was a handsome teenager; I thought he was way out of my league. I followed him to see where he was going, if he was meeting anyone, but he was just walking a dog. Thomas never knew I was following him, but then I never saw him again for months. It wasn't until I saw him walking past the house again at Christmas that I realised he was related to the family next door. All the times I followed him and bumped into him again after that, he thought it was all accidental. I just needed that one moment to get him chatting: I knew I had to make a good first impression.

What finally brought us closer together was Thomas moving down to Plymouth for the whole of the summer. He had considered that the University of Plymouth was an option because of having family down here. I used to chat to him for hours next door; we'd sit on the doorstep and talk about our lives. I knew he could see how evil my mother was, he saw the look on her face when she'd come home and see us chatting. The amount of times she called me a slag for that. But nothing happened between us. He could see how difficult my home life was and I think that only brought us closer together.

He wanted to help me.

I knew getting pregnant would be the only sure-fire way to ensure he wouldn't stray to other women. I had to trap him; nobody had ever shown an interest in me like that before. I didn't want to lose him. The joy on his face was perfect when I announced the pregnancy after an argument about other women I thought he had been sleeping with behind my back. That look he gave me was a mixed reaction of disbelief and utter shock, but when my announcement sank in, he was thrilled. You could count on one hand how many times we had slept together. I'd told him I was on the pill; he believed me.

'It's true. I can't hide it any longer.' I remember my words even now, just over twenty years on. 'You're going to be a dad; we're going to have our own little family.'

'It's too soon, way too soon,' Thomas replied when he was finally able to catch his breath. 'We're still only dating – aren't we?'

'A bit late to worry about that now,' I replied, smiling as I held my stomach, edging myself closer towards him. 'You're the only man I've ever slept with.'

I had missed my period that month, but I put it down to my poor diet starting to affect my cycle. I barely ate proper meals, just snacked in private and took bits of bread here and there from the cupboards while my mother wasn't looking. She used to like us all to sit down as a family when I was younger, but with all our working hours varying it was as though I was living with flatmates.

'Remember to pay for that,' my mother would shout if she ever saw me eating. 'I work hard for this family while you contribute nothing.'

I didn't earn very much in my training days because it was student finance loans, yet I was thankful I wasn't made homeless. The only reason I believe I wasn't thrown out onto the streets was because of the impression she wanted to give all her friends. If I wasn't around, then how could she talk about having such an evil daughter?

'Look at me, feeding, clothing and still having to support my failure of a daughter.' I can almost hear her talking to me at times, the voice remains in my head. I can't shift it some days. 'My little bitch still needs me.'

I grew apart from my father after the abuse started; I was convinced my mother made him hate me. She hated the attention he gave me and was jealous of it at the time. As I grew into my late teens, she had caused enough lousy feelings with her lies that he barely even acknowledged me anymore. I cling on to the happy memories though, those times when it was just me and him, before the sexual abuse when he became an alcoholic – the times when he treated me like a daughter.

My mother ruined him.

Thomas barely saw the surface of my emotional abuse when we first got together, but knew that something wasn't quite right with me. This wasn't in his words *an average family*. I confided in him about the sexual abuse after my parents died. He doesn't understand how I can still say I love my father after that, but he doesn't realise the abuse we all suffered at the hands of my mother. She drove my father to drink; I blame her as the root of all our evil. My father was the only person to ever show me affection; at least one of my parents wanted me.

During the early stages of my pregnancy, Thomas had eventually got used to the idea of being a father. Every day our discussions were about his wish for a son. The pressure I was under was incredible. He talked as if girls didn't exist just because he wanted to make his father proud. I was convinced if I had a daughter, he would leave me – it was not what he wanted. All because of the importance of carrying on his family name. I didn't want to disappoint him. It was mentioned so frequently that I thought the baby's gender would be the make or break of our relationship.

When I confirmed to Thomas that we were having a boy, he proposed to me. Right there and then, on one knee and everything. He said I was all he ever wanted. He didn't have a ring as he hadn't prepared to do it in that manner. That didn't matter to me – my heart melted. I had a man who wanted me, loved me enough to make his wife. I couldn't have been any happier and I was committed to making everything work.

Due to the upbringing I had, thanks to my mother and the disappointment I was to her throughout my whole childhood, I convinced myself that if we had a daughter, our lives would be ruined. I had to have a son. I wished and I prayed for a son.

I couldn't let him down.

I hate myself at times. I feel victimised by my own mind because the hatred is starting to get out of control. I blame myself for everything. I have become a shadow of my mother. An evil I can't forgive myself for. The resentment towards Thomas for so desperately wanting a son was another factor to drive me to alcohol again when Andrew walked out on me. All of this has been for nothing.

I should have kept my little girl.

Nineteen

Wednesday, 12 September 2018

It has only been a few days since I dropped the necklace into her hands. Patricia must have had the shock of her life as I gave her back a memory. My instinct was that it would send her over the edge. I intended to push her to the point of being frustrated and filled with regret. I should feel sorry for her, but the hatred burns too deep. I wanted her to feel how I feel.

I'm back in my favourite spot in the woods where the crows congregate to spy on their surroundings. It is as if I am in sync with the birds that flock above me as though they are looking for trouble. It's not just trouble I seek, but revenge.

This secluded pathway that leads on to the back of their house is perfect. Equipped with my binoculars I can take a good look into each window as I fuel my rage. I want to watch her die, but it has to be slow and painful. She should suffer for her actions because this despicable bitch is pure evil.

The chill in the air is keeping me awake as darkness is edging slowly into the night sky. I've been watching her for a couple of hours. The slow movement from one room to another, a little unsteady on her feet. I see she has been drinking again. I should pity her, but the devastation she caused in my life is unforgivable. I once trusted her.

Twenty years ago, Patricia befriended me in the hospital when I was heavily pregnant. I was only sixteen years old and being in the hospital was the first time in months I was able to stay warm, have a comfortable bed and eat food regularly without begging for it in alleyways, or near shop entrances in the city centre.

I thought she was going to be my midwife; I trusted her. She came across as though she was my best friend. Patricia was like the older sister I never had. She told me a few issues from her past with her abusive mother. I believed her; I opened up to her and gave her details of my drug addictions. These were all things I had managed to cover up with the doctors. I lied to them, but Patricia was like a best friend, she was understanding and so warm to me. She even managed to slip me some methadone she had acquired. I never knew how she managed to get her hands on so many drugs. I assumed it was due to her working in the hospital. I was so thankful at the time because my body craved it. I yearned for more, it was like a guilty secret between us. Wrong in so many ways because I hadn't even given birth, but the dosage was always so minimal to begin with.

Her smile, her warmth, her persona was that of a woman I thought cared about girls like me. All the time that I knew her, I was being cheated. I hate her for feeding me drugs that made me more addicted than I ever was before knowing her. Patricia had succeeded in making me hooked on methadone after I left the hospital. By the end of a couple of weeks, she was not only my friend but my dealer. I needed her because no one else could give me the drugs in quantities that she could get hold of. My naivety was my downfall.

I had no idea that all Patricia wanted was to get her vile, dirty hands on my son. I nearly died because of her, and it has taken years of hard work to get back on my feet again. Even now, I still have the cravings, but I have the willpower to live. I am more driven now to stay alive because I will not let that bitch win.

'Our lives are very similar,' Patricia once told me from the side of my hospital bed as I recovered from an attempted overdose. I was barely twenty-weeks pregnant and only took a handful of ecstasy. With the father nowhere to be seen and a family that had abandoned me to a foster home; I can see how ripe I was for her pickings. 'I had a troubled upbringing too.'

At the time, I had taken an overdose because I had no support, with the world feeling like a weight on my shoulders. I was expelled from Plymouth Central High School for misbehaving; the downfall was the drugs and getting in with the wrong crowd. My family disowned me when they knew I was pregnant. My father said it would bring shame on the family.

How could I cope with a child on my own?

I was still barely a child myself, who wouldn't even be able to recognise my child's father because I'd been high on drugs. Sex whilst on drugs was the only time I had ever felt closeness, albeit for a short time before the real emptiness set back in motion once more.

I know I am alone in the darkness as I watch their house. Standing under the branches where crows and magpies watch me, I am in the same spot I was two days ago, feeling the same hatred. I want to confront them, but I am afraid of what I might do to her.

A couple of years ago, I just used to follow them, writing notes in a book about their typical daily activities. I would watch only once a month, sometimes just barely a handful of times in a year. Now my urges are starting to surface as a reminder of my past addictions. I blame her, I blame them both, and I can't stop myself from indulging in the torment of watching Patricia even more. I may never see my son again. She failed me, and she failed herself. I trusted her to look after him.

Thomas is out in his taxi this evening as he works almost all the hours under the sun to pay for their home, from what I am assuming. Unable to work because of her depressed state, I can see Patricia relies on Thomas to provide her with everything she wants. The house, the ability to sit at home most days without having to work – basking in the misery of missing Andrew, my son, my boy that she stole from me. I was denied being a mother because of the misfortune of meeting her. She has never had to suffer as I have.

How dare she act the victim in all of this?

For years I felt saddened that I once believed her. This woman that I handed over my son to was supposed to have given him a better life, a life I was unable to provide for him. I did not want my son to grow up addicted to drugs and living out of different foster homes as I did. I wanted better for my son, and she was supposed to look out for him. I trusted her with his life. I cannot forgive her or myself.

I remember that Patricia said she had an accident during her pregnancy, which led to her miscarriage. It's all a bit vague, but she said she'd fallen down a flight of cement steps not long after she found out she was having a little girl. Unable to tell her boyfriend, Thomas, she led him to believe she was still pregnant after I agreed that she could take care of my son. I remember her telling me that he had always wanted a son. Thinking back, I am not convinced she didn't throw herself down those steps intentionally. It felt like she was desperate for my little boy.

I bet that she wouldn't have been anywhere near me if I had a little girl.

That fucking evil bitch was supposed to have kept in touch with me. We were meant to be meeting up for secret days out, trips to the seaside, birthdays that would have included me in his life. She said I could be his aunt and be a more stable part of his life once I was off the drugs. I should have been introduced to him as a distant relative from her mother's family. Instead, she just disappeared and left me to fend for myself. I went through hell and back in those years. The drugs almost killed me.

All these years, this feeling of loss was down to her. She took him, and I was never able to see him again. She stole my son, and there was nothing I could do about it. I was so fucking high on a cocktail of drugs and sleeping about in all the wrong circles. I was in no fit state to be a mother and Patricia ensured I was falling into lousy drug habits.

I bet she thought I had died years ago.

Throughout the last couple of decades, I have had shit boyfriends, abusive relationships, periods of managing to keep my self-control and sadly, other times, when I had to give in to the temptation. The days when I am down, I am really depressed with what seems to be no way out. I become trapped in a tunnel of darkness with no light at the end. I was merely surviving here, there and wherever I can. I existed with a life that could have been cut short at any given moment. No one would remember me; my son doesn't even know me.

It has only been within the last five years that I really turned my life around. Knowing that my son was going to turn into a man, I wanted to be sure that if he met me, and I was in a position to call myself his mother, he would be proud of me. I've managed to keep myself in part-time employment, I even studied my English and Maths GCSEs that I should have taken when I was at high school. Then I discover my son is missing three years ago after reading the newspaper stories, another setback because of Patricia.

I want Patricia to pay for the twenty years of memories that she has robbed from me. It is a shame that I can't inflict twenty more years of hell in her life. There have been times when I would stop people in the street to ask if they knew of Patricia and my boy. Days and nights, I would walk through Plymouth housing estates while stopping and staring at families looking for hope. Those times when I was physically and mentally strong enough to reveal myself as his real mother, no one would ever give me the time of day. I had contemplated contacting the police, but I know they wouldn't be interested. I've had my dealings with the police in the past, they wouldn't listen to an ex junkie like me. I don't trust them.

Having given up all hope, I even accepted the idea that they had moved abroad. If they had all died in a freak accident, it would be easier to accept, but in reality, they were less than ten miles away.

Ten fucking miles away.

I hope that both Patricia and Thomas liked the gold chain I delivered to their door a couple of days ago. I was able to find an exact replica on the internet; one of those online second-hand jewellery shops. I couldn't believe my luck, and it wasn't all that expensive either. I kept looking at the image I saved from the newspaper cuttings showing a photograph of Andrew at college. I knew I needed an older chain because the one around his neck in the images appeared worn.

The image of his face haunts me due to the lack of expression. The local paper showed a boy who was supposed to be among friends, yet the highlighted image of Andrew was that of a late teenager who didn't look quite right. Unable to put my finger on it, I have perhaps read too much into the image because I cannot un-see the face of a boy looking like he needs help. He looked fat and miserable.

When the local papers reported Andrew as a missing teenager three years ago, this is when I first saw her face after all this time. My heart stopped with fear, I recognised her instantly. The distressed faces of Patricia and Thomas were side by side. I distinctly remember how strange it was not to see a photograph of them together as a family, but instead three separate images. I rubbed my hands across the pages because it brought back so many bad memories. Memories that had buried themselves into my past that should have stayed long forgotten. I struggled daily to forgive myself, which took me further into my drug addictions after I gave my baby away. All that pain and suffering was starting to come flooding back to me.

'That's my boy,' I said out loud to myself while coming to terms again with the memory of giving him up to her, that bitch. 'They called you Andrew. I have a son called Andrew.'

Knowing his name made it feel more real. I felt connected to him in ways I hadn't before. All the images I conjured in my mind evaporated with the reality of his actual likeness. Saddened that before this moment I would never have recognised him in the street, I wondered if our paths had ever crossed. I was surprised that they were still living in Plymouth, albeit on the outskirts, where they show minimal signs of travelling beyond their village. My little boy had never been all that far away from me.

I cannot forgive them for denying me the right to see my son. After I handed him over to her at the hospital, shortly after he was born, she begged me to keep her secret.

'You must never tell my husband our plan,' she asked of me. 'I'll give your son the best life he could ask for. He will never end up like you – that's exactly what you want, isn't it. You want him to have a mother who will look after him properly?'

She handed me the drugs, I handed her the baby. I knew that Social Services would want to get involved, so I ran away where no one could find me in the confines of my junkie friends at the time. I made them lie for me and tell anyone that knocked doors that I had moved away. It's what my parents thought anyway.

From that day to this, I have no idea what search efforts they put in place. I was travelling around the less desirable areas of Plymouth from one squat to the next. I cried for days on end and ran away to a local squat to meet up with old friends who I knew would welcome me with such vast amounts of methadone. We could sell it to buy harder stuff on the streets.

As I look back on my life, I accept that these people weren't friends at all – they used me. They used my body. I told everyone that I had given my baby up for adoption, that because of my drug problem he was taken into care.

They all believed me.

The temptation to take a methadone overdose with a cocktail of painkillers had crossed my mind, but I needed money badly and was able to sell it in small doses on the streets. A turning point for me was when I was mugged. I was badly beaten and left in an alleyway after I offered a guy a hand job for some money. I struggled to defend myself, which left me wondering what the point of my life was. The point was, I should have been a mother. If I had kept my little boy, I would have been given support for social housing. Our lives could have been so different. She robbed me of him.

Patricia took my number but had never called. I put my trust in her, yet she ruined my life in the blink of an eye with such disregard. I could have gone to the police, but no one would listen to a drug addict. I could barely open my eyes back then let alone speak without gurning. With no self-worth, I was helpless.

It is ironic that my finding the son I had lost for so many years was due to him being missing. My persistent watching of this house has been to see if he would return. More than three years have passed without so much as a single sighting, but the hatred refuses to leave me because

I cannot ever forgive her. I have so many unanswered questions.

Did he go because he knew she wasn't his birth mother? Was he trapped in a life that was so cruel he had to vanish? Do they know more than what the newspapers at the time suggested?

I remain here, silent and watching their house from a distance. Like clockwork, Patricia is walking to the kitchen and I witness her stretch to take out a bottle of vodka from the cupboards. My stomach has that sinking feeling: I can't fully look at her without feeling anger. Tonight could be the night I confront her face to face. I know that Thomas will be away all night with his taxi, and these nights alone for her appear to be her worst. I've watched her so many times, I know her every move.

I hate that vile bitch.

Patricia stole my son from me and as much as I tried to move on with my life in the beginning, she took advantage of my vulnerable mental health. She ruined my life, destroyed any chance I had of motherhood while leaving me in the dark. I know it's time I come out of the darkness now, I need to have my time with her. I'm going to destroy her, ruin that life she built for herself and expose her lies.

I want her dead.

Twenty

Wednesday, 12 September 2018

The darkness of the room confines my loneliness while the tears stream down my cold cheeks. My breath is making an echo as the silence lingers before I start breathing heavier with the anticipation of my decision. I want to do this; I'm entirely sure of my fate and the guilt ravages my heart with an ache I cannot forgive myself for. I'm going to commit suicide tonight. Alone.

Thomas will be out all night on the late shift with his taxi, so I know he can't walk in and disturb me or persuade me to change my mind. I don't want to be stopped. In fact, after what he told me today – I want him to find me here. Dead.

I hope he can live with the guilt.

'If you don't see a psychiatrist, I will go and take you there myself,' Thomas said. 'Our marriage is deteriorating. I can't take any more of your behaviour. We need a long discussion about our future.'

He's leaving me too. I know it.

I've got nothing left. My son has walked out on me, or is possibly even dead. My husband has had enough of me and wants me to get professional help. I'm disappointed that he doesn't understand me. I can't meet someone and explain what has happened. It's not just about my mother, my father, my love for Andrew. They'd lock me up and throw away the key by the time they'd heard everything.

I am evil. My mother was right. I'm good for nobody.

My depression is reaching the point I can no longer cope with it. I intend to end my life tonight because I have nothing left to live for and I've always had an idea in my head how I would like to do it. I'm going to leave this world with a concoction of vodka, old antidepressants I have left in the cabinet, and all the painkillers available from the kitchen. The cocktail of drugs has always been there waiting for me to decide that the time had come. I can't keep living my life like this, there's no way out.

That time is now.

The candle that had been lit in memory of Andrew is still on the mantelpiece. I hadn't put it away in the cupboard because it is another item I can't part with. Every year I light it in his memory as a means of giving me some hope. I pray he is alive, but I can't forgive myself for what I have done.

I've lit the wick to symbolise how it joins us together, and I have his gold necklace in my shaking hands. The chain is cold to touch, but I slowly place it around my neck while holding it with one hand near my chest. There is no coming back from my loss.

The mental suffering that I feel daily has me confined within the walls of my home – a house that once housed us a family. I love my husband, but our marriage is failing. Thomas is right, our marriage is doomed. I can't bring myself to see a shrink, and now that Andrew has gone, our lives are in ruins. I have nothing left to live for.

'We need a fresh start. You need to let go,' Thomas constantly reminds me. Thoughtless words. 'Move on and let him go. He doesn't want us anymore.'

Thomas deserves a life without me.

'Nobody could ever really love you or want you.' I hear the words of my mother haunting me further. 'You're useless Patricia – you've done nothing but bring shame to this family.'

Anger, shame, rejection, sadness and disconnection. I feel so many emotions but am numb to happiness and self-worth. I am trapped in my own mind with the desperation of escape. All this time my mother was right. Nobody wants me, nobody could love me because I am damaged goods.

I am evil.

I wake up daily, and it is fast becoming a struggle to get dressed or motivate myself with a constant lack of energy. I shake with worry that Andrew knows the truth, secrets that were always meant to be kept safe. Secrets that have now ruined my life because I thought I had it all under control. He was never meant to leave us.

Did he find his real mother?

Twenty years ago, I knew I would disappoint Thomas if I were to tell him we were having a little girl. As soon as the news of my pregnancy reached his family and friends the discussions centred on his dream of having a little boy. When I discovered I was having a girl, I cried because I hoped and wished for a boy so desperately to keep him happy. To keep him by my side. Giving him everything that he wanted would end his womanising ways – he owed me for his wish, and I had the perfect family. For most of the last twenty years we were happy together, or at least I thought we were.

I hope Thomas is happy without me.

I never did give my little girl a name. I couldn't allow myself to keep the pregnancy; for the sake of holding on to the life I desperately wanted – I had to ensure everything was perfect. I needed a little boy to cement this relationship. It was the only fucking thing that Thomas talked about over and over. He drummed it into me.

I will never forget the day I saw the wall and the daunting drop of a set of concrete steps that led into the water. Plymouth Barbican had many slippery cobbled streets that could make any fall look entirely accidental. The wall was inviting, but I could feel the pain from just peering over it, knowing it would hurt. I knew it had to be hard, fast and on my stomach with an intense pressure. I knew it was really going to hurt.

I waited until the dead of night while Thomas was at work. I took one gulp of air before throwing myself over the edge, and caused enough trauma to terminate my pregnancy. No one noticed, but the blood slowly escaped from me as the cramps, pain and internal suffering slowly worked its way out of me. I never felt her, looked at her or connected with her after a short labour I endured in the backstreets that continued at home. I flushed my daughter away while Thomas was working a night shift. To me, this was something I just had to do, and the bruises soon vanished. Afterwards I relied on painkillers to ease the cramps, but I managed to slowly reduce the dosage after a few weeks. A colleague scanned my womb at the hospital although I already knew the outcome. She was gone.

'You're sick in the head,' my mother would shout at me some days until I would believe it at times. 'Something about you isn't quite right. I gave birth to a monster. If your father ever saw this evil, he would have swapped you.' My mother tormented me with her tongue. 'No one will ever want you.'

The guilt hit me hard after a couple of days of still pretending that I was pregnant. Keeping up this lie was difficult, but I had my eye on other babies at the hospital. I befriended the mothers who bought into my over-friendly persona. I was desperate to find a mother who wanted to give her baby boy away for adoption, but nothing ever came of it. If they weren't having girls, they were too much infatuated with their boys. I thought it would never happen.

There was one pregnant mother who stood out though, a young girl who was pregnant with a little boy. A junkie with no family, who couldn't care less about her baby – she didn't even know who the father was. That girl didn't deserve him. I remember she wasn't even eating properly. She didn't care about her pregnancy and wouldn't have cared for her baby boy; all she wanted was the drugs. Here I was, pregnant with a little girl, and I would have done anything for a little boy. I saw how weak minded she was. I knew that all she needed was a mother figure to persuade her and get in her mind. I knew then that I had found my Andrew at the hospital. That boy was mine; it was meant to be.

To start with I knew I had to gain weight so I would eat fast food – as much as I could handle. Pizza after pizza, biscuit after biscuit and burger after burger. The weight gain was slow with padding across the stomach area helping at times to give an impression of a small bump. Thanks to Thomas working all the hours under the sun to get extra money for our house, baby clothes, much needed furniture, he was never around much to even notice I had fabricated such a lie.

I am evil.

It was easy to convince him of the baby kicks; he was so simple-minded, and I will never forget the look on his face when I told him we were having a boy. He was angry that I had not invited him to the scan, but it was easily done because I was a trainee midwife. I informed him that I had just got a colleague to perform a quick peek of the baby's sex. I knew, of course, that he would be livid that I had it done without him, but the joy of having a boy would soon help him overcome his anger. He was so predictable; I knew him so well.

The hardest part through most of the fake pregnancy was the bump. In the early months the padding and clothing strapped around my waist gave a decent impression, but I knew it couldn't last for long. In my later months, I stole a pregnancy harness from the hospital – one of the ones midwives use to demonstrate the pressure of the bump on your spine. I'd have to wear it to bed constantly and only have a shower while Thomas was at work. I never let him near me, but I distracted him with fake sicknesses.

Sometimes I forgot that it was all a lie.

Every single day for nine months my mind was in overdrive so as not to give the game away. This intense stress added to my mood swings. He believed every part of it; it was perfect.

I cannot remember what her name was because my memory is so terrible now, but as I sip the vodka, I am sure she was called Mel. Andrew's birth mother was desperate to get rid of him. She never wanted to be pregnant – it was an accident, and the timing was perfect. I needed a baby boy, and she needed to know he would go to a good loving family with a woman who wanted to be a mother. I was so overjoyed to get Andrew; I felt that with our paths crossing it was a sign that it was meant to be. This random drug user, who didn't deserve to be having a boy I so badly wanted. I had to keep her close. I needed her to need me as much as I needed her. She was vulnerable, and I manipulated her enough to need me. She became desperate for the drugs I could provide.

I remember that Mel came from a really well-off family, unlike myself, and she had gone to a posh high school, whereas I was a more common comprehensive girl. Although it is a struggle to think right now and it's all a bit vague, I am sure she also told me that her family kicked her out when they discovered her teenage pregnancy. It brought shame to the family. The drug addiction then followed. I know we came from two completely different backgrounds and upbringings, but still the world shit on us both.

It was my gain. I couldn't help myself.

Months passed and I managed to eat enough to gain a few more kilograms in weight, and during this time I formed a trusting friendship with Mel. I became a motherly figure she'd never had, but I knew what she really wanted from me. I regularly supplied her with drugs I had managed to acquire from the hospital I was working at. They were meant to be disposed of, but they weren't accounted for as accurately as they are now – computers and delivery methods weren't as great all that time ago.

I was so quick that no one saw me taking the odd bottle of methadone here and there. Boxes would sit opened behind the scenes in administration areas, delivery areas before being sorted and stored. Taking small amounts to start with went unnoticed, but by the time I left, I am sure they doubted me. Without the evidence, there was nothing they could do. I often feared that my baby boy might have been born with complications due to the methadone she was taking. But in the end although he was smaller than I expected, he was perfect in every way.

I quit my training in the hospital shortly after Andrew was born. I was there at the hospital watching Mel as he came into the world. Every breath she took, every pain she felt, I was there by her side for the whole ten hours of labour. When the umbilical cord was cut, I placed Andrew in her arms while jealousy tore through me. Ten hours I had waited for that precious moment to hold my boy. So as not to disclose my plan in any way, I had to smile and watch while I waited for my turn. A few minutes later I placed his head next to my raging heartbeat. That moment was the most special I could ever describe, knowing that I was going to take him home and be his mother for the rest of his life. My little Andrew.

I will always be his mother.

I felt a connection to Andrew, not only because I had watched him take his first breath, but for two days I visited him regularly until I finally carried him out of the hospital and into a taxi. I remember Mel's grief as she accepted that she was going to give him up, and it being eased by knowing that she couldn't be a mother to a son from a squat. A mother so hooked on drugs that Andrew had to go cold turkey when he was born. It was a miracle that we kept her addictions so secret, but the hospital thought I just had a soft spot for her. My colleagues could see all the special treatment she was given, but no one questioned me for helping such a poor girl in need. I assured her I would give him the best things in life. He would never go without love, parents that wanted him and a good home.

I have failed as a mother.

I fucking failed so bad that I hate myself. I have conned, lied and manipulated my family over the last twenty years and I fear I have fallen victim to becoming the shadow of my mother yet again. I hate that she was right. I hear her words and they send fear to my soul.

'We'd all be better off without you. I didn't really want you but kept you because it was too late to correct my mistake. You're a sick child, Patricia, and nobody could ever love you with that bad attitude of yours.'

Didn't my father love me?

I love my father, and I miss him terribly at times because I focus on the good memories of him. I have forgiven him for his part of the abuse I suffered because I have always blamed my mother. If she had put out more and treated him like her husband rather than a doormat, he wouldn't have climbed into bed with me drunk some nights. It only happened a few times, a handful at most, and it was very quick, but he told me that he loved me afterwards. I believed him too; in a twisted way, I liked the attention at the time, even though I would cry with shame for hours. I should have spoken out sooner, but I was only a young girl. My mother would have only blamed me.

There were other times my father would start commenting on how I reminded him of a younger, better-looking version of my mother. He said this in front of her and I took the compliments. I watched her face shrivel with rage during these conversations, which gave me a sense of satisfaction. She was jealous of me; she hated my youth. I don't think that she ever wanted my father to love me.

I'm not convinced my mother ever knew what was going on between my father and me, and I forgave him because he was a drunken mess. I knew it was wrong and I managed to push him off me one night. I remember the smell of his sweaty body trying to force himself on me. The smell of cigarettes on his breath and the feel of his hardened penis rubbing against my legs. I felt sick to my stomach. I knew that this shouldn't have been happening. It was wrong. I hit him hard in the face and he fell off my single bed onto the bedroom floor.

'Get off of me,' I whispered through gritted teeth. 'Fuck off, and stay away.'

After that we never spoke of it again, he kept his distance from me, but I still blame my mother. She was damaged to the core.

Finding the gold necklace again has brought so many memories of my childhood despair to the surface. My mother hated that my father could give me anything decent and sentimental. Those times when I tried to speak up against her, she would scream at him that I was a liar. I know he believed her, as I could never forget the disappointment in his eyes when she told him the bruises on my body were because she had to defend herself against me. She convinced him I was a problematic child with behavioural issues; I even overheard her friends say they felt sorry for her for having such a difficult child as me. I was trapped inside a home where I had no one to turn to, where everything felt like it was my fault with no way out – until I met Thomas.

Looking at the vodka and all of these pills I sense that my mother has won. I've lost. I've given in to her and she has won this battle, but she is right.

I am evil.

I doubt Thomas will grieve for me since he is barely here as it is and our lives centred around Andrew so much that we no longer have anything in common. I have gone from mother and wife to a wreck. The necklace hasn't helped – in fact it has brought home the memories of my despicable childhood, the happy memories I had forgotten about my father when he gave me this for my own birthday. I gave it to Andrew to remember me forever. It upsets me to know he doesn't have it. I'm still convinced that somebody must know something. Thomas refuses to believe that someone dropped it outside our back door. I've given up caring, but each time I look at it, I am engulfed in heartache.

I haven't stopped thinking about that necklace. I know Thomas thinks I am crazy, but I believe it was Andrew that left it on the doorstep. He might not have the confidence to confront me after all this time. I see it as a message to let me know he is alive, but still rejects me. He didn't stay around to see me, speak to me, or let me apologise for the outbursts with him. It was the necklace I gave him to remember me by and now he's given it back. It's unwanted, just as he doesn't want me as his mother.

The pills are sliding down the back of my throat too easily. One, two, four, six, ten, fifteen, twenty, thirty; I lose count, and I am starting to feel sick. The vodka is easing the urge to vomit as my stomach is in knots. I can feel the muscles contract as I hold back. My throat is lining itself with saliva in preparation for the need to violently release the contents of my guts. I need to hold back: *breathe, breathe. I t*ake a few deep breaths and it eases up slightly as the drowsiness is making a welcome appearance.

The nausea is showing signs of wearing off, but my vision is blurry. I am watching the candle flicker; the light is shimmering, glowing at me yet I can hardly make it out. I know that soon I will feel no pain, no suffering or mental torture. This is not a life I want to live. I ruined my family. I destroyed every hope of being the mother I had always wanted to be. My mother was right. I'm fucking useless.

I'm so sorry, Andrew. Forgive me, Thomas, my handsome husband. Thank you for being there. Forgive me, Andrew, for all those times I shouted at you and locked you in your room. Forgive me for those times I said I hated you and those times I lied to your father about you. Forgive me, Mother, for holding you back.

I tried so relentlessly to be a good mother and a decent wife, but ultimately I have lost control. My breathing is getting slower and I can hardly keep my eyes open. I have a sense of peace upon me knowing that for once in my life I have made the right choice. I know my suffering will end and I hope Andrew can forgive me. I hope Thomas can forgive me too.

The candlelight is starting to appear dimmed, my vision is blurring, but I am sure I can see a face staring at me from outside the window. I feel too weak to move or even stand as my lungs are struggling to produce such small, shortened breaths. Is that you, Andrew?

But the vague apparition is a woman. She's staring at me. I do not recognise her. *Is this the afterlife?*

The darkness is almost covering my vision and my consciousness is on the edge of shutting down. She is waving at me. I see the light in the darkness. It's becoming brighter the more I stare at it. A feeling of relief is warming my body, but the tingling sensation across my arms and legs is worsening. I'm accepting that this is death. By the time Thomas comes home I should have quietly passed away. I've given up and succumbed to the decision that I am worthless. My life has no purpose, and soon this mental torture will end.

I love you, Andrew.

Every time I close my eyes, I can still see his face, but as the darkness grabs hold of me, the candlelight is visible no more. The nothingness has consumed me.

I am free.

Twenty-One

The Watcher – Now

Wednesday, 12 September 2018

I'm mesmerised by the look on her face as I stare through the living room window – I had to get a closer look. Due to shock and disbelief, I feel a shiver through my spine. I cannot move from this position. It is as if time itself has frozen with only Patricia and myself in the world. All those feelings of hatred, anger, despair wave over me in different strengths. The anticipation of her bitter end is drawing too close while I fix my glare on her window.

I stare at her as the reality of the situation hits me. This bitch has finally dared to do it. To end her life where I can witness the end to the suffering that she brought on me and my son. I watch her every moment, and I start to shake with fear.

'Die, you evil fucking bastard,' I mutter through the window. Her eyes are fixed on me as she appears to drift in and out of consciousness. 'Fuck you.'

I doubt after all these years she will recognise me, but I hope she can see in the final minutes of her life, the pain on my face. The expression lines that have engraved themselves across my forehead through the worry and fear of what she has done to my son's life. The torment that she put me through, as my only focus was to become a better person so that I can be in my son's life. Patricia has destroyed all my hope, all of this effort for nothing. She ruined everything.

My son is missing, and he doesn't even know I exist.

She's looking at me again. The candle flickers in the background, but there is something about her glazed stare that lets me know that I am in her view. I start to wave to catch her attention, but her face remains expressionless. I want to laugh, cry and scream all at the same time. I hate her, but can I really watch her die without the bitch hearing me out?

'Die,' I mutter and I hope she can read my lips. The sound of the crows and the magpies has dimmed. 'Drop dead, you evil piece of fucking shit. Worthless, manipulative bitch.'

I agonise because I wanted to take control of this moment. I have watched for months and spent hours fixated on my plan of trapping her into a corner and confronting her. I want to kill her; it was meant to be me.

Initially, I had planned to kidnap her, tie her up and force her to come clean about everything she had done. I thought about videoing her telling the truth so that I could show the police what she did to me. All her lies would then be exposed and I could finally be acknowledged as Andrew's real mother. When I realised the unstableness of her mind, I knew the necklace would potentially break her.

I know she didn't really care about me. I know she is more than likely to think I had died from my addictions all those years ago, but I despise that she never once came looking for me either. Patricia denied me the chance to become a better person, a loving mother, and for that I resent her. I hate her, and even death itself is not cruel enough for the vindictive manipulation she had worked on me. I was young, troubled and I trusted her.

Do I call the ambulance or watch her die?

In these final few seconds between life and death, I still have a choice to make. Would it be crueller to let her live, and make sure that she knows I was the one person who refused to let her die? Or, should I sit here and watch with joy as she dies in my vision?

The drowsiness is clear on her face as she struggles now to lift her head. Drool is dripping from either side of her mouth as her chest is heaving deeply. I can see she is almost gone. The struggle in her body to breathe is worsening, but I am enjoying the view. Her death excites me.

I am troubled by the idea that this bitch has not heard me out. She has annoyed me by deciding her own bitter end. And not once has she contacted me. Not once has she fucking heard my side of the story, and I have no idea where my son is or what she might have done to him.

Something drove him out of this house.

'Why?' I mouth at her from the window. Unsure if she can see me, hoping she can read my lips. 'Where is my son?'

The wind is whistling and the moon is visible in the night sky. It is cold, and I feel every whisper of the breeze blow against my skin. The fine hairs on my arms tingle as I have minutes to make a choice.

Do I allow her to live, or die?

Holding the mobile phone to my ear, I dial the emergency services and know that there is no going back. In the blink of an eye, it could be too late, but I want my encounter with this woman; she owes me the right to listen to my opinions. As much as I am enjoying watching her fade from existence as she is sat in her own misery and torment, I'm not ready for her to die right now under these circumstances and certainly not without giving me an explanation.

'I need to report a suicide attempt. I can see from the living room window that a woman in her forties has taken an excessive quantity of pills and alcohol. It appears to be vodka. Her address, yes it's the first house on the corner of Elm View.'

I sound helpless and in shock. I don't want them to hear the regret I have in calling. Yet I get pleasure from knowing that her attempt has hopefully failed.

'I'm sorry, but I can't give you my name. She needs help and soon. Her breathing is slowing down, and she's foaming at the mouth. Barely looking conscious, if even alive by now. Please, just hurry.'

I cannot stay here, and I have to move without being seen. I hang up the phone and run towards the woods at the rear of the house. Keeping everything crossed that no one has seen me, I try to make as little noise as possible. I move quickly while hugging into the sides of the bushes to conceal my appearance in case I am spotted by a neighbour.

The minutes are ticking by as my thoughts are consumed by Patricia's possible death.

Will the ambulance come in time? Will the police suspect me of anything? They will trace my call – should I confess my presence now?

My gut sinks as the reality of what I witnessed takes hold of me. This will become a big deal if the police start an investigation. I start to regret calling them, but my need to confront her face to face will end the suffering and guilt that I place upon myself. I hate her for convincing me that my son went to a decent home, a loving family who would give him all of the care that I was unable to provide. I gave him to that vile woman, and I hate myself more for believing her.

The sirens of the ambulance fade in from a distance as the flashes of lights start to become visible in the sky. My nerves are on edge because I know this is a moment of life or death for Patricia. I want her dead, I would take great pleasure in seeing her taken out in a body bag. The look on her face and the foam dripping from the corners of her mouth did not give me any assurance she would survive. If she dies, the suffering for her has ended, but my life, my son's life is still in ruins. I won't get the answers I need, nor can I begin to find out where my son is hiding.

They arrive within minutes.

A male and a female paramedic run from the ambulance to the house. The man has a torch and is trying to get into the back garden. I can see him wandering around to the window where I was standing less than ten minutes ago. He is peering in; with a flash of light he runs back to the door. The force of his kicks doesn't budge the door, but his concern is enough to send me into a state of panic. The woman is carrying a heavy-duty bag, and I can still hear the sound of the engine running in the background. A police team rally around the door to gain access.

They can't see me.

The neighbours are starting to put on their lights and congregate together near the property. I should use this moment to blend into the crowd but, looking around the scene, it would be a challenge to get near the house without explaining why I have appeared from the bushes. I need to remain in the shadows and be vigilant.

I need to dump this mobile phone too. They will soon know that I was near the property; they will see she took the pills herself. I should only be a missing witness since there is no foul play. As I reassure myself that I am still unknown and anonymous, I hear the shatter of glass as the police smash the back door. The panic within me still has me shaking like crazy.

Slow, short breaths push through my lips as I raise a hand to my head.

What the fuck has she done?

I witness Patricia being carried out on a stretcher, which is enough to assure me that she hasn't died. Her face is uncovered, as they move slowly from the back door through the small gathering of locals who watch on in horror.

I dare not go near the house now that there is a focus on it. I bet the attention she has attained will be right up her street once she arrives at the hospital.

I need to go to the hospital. Has Thomas been informed?

Among the feelings of panic, hatred, despair and torment, I have one thought: this can't stop right here. I need to confront her before it's too late. I need her to know that she has destroyed my life. I want that bitch to know how I feel; how she has taken my son from me and now I might never know where he has gone. I need answers.

When the fuss has died down, I will slip away and head into Plymouth – there is only one hospital, on the outskirts of town. I shall make my way there tonight to find out the extent of the damage she has done, or if she'll even make it through the night.

This is not over, Patricia. Your last breath should be mine.

Twenty-Two

Thursday, 13 September 2018

The telephone call from the police officer sent my mind into overdrive. At first, I thought Trish had died in a terrible accident, yet I was reassured she was still alive at the moment he called. It was as though time stood still with the world around me closing into a dark blur. Every second felt like a minute, and my breath was heavy. I was shaking head to toe with the tension rising because I was desperate to know what had happened to her.

'It appears to be an attempted suicide, Mr Mullner,' the officer told me. 'The ambulance crew have taken her to Plymouth Central Hospital. They're doing all they can for her.'

Trish's life was hanging in the balance, if not by a single thread, as I waited by her side all through the night. For hours I just kept talking to her about my day and other random little thoughts that crossed my mind. I wanted her to sense normality, however far the situation was from it. I apologised for asking her to see a psychiatrist. I only wanted her to get help.

This proves I was right.

My nerves aren't holding up to much as I walk around with head lowered and occasional uncontrollable body shakes with the anxiety this has caused.

Trish has been placed into an induced coma after a stomach pump to rid her body of the contents that remained to poison her system. I was informed by the medical professionals that the chances of recovery are very slim. I was also advised to prepare for the worst, but I'll visit her again this afternoon after I manage to get some sleep. They told me in no uncertain terms that the potential damage to her liver could be irreparable. Sadly, all the years of drinking have damaged her liver, but the pills were the final straw that have fatally weakened it to the point of failure. Trish had already been slowly killing herself all this time.

I knew her drinking problem was potentially serious, but I had no real idea of the depths of her addictions. All those sleepless nights, all those days she promised me she hadn't touched a drop – all those lies she covered up, now come to this single moment.

Alcoholism, liver damage; did I notice the change in her behaviour leading up to the overdose? How long has she been taking painkillers?

I have been ignorant of her condition; I never guessed she would have taken it this far. I am floored emotionally because this family has been driven to the brink of hell and back, yet she still wants to selfishly inflict more misery upon me. I love her, yet I hate the control she has over me. That fine line between love and hate has been tested this week alone. I do not think we can continue. If Trish survives this ordeal, I have no idea what the future holds for us. I don't think I can live with the uncertainty that she might cause herself some considerable harm.

Did she do this to torture me? Was it to make me suffer?

Although she never was able to get over Andrew taking the decision to walk out on us, I begin to wonder if the overdose was related to our arguments that have been happening more frequently. I made it quite clear to Trish that our marriage is strained, and we needed to talk about our future.

I didn't mean to end it all.

I feel like shit for not being more firm with her. She should have seen a psychiatrist; she should have had professional help sooner. Now it may be too late.

I wouldn't have any idea where to begin to rebuild my life again since half of it has been spent with Trish, but I know I would be free of the emotional blackmail, the turmoil and hatred, the coming home from work and not knowing what mood she would be in. I feared that leaving her would spiral her mental health to an all-time low. I also feel that if I leave her, the whole of the last twenty years has been for nothing. I don't want that failure on my shoulders.

Did she suspect my intentions?

For the last three years, every day has been about how Trish feels, how she manages to cope. I feel for her at times, I really do – yet the alcohol was an easy way out for both of us. As much as she was willing to drink it, I was ready to keep her topped up with more vodka, gin and rum because it was easier. Knowing that she would quietly sit sobbing on the sofa all night sometimes gave me a night off from the arguments. I am as much to blame for all this anguish as she is, but she always has to take it one step too far. I feel guilty, yet the anger is starting to control me.

Maybe it would be better for all of us if she was dead?

Growing up, I thought that when I got married I'd have two or three children, maybe even four. I expected to have a professional working wife and a life where we could afford many holidays. That we would earn enough money to give the kids a great life and the best education too. I had so many fucking dreams and now they're in tatters. I can't blame her entirely, but when she was pregnant, I had to put her first. She knew that too, and at times I am sure she played on it.

She should have fucking died. How dare she put me through this!

No, no, I can't think like this. I am angry at her, but maybe Trish will get the help she needs when she recovers. She has to recover from this. There must be more the hospital can do for her.

They can get her body functioning again, surely?

Trish needs professional support, and now this is the wake-up call we both need to get her fully motivated to live her life and return back home again. I need to take control now. I need to support her more and be around. We've spent so long focusing on Andrew that we have become too far apart from each other.

Do I really love her?

I am under no illusion that she will ever be the same woman that I met all those years ago. However, I just want a glimmer of the Trish I once loved to make a reappearance. In the early days, everything was so uncomplicated. We used to listen to each other, understand each other, have fun. From the birth of Andrew, every year we just seemed to slip further apart.

I failed. Why do I feel so guilty?

I feel utterly useless as I lie here alone in our bed. I wanted to stay with Trish at the hospital, she's all I can think about. I need to be by her side, but I was advised to go home and get some rest. How can you rest in a circumstance such as this?

My wife is dying.

I'm stroking the sheet where she would normally be by my side, followed by the pillow beside me as I come to terms with the fact that maybe my wife will never be by my side again. As she lies in the hospital potentially dying from the cocktail of drugs that she poured down her throat with the vodka, I wonder if I really loved her would I feel more saddened. My eyes are heavy from the lack of sleep, but I feel resentment that she brought this on herself. This trauma could have been avoided. I wish she had sought professional help before it got to this point.

Should I be crying? Why am I not crying and why am I so fucking angry with her?

All of these mixed emotions that combine grief, guilt and sorrow confuse me. I should be in an absolute emotional breakdown, yet I cannot feel what I think I am supposed to feel.

On the television, actors often portray situations like this with distraught breakdowns, and the idea a person's life cannot continue without their loved one. I would miss Trish, but I feel like I lost her years ago, when her priority became trying to find Andrew.

Andrew is not dead. They never found a body.

I'm numb and confused about whether I love my wife or not. I now understand the term going through the motions.

Maybe I am just too tired and need to rest?

Deep down, I have already accepted my loss. Sometimes Trish was dead to me already as my daily routines continued to have me just existing within our marriage as that guy who gets up in the morning, drives a taxi, comes home, eats, sleeps and repeats this sequence almost every day. Among the nothingness of our relationship was the ferocious worry about not upsetting her, all before I even had time to think about what did actually happen to our son.

Andrew walking out on his family – I have had no choice but to accept it and force myself to move on from the depression it could cause. I may never have all the answers I want about the circumstances, but I am convinced that Trish lives with some kind of guilt that she has never discussed with me.

There have been sightings of him randomly across Devon and Cornwall, but no real concrete evidence that it was Andrew. We have tried pleas, posters, cards in telephone boxes, pictures in shop windows, but to no avail. No known contact, no body found, no one with any motives – he is just classed as a missing person not willing to be contacted or found. That we are a family with a missing person was itself hard to come to terms with after the first few weeks of his disappearance. You always hear this with other families on the news, but you never think of the consequences or the distress of the relatives behind every face on every poster.

The tiredness is starting to relieve me of my constant thinking process as I struggle to keep hold of my consciousness. My eyes are heavy, but I remember one last thing the police officer said to me as I held the hand of my unconscious wife at the hospital.

'You may have a guardian angel,' she dropped into the conversation before explaining that there do not seem to be any initial suspicious circumstances. 'A woman called the emergency services. She seems to be the only witness to your wife's overdose. There was no evidence to support anyone else being in the property at the time, but she saw enough to try to save her life by calling us.'

Someone was out there watching her take those pills.

I drift off to sleep, wondering who that person was and what exactly did she witness. I informed the police that I have no idea who she was and can't seem to fit all the pieces of this jigsaw together. How could she have seen her from the living room window, which is at the rear of our house?

Who was watching our house from the back garden?

Twenty-Three

The Watcher – Now

Thursday, 13 September 2018

The realisation of her suicide attempt still delights me every time I remember the frothy drool falling from Patricia's mouth. It is as though after all this time, in a weird twist of fate, we have collided full circle back to this moment of just the two of us.

This very hospital where I was once convinced to hand over my beautiful baby boy; I now stare into the face of my demon. The monster that has stood behind me my whole life with her guilt, deception, deceit and depravity – Patricia Mullner is an evil I have to face.

'Can you hear me, Patricia?' I ask her gently. 'Can you fucking hear me, you manipulative, selfish bitch?'

The lack of response angers me again and I am conscious of how close I am getting to her. I want to strangle her.

'I've wanted you dead for years,' I mumble. 'For taking my son from me. You were supposed to be looking after him. Not losing him. Where the fuck is he?'

Her body lies motionless, as not a whisper of response comes from her mouth. I feel powerful. I want her to wake up; I want that fucking woman to listen to me. For years I have tried to let go of how I feel and move on, but I can't. I will not be free until she listens, explains or just outright dies in my hands. I want to make that choice, not her. How dare she deny me an explanation by swigging back all those pills.

Selfish fucking bitch. Even after all this time, it still seems to be all about you and your loss.

I need closure for the loss that has haunted me my whole adult life – my son, who doesn't even know who I am. I want revenge, and to inflict more prolonged suffering and distress. How could I ever have known the necklace I dropped off would send her into this much of a shockwave?

'Open your eyes.' I raise my voice. 'Open those fucking piss holes of yours.'

The rage is burning up inside me as I try to hold back. I want to run at her and smother her to death, but I also want that bitch to feel punished. I want Patricia to know how I feel. I want her to see and hear me. I need her to acknowledge that she fucking stole my son, the bitch.

Wake the fuck up.

The temptation to place a pillow over that rancid face and use both of my hands to press it into her is real. Nothing would make me happier than to sit and listen to the whisper of her last dying breath. But I have to find out the truth: I need answers.

I remember there was a time I nearly died because of my addictions. If only I had been included in my son's life, I could have had an incentive to live. I needed a purpose to ease me back from the dark side. I could have been a mother, or at least included in his upbringing to give a new meaning to my life. I had no purpose, no family, no support, and no son.

I can never forgive her. She took Andrew from me and knew she would wipe me out of his life completely.

I have a son who knows nothing of my existence, a bond that is potentially forever broken between us – and I can only blame her. That pure-evil piece of shit is virtually lifeless in my hands. If I hadn't needed a face-to-face confrontation with her, I would never have called the ambulance last night.

I've been awake all night thinking about the story I needed to create to get this close to her in the hospital. I still can't believe it worked. The distraught-sister act had me whisked through the Accident and Emergency department in no time. I had spent at least an hour perfecting my performance before putting it into action.

My plan was to have an emotional breakdown in sight of everyone waiting at the enquiries desk. I had even considered self-harming as a means to display my troubles in front of the nurses. The trauma I showed, and the information I gave was substantial enough for the staff to believe me.

The Intensive Care Unit was a five-minute walk away, during which I lowered my head to look distressed. The closer I got to the ICU, the more my nerves were on edge. I had actually pulled this off, and I thanked the very little sleep I'd had through the night for giving me an unkempt, distressed appearance.

Not one member of the hospital staff had challenged me during my performance, and I was patient enough to wait until Thomas had left the hospital. Waiting in the bushes or behind walls is something I have mastered over several years. I had taught myself manipulation skills in my days of dependency on various drugs. Being able to get what I want has always been top of my priorities.

Every time I look at her face, I am reminded of our past. The drugs, the deception, the old me that I have tried to improve drastically. I had partially succeeded, until I discovered my boy had vanished. This vile, evil bitch had denied me twenty years of happiness, and I could never forgive her. Now that Andrew has disappeared, and could have been murdered for all we know, I can never forgive her. My life is ruined. My life is over.

What must she have done to him?

If she manipulated me in that way, then what damage could she do to a child? My child; my son. I can't imagine how bad his upbringing must have been. All this time I was meant to believe she had taken him to give him a life I could never provide – and it might have been so bad that he had to fuck off and leave her.

I'm so sorry for giving you away.

Five minutes ago, the doctor informed me Patricia had been induced into a coma after she was admitted. It's something to do with checking the level of damage to her body. Fortunately, he has told me there's likely to be considerable irreparable liver damage, in addition to kidney damage, stomach bleeds and high blood pressure.

Patricia was given activated charcoal treatment to bind the poison in her system. I could have told them without the tests that she is poison to the core.

I am still holding out hope for a slow and painful death, but it appears to be touch and go. The damage to her internal organs means that she has at most a few weeks or even days to live.

She has come out of the coma.

The nurses have retaken her blood to measure the levels of drugs that are pumping around her body, and they will return to repeat the process in two hours.

The curtains are closed, the room is cold, and the beep of the heart monitor echoes in the space around us. I am conscious that Thomas might appear at some point today, but I am tense because I really need to speak to her, and I am desperate for this bitch to answer my questions. Her body may be a damaged wreck following weeks of drinking vodka and the massive ingestion of tablets, but she still owes me an explanation for everything she denied me in my life.

'You fucking owe me an explanation,' I say. 'Why the fuck did you ruin my life, and what drove my son to walk out from you both?'

I hold back my overwhelming urge to scream to release this tension; instead, I walk closer to her, and my eyes are fixed on every inch of her face. I keep getting recurring flashbacks of the day I allowed her to take my son away from me. Still, I want to scream, and again, I need answers.

She was supposed to be my midwife; how could I have allowed her to manipulate me?

I was not even an adult at the time, nor in any fit state to make sensible decisions. I know she spotted these flaws, recognised my weakness and used it to convince me to give my baby away. Patricia used her manipulative friendship with me to encourage me to keep our plan a secret. I knew for the sake of Social Services that I would have to run away and hide in the squats. They could never have known I gave my son away, but Patricia had my mobile phone number. She was meant to stay in touch.

I am a victim of her evil plan, yet the only relatable circumstance I have with her is the overdose. I know how hard it can be to feel that the only way out of the depression and constant mind-fuck of negative thoughts is to end your own suffering. At least she knows what that feels like. I struggle to show any sign of remorse because I struggle to feel anything other than hatred.

Standing in the shadows of the trees, lurking around the corners of her house, it has taken me years to understand the workings and the routines of their daily life. There were times I stood at their door desperate to knock it in the middle of the night and confront them, but I would stand there frozen in fear. Other times I would think about dressing up as Andrew and walking past the window, but my greatest fear was returning back to my old drug habits. I have to be clever, yet I am addicted to watching her. I enjoyed that she didn't know I could see her every move.

I noted every minute they left the house. I watched them cook, eat, shop and realised the relationship was starting to show its cracks. I watched arguments from a distance; I saw tension, and I felt rage. I never had the confidence to confront her, but the anger at times drove me to watch them both, it fuelled my hatred towards her.

When Andrew vanished, and the newspaper headlines focused on my missing boy, I kept scouring the papers on a daily basis hoping to read as much as I could about him. It was the first time I built up a knowledge of his life. He became real again to me, and not that little baby I let slip into her hands. Patricia had described her turmoil and constant recollection of the weeks and days leading up to his disappearance in case she missed anything. I remember reading that Andrew had left no note, which was weird, but Thomas's version of events focused on how Andrew was bullied at school and always isolated himself in his bedroom. I don't understand why Patricia painted a rosy comfortable home life, while Thomas described the complete opposite.

One of them was lying.

I still have confidence that Patricia, deep down, knows why Andrew left home. This was the mother he trusted to do the best for him. I do not believe that he simply walked out of the door one day for no specific reason. Something or someone drove him out of that house of hers.

She's a fucking liar.

I can't stop twitching or fiddling with my long curly hair as my brain keeps wanting me to keep my body moving in directions that sometimes are beyond my control. The disorder I have, following years of drug abuse, leaves me realising at times I am walking the streets talking out loud to myself. I see the people around me staring or suddenly switching directions, but they don't know how I feel on the inside.

Passers-by have no idea about the circumstances that drove me to develop the signs and symptoms I have as they stare in my direction, but if I had been in my son's life, everything could have been so different for me. These twitches, the feelings of loss and emptiness, my life would have been so different if Patricia hadn't taken him from me.

Further fuelled by my hatred for her, I struggle daily to hold it all together. Any given moment, I could snap. I just don't care anymore and looking at her body in front of me makes me want to cause her some harm. I sometimes have to remind myself to eat, sleep and function because the obsession I have with her suffering drives me to watch her.

She still hasn't woken up. I don't know if she can hear me.

The heart rate monitor's beeps are closer together than before. *Beep*, I count three seconds, *Beep, Beep*; I now count two seconds between them. Something is going on.

Is she waking up?

My eyes are alert for signs of movement. Nothing but stillness from her limp, despicable presence. I bite my tongue so hard not to say it out loud.

'Die, you vile, evil bastard.'

The beeps are now consistent and louder, faster. The noise is screeching, piercing my ears, but it is as though I am frozen. I see a rush of nurses flood the room, surround her bed. I am panicking as a hand drags my arm to pull me outside while doctors continue to run past me. Then I hear it, that one singular tone followed by counting as they desperately try to revive her. It's happening so fast, all at once I am excited and nervous at the same time. Eager to know if that bitch is dead.

As I am led away down the hall, I hear voices talking to me, but nothing is registering. I nod my head in agreement as I assume that I am to wait here outside her room.

'She's back with us. She's stabilising.'

The voices echo to confirm she has survived yet another near-death incident. With her body in such a damaged state, I doubt I have much longer to confront her. The nurses start leaving the room as I faintly listen to the beep of the heart monitor again.

I'll come back to you, Patricia.

Twenty-Four

Thomas Mullner — Now

Thursday, 13 September 2018

I answer the telephone after its continuous ringing rouses me from the state I am in, staring into the corner of the room, lost with my own thoughts. Unable to drift off to sleep on the sofa, my mind had wandered to the worry and the burden that my wife has become.

The stench of Trish's urine still lingers in the air as I cannot bring myself to wash her chair, where she thoughtlessly attempted suicide. The vodka bottle and the empty pill packets are still strewn across the floor, reminding me of my wife's torment. The thought of losing her horrifies me to the core, but we've been through too much not to fight.

How could she try to end her life like that? Have we not been through enough torment together these past few years?

So many questions run around my mind without answers. I blame myself. I have lost my son; I cannot lose my wife too. All the control I had over my family has died. First, Andrew disappeared, and the consequences of his actions have spiralled Trish into a tormented world of her own, while our marriage slowly disintegrates.

I could have done more for her over the past couple of years. I could have been there for her. I shouldn't have let it get this far after Andrew vanished.

'Mr Mullner, are you sitting down?' the doctor repeats the question. 'Mr Mullner, I am sorry to inform you that your wife has suffered a cardiac arrest. We have her stabilised, but are you able to come into the hospital; it's so that we can discuss her condition with you face to face?'

With very little sleep and a building sense of loss, I do not know how I manage to compose myself through a forty-five-minute journey from one end of Plymouth to the other. I should have called a taxi, which is ironic, and I don't know how I am going to cope with the current situation. At least I make it here without crashing the car.

I look at the doctor, who has whisked me into a room opposite my wife's bed.

For the whole journey, I was convinced she would die before I arrived. There is so much I have to tell her, so much I need her to know.

'Mr Mullner, the team were able to perform cardiopulmonary resuscitation. Your wife has regained consciousness but, having done some extensive testing, it is evident there is fatal organ failure. The charcoal has stopped some of the toxic ingestion, but it was too late. Her body is not responding to our treatments.'

I stare directly at him. I feel numb from head to toe, yet the emotion is building to cause my breath to speed up as the tears hit the corners of my eyes. There is a gentle tug at my stomach due to the fear that starts to ravage my senses.

Organ failure. This is serious shit. I'm losing her, aren't I?

'Is she going to die?' I ask. 'How long do we have left with each other? Can she come home; can I look after her? Are you sure?'

I am panicking, but relentlessly looking for hope. Where there is life, there must be some kind of positivity; she's still breathing for fuck's sake. I am starting to tremble, the hairs on my arm standing to attention. I can feel the breeze from the open window blow past me. I can't describe how I feel emotionally, but it is as though I am dreaming; almost as if I can see myself sitting in the chair looking at him. Everything around me has transformed into a third-person view for just a few seconds as the doctor replies. This cannot be happening to me, to us, this family is ruined.

'A few days or maybe a few weeks at best. I am very sorry, Mr Mullner, but we will try to keep her as comfortable as we can with palliative care. She is able to speak a few words at a time and hear you, but she does drift in and out of consciousness. We have a team in place to manage her pain and symptoms, which you may find distressing to see. Is there anyone else we can call for you at this difficult time – Patricia mentioned Andrew?'

I am lost for words. My body aches as I feel the weight of my head wanting to hit the floor beneath my feet. The room is closing in on me as I start to struggle to breathe with the stress this life-changing fuck-up has caused.

'Andrew is our son,' I reply with tears now dripping to my chin as I realise my wife is dying in front of me. 'He hasn't been seen for years. He vanished.'

The doctor leans forward with a solemn look on his face. His glasses, I notice, are slightly skewed. I am looking around the room, not sure what to do next.

'Blood tests have indicated high levels of creatinine in her blood. This is common with kidney failure. In addition to this, there are enzymes in the blood from the liver that should not be present. Are you able to confirm if she has had any previous history of painkiller addiction, because her body is showing signs of severe damage likely to be caused by substantial long-term abuse.'

I stand up, wipe my tears with the backside of my hand. I can't even look him in the eye. I have been ignorant of this for so long, and the signs were staring me in the face for years.

I'm meant to be her fucking husband.

'I should be with my wife. Can I see her now?'

I ignore his questions because if I discuss her constant abuse of the vodka bottles and my lack of awareness of the painkillers it could lead to more interrogation.

What a neglectful husband must he think I am.

'Mr Mullner,' he says as I show intent to leave the room, 'we are still doing more tests, can you please sit back down?'

I return to my seat. Nauseous and breathing heavily, I have mixed emotions.

'What about transplants?' I ask. 'Liver, kidneys, would that make any difference? Could it help her?'

'There would be a waiting list, but by the time one or possibly both organs arrived, your wife would have deteriorated further, possibly to a fatal extent. The serious issue we are currently facing is the long-term damage caused by the painkillers.'

'How long-term?' I ask the doctor. 'I don't think she's been on them that long?'

'Her yellowing skin, hypocalcaemia and cardiovascular issues suggest she has an addiction.'

'I've known her to take painkillers after her binges on the booze,' I reply. 'It shifts the headaches. Perks her up sometimes. I had no idea that she had been taking them constantly.'

I need to be with her.

'I need to see my wife, Doctor.' I ask, 'Can I see her. Is she even able to talk?'

'Yes, she can hear you, and she has muttered a few words, but she is sleeping quite heavily. I suggest that she does get all the rest she requires and myself and my team will ensure she is kept as comfortable as possible.'

As the doctor stands up to lead me out into the corridor, I try to accept that the next few days or weeks will be precious to me. The tears are starting to stream again while I hold my head in my hands. This internal ache lingers within my soul as my heavy heart tries to accept the loneliness of my current world. How our lives have changed over the last few years has been nothing short of a rollercoaster ride.

'I'm losing her, aren't I?' I ask the doctor; he looks at me with dread having told me her death was imminent a moment ago. 'She's dying?'

He doesn't reply, but instead tightens his lips and nods his head. I have no idea how my body can feel so weak and heavy at the same time. I struggle to accept that my beautiful wife, Trish, is dying. Together we had come so far and the obstacles in our relationship from the early days are now nothing short of a disregarded mishap.

How dare she not fight this torment.

I walk beside the doctor as he leads me to my wife's bed.

'She's still sleeping,' he says. 'If she wakes, she will be able to speak slowly. Patricia was able to respond to our questions earlier.'

Questions? What questions?

The doctor places a hand on my shoulder before walking away. I see him from the corner of my eye as he approaches the door behind him.

'Also, your wife's sister has been in with her most of the morning. She appears to be struggling to accept the effects of Mrs Mullner's suicide attempt. Naturally, she too is coming to terms with the fact that her sister is not responding to any of the treatments.'

For one split second, I don't realise the enormity of what he has just said to me. I nod to signal that I've heard, shrugging my shoulders for him to leave me in peace with my wife. Then it hits me like a ton of bricks. My eyes widen with the confusion I am now faced with.

Sister?

'Patricia doesn't have a sister,' I reply firmly, but I'm getting more and more confused.

The doctor looks at me like I have completely lost my mind. He can see I am struggling to take in the information, but I see him hold on to the door handle, ready to open it, he turns to face me and leans forward.

'Melanie,' he replies. 'Melanie was here when your wife went into a cardiac arrest. She's gone home for some rest, but she informed the nurse down by the entrance to the ward that she will be back later.'

'Doctor, I can assure you again that my wife does not have a sister. I have never in my life heard of anyone called Melanie in her family.'

There is an awkward silence that creeps in while the echo of Trish's heart machine beeps a steady tone in the background. I take a deep breath to compose myself. My eyes are fixed on my wife, yet the confusion focuses my attention on the doctor's claim.

'I just want to sit with my wife. She needs me right now, it's important I talk with her alone. Every minute now is precious for us both. Whoever this Melanie is, she is not her sister. Her mother and father died years ago in a car crash; she doesn't have any family except for me and our son, Andrew. I don't know what else to say.'

'She will be back later; maybe we can discuss it when the woman who is claiming to be your wife's sister returns. In the meantime, I will speak to anyone she has come into contact with to gather more information and see what I can find out for you. If you are absolutely certain, then I may need to contact the police. They too will want to question you.'

The doctor leaves the room and closes the door behind him. I stare at my wife, who is lying on the bed with her life creeping out of her at every minute. These moments could be our final goodbyes. I start to wipe my eyes as I shed tears of sadness. These tears that drop into my guilty hands.

'Trish, I am so sorry.' I look at her for a response, her mouth moves slightly, but still, I am unsure if she can hear me. 'I feel so guilty.'

I can't hold back the emotion any longer as the responsibility for Andrew's disappearance looms over my thoughts. It was never meant to go this far.

Now I come to terms with the sense of losing both my son and my wife.

'Look at us, Trish,' I mutter into the air as I raise my head. I've never been very religious, but I stare upwards just for the hope that maybe in this split second I can be heard. 'I'm sorry for everything, absolutely everything. I truly mean it too. I love you. I love Andrew, I miss him, but how could you do this to all of us.'

Trish mumbles under her breath. It's such a faint whisper I can barely hear her, so I move closer to be by her bedside.

'I love you, always remember that,' I say quietly as I bend down to her ear. The machine she is attached to is still beeping in the background, an annoying tone that distorts my hearing. 'Trish, it's me, Thomas. Why did you do this? Why, Trish? I can't lose you too.'

The mumble sounds short and distorted, but I heard it more clearly this time.

'Kill me,' she whispers, her eyes still not fully open or focused on me as I stare at her. 'Let me go.'

A sudden coldness snaps down my spine. Again, seconds feel like minutes as my world closes in on me, once more confining me to the room as if it imprisons me. Trish says it loud and clear this time with what must take every surge of energy she has within her.

'I want to die.'

I stand there in front of my wife looking at her as if she is a complete stranger.

Twenty-Five

Patricia Mullner – Now

Thursday, 13 September 2018

I can hear Thomas. His voice rings in my ears as I drift in and out of this deep sleep.

Please kill me. Help me release this torment and let me go.

'Do it,' I ask him, begging to be let free from this world. 'I want to die.'

I wonder how I survived as the weight of my body feels chained to the bed. I open my mouth to scream with an agonising pain stretching across my waist, through to my stomach that reminds me of when I had my miscarriage.

In this strange moment, I think about the little girl I could have had, the little girl I let slip into the water while I mopped up the blood with some clothing I later discarded.

I bet she wouldn't have walked out on me. Thomas so desperately wanted a boy. I know he would have walked out on us if I had given him a little girl. He was so thrilled when I said we were having a baby boy. His face could have lit up Plymouth lighthouse.

I lay all the blame on my mother. I had to escape her clutches, her control over me and that low self-worth she had bred into my thoughts. Every negative issue I have with myself is her voice coming back to haunt me. I feel so tired and drained. Sometimes the room darkens, and then I reawaken with that constant voice telling me that I am worthless. I know she was speaking the truth. I have no purpose anymore. No fight left in me to live.

It's over.

Thomas was an escape from the hold she had over me. If *she* hadn't been so cruel to me my whole life, I never would have needed to manipulate that deprived teenager to hand me over her baby boy. It was so much easier than I anticipated, but her youthful naivety helped me in more ways than I cared to imagine.

I miss you, Andrew. Please forgive me.

Thomas only ever discussed having a boy during the early stages of my pregnancy. His disappointment at the idea of a little girl ignited a switch inside of me. I knew I had to obtain a baby boy through any means. Manipulated theft on an unsuspecting drug user who shouldn't have even been having children was so easy for me. This became my sole purpose for weeks on end until it was as though Andrew had landed in my lap from that helpless drug-addict creature. I became fixated and obsessed with succeeding in my plan. She was in no fit state to ever be a mother.

Working in a hospital put me in such a prime position around vulnerable mothers-to-be. When this young, fragile teenager needed support, I had to put myself in the forefront, especially when I knew she was having a baby boy. I persuaded her that I could give him a better life away from the world that she lived in. The more she trusted me, the more she bought into the idea. I seized the opportunity because without her baby my lies could have all been exposed. The handover was smooth and faking my pregnancy to Thomas was another challenge to overcome. All along, I asked myself the same question: what would my mother have done?

I am very sure that Thomas was sleeping with other women behind my back before we were married. I remember the smell of the women on his clothing, the perfume on his jackets and that one time I saw the lipstick marks on the back of his neck. I have always kept my knowledge of this from him because I was confident a baby boy led to his exclusivity to me and only me. I had no doubt from the moment I announced we were having a baby boy that Thomas was all mine, and mine alone.

I will always miss you, Andrew. Regardless of what you think of me, I only ever wanted the best for you. I treated you like a real son of mine.

My mother was right about me all this time. I tried my whole life to rebel against her abuse, yet she knew it from the beginning. I am evil. I do not belong here; I should have slipped away from my mother's womb long before birth. I've never felt good enough at anything I do. I want this suffering to be over for everyone's sake.

If I'd had my baby girl, it would have been disastrous for everyone, not least for the girl who would have grown up to hate me as much as I hated my own mother. I convince myself that I did the right thing by throwing myself down the old stone steps.

That little girl was better off without me as her mother. At least she'll never know.

The regret of inducing a miscarriage on the deep steps of Plymouth Barbican have never before led me down a path of guilt. Only now in this moment of agony as I reminisce about the pain from all those years ago, I wonder how life could have been so different.

Would she have loved me? Would she have not walked out on me like my son?

Thomas would have walked out on us both as he would have supported some shrew who could give him the baby boy he had always wanted. No other man would have wanted me as a single parent with a child born from pure evil genes.

I don't hear my own attempts to scream because I am unable to gather the energy to release anything other than whispers. The pain returns, only this time stronger than before, yet I am unable to move or yell. I desperately need some more painkillers.

'Help me,' I whisper as Thomas holds my hand. 'Let me die.'

Trapped inside my own body, I am aware I am at the hospital. My vision is blurred, and every attempt to squirm in this agony feels like an effort. The heart monitor continues its beeping as I focus on its tune of my heart rate. It doesn't sound great. My throat is sore, and I can feel tubes wired up to my nose. I no longer care what is happening, I just want this life to be over with. That massive pain in my chest is consistent with the aches down my left arm.

Hopefully, I am having another heart attack. I have come this close, how am I not dead yet?

A flashback memory has entered my mind. I remember sitting on the sofa, drowning in the vodka and tablets. I felt my life fading, and I knew I would be alone for the whole night as Thomas was out on his taxi shift. I can still feel the dryness of my mouth with the aftertaste of the drugs. I remember the candlelight fading into darkness as I gave myself up to the incidence of death. I thought I was gone – almost relieved I would be non-existent.

How did I end up being admitted to the hospital, because no one was meant to find me except for Thomas in the morning. I should have been dead by then.

'It hurts. I want to die.'

I start to feel more awake and muster enough strength in this despair to mutter a few more words to Thomas.

'Suffocate me.'

Thomas leans forward towards my face. Unable to see him clearly, I spot the mole on his chin, and I recognise the shape of his face. In this moment of urgency, I remember how handsome he is, my loving, selfish husband.

'They're keeping you comfortable,' he says in my left ear. 'You're not going to survive this anyway, Trish. It's only a matter of days or weeks. We don't have much time together. Your body is shutting down.'

Weeks?

'Kill. Me,' I mutter, now louder and clearer as my body gives me a surge of strength. 'Fucking kill me.'

I hear Thomas crying his eyes out. I have accepted my own fate and wish for him to give me this last push. Surely a pillow over my face will succeed in a less painful death. I hope he hates himself for watching me suffer in this way. That family life we created together has gone; I am emotionless and numb. Mentally I have been prepared in the last couple of days to do this. The world doesn't need evil like me. A bitch who can't keep her family together, a vile child who got in the way of her mother's happiness. I'm worthless, selfish, and I deserve to die. I want to die.

My body is all but on its last legs; but I have accepted my situation. I am calm, I am ready, but I am too fragile to walk off a bridge. In hindsight, it would have been quicker, but all the ingredients I needed to knock myself out and die were in my house the whole time. The emotion and guilt have created a mountain of issues within me that I cannot resolve as I accept my death.

I need vodka and more painkillers. I'm so restricted in this bed.

'It's not happening,' Thomas blurts out. 'I can't do it. I should get the doctor back.'

I struggle to croak a few words together. 'If you love me, you'll do it. Thomas, set me free. I'm dying. This is the end. I beg you because I can't live anymore.'

I smile at him and nod my head gently to signal an assurance that I mean this, and I am ready. Our eyes lock on to each other, and I can see from the look he gives me that he is suffering. The sadness is prevalent across his expressions, but I know he will accept his loss in time. The greatest gift I can give him now is a new start; it's all he has been mentioning for the last three years. I could never leave our house in case Andrew returned, and I wasn't there to welcome him home.

We need a new start, Trish; we should move away. A fresh start would do us both some good.

Thomas lowers his chin to his chest as he starts to remove the pillow from behind my head. I feel him stroke my forehead with his hand as he gently raises me before holding the pillow in front of my face. I am silent but nodding. I want him to read the signal in my eyes.

Do it. Do it. I've never been more ready.

I am sure to face my final breaths. He should finish what I started and let me go in peace. I see his face has reddened with the constant crying; his arms are shaking as he contemplates his next move. I try to raise my head in the direction of the pillow, but I struggle due to the heavy pressure and pain on my body. Life is fading as I feel the loss with almost all my breath. This world is now my struggle.

'Let me go,' I whisper to him again, less frustrated. I now close my eyes to feel him lean over to kiss my cheek. A salty taste of his tears reaches my mouth as he cries into my face. Emotionless and accepting, I still remain calm, although I want him to hurry before anyone catches him in the act. I want this to be over with and soon.

Thomas looks into my eyes once more and stops dead, shaking his head at me furiously. He is lowering the pillow further into my face; this time covering my nose. His cries are louder, I can hear him sobbing over the beeping of the heart monitor. My heart rate increases as the anxiousness of my looming suffocation both scares and excites me. This is it.

'No. I just can't do this.'

Thomas removes the pillow from my face and throws it to the ground in a forceful shove. He places his hands over his head and then drops to his knees on the floor in a hysterical mess.

Fuck it!

I feel a small tear form in the corner of my eyes. Saddened by Thomas's weakness, I do know that he loves me. He should have finished this to stop me from the painful death my body has induced.

In the short few seconds that pass by as he returns to his seat, I wonder if I ever really loved him, or whether it was just that he was able to provide me with an escape from my vindictive mother. I loved what we had together, my purpose was to give my child hope and direction. To not ever feel how I felt growing up. I wanted the best for Andrew.

I just want an end to my suffering. I do not have the strength or power to eat anything. The only control I may have is to try and starve myself to death, but I don't think I will last the next few days. If they want to feed me through a tube, I will rip it out and refuse treatment.

'Andrew,' I mutter as loud as I can manage. Albeit not very clear. 'About... Andrew.'

I cough to clear my throat as Thomas returns to my bedside once more. His tears have dried, and he holds my hand. He squeezes my fingers, which reminds me of the days when we had happier times at the start of our relationship. He would continuously touch me, cuddle me, squeeze me. I smile at him; although his world is about to be shattered even more. I have to do this for his sake. I have to be honest before it is too late.

'He's gone,' Thomas replies. 'Andrew left us.'

'It's not that,' I reply, stopping to take a deep breath. 'Andrew.'

'What about Andrew?' Thomas snaps, removing his hand from mine. 'What is it, Trish?'

'He's not your son. He wasn't ours.'

Thomas frowns at me, shakes his head. I continue to stare at him with a seriousness I know he will recognise from me.

'You are not his father. You never were.'

My voice crackles, but I want to finish my sentence. Thomas stands to attention.

'You were never his father. He was given away by his young mother.'

I take more breaths; I'm running out of air.

'I took him, Thomas. I took him from her.'

I watch as Thomas starts to walk backwards. His body language appears repulsed, but I sigh with relief that after all these years I have given him this honesty that he deserves. In this small room that binds us together, for once, I have been able to look him in the eye and be honest. He deserved to know the truth.

'What are you going on about? You're lying. Is this your bad memory again?' Thomas asks me. 'Andrew is my son. Who else could have been his father? So, you're saying you're not even his mother?'

I do not have the strength to answer, but I close my eyes and shake my head. I cannot be bothered to live through this suffering any longer.

'No,' I mumble at him. 'It's not a lie. It's why I could never take him to the hospital when he was ill. It's why I couldn't go to the police with the necklace. Someone put that necklace there. Someone knows.'

Through a squint and blurred vision, I see him raise his hands to his head. The cries continue as he sits back down. The realisation will soon set in that he has fathered another man's child. Mourned the loss of a son that was never his and yet I still know that he is kind enough to forgive me. I never deserved a man like Thomas, which reassures me that he will be better off without me. I hope he can move on after my death.

My heavy breaths send me into this overwhelming tiredness, but the pain still screams its way across my dying body. Helpless and restrained, all I can do is listen to Thomas as he sobs louder and louder.

I'm sorry, Thomas.

'Trish,' I hear him say through the sobs, but I can barely keep my eyes open, 'you're not the only one keeping secrets.'

Twenty-Six

Andrew and Thomas Mullner – Then

Friday, 21 August 2015

Trish was out for the count on the sofa. I saw the vodka bottle down beside her feet, which answered my question as to why she was snoring so heavily that early on in the evening. She was supposed to have given it up. I wondered then whether with Andrew being older, she was finding her duties as a mother were no longer required.

Could she cope knowing that she wasn't needed as much?

I'm sure she was struggling, but we didn't communicate very well then as husband and wife. Trish seemed to have good days and bad days, but as the years went by, the bad days came around more frequently than the good days. She blamed it on her headaches, which were getting worse and more frequent.

'If you're getting this many migraines,' I told her, 'go and see a doctor. I'm worried about you. Maybe it needs looking at.'

'No, I do not need a doctor,' Trish responded. 'I know all of that medical shit from my training days. They just give you painkillers anyway, and I can pick some up at a chemist. It's stress, and I'll deal with it in my own time.'

I had given up arguing with her; I'd had the bruises and the ear-bashing moments to prove that I wasn't getting anywhere fast. I had my suspicions that she was bordering on the brink of a breakdown, caused by something so great she couldn't even talk to me, her own husband, about it. She knew I loved her; she knew I would be there for her no matter what. When we married, I knew she had me for the rest of her life. I meant every word of my vows. Every word. My mother and father brought me up to respect marriage, and to make it work. I had watched my own parents have their squabbles, but they were together for life. I had my tough times with Trish, but all I ever wanted to be was a family man with my wife and kids. I wished we had more than one, but I was grateful to have Andrew to carry on the Mullner name. I had always wanted a son.

Together, I thought we could work through things as a family.

The weekend trip we took to Wales was meant to bring us together as a family, but over the twelve months since then, we had drifted even further apart. Something changed Trish's mood that weekend, although she always denies it. I knew something happened that she was keeping from me. I don't like her keeping secrets. She knows that she can tell me anything.

When we came home, we had a huge row that same Monday evening.

'I know you're hiding something from me,' I said to her in one of her drunken states. 'I know you, Trish. What is wrong with you? Look at you, your drinking is getting out of control again. Whatever it is, it is better that you're honest with me. I'm your husband for fuck's sake.'

Andrew stayed upstairs in his bedroom while Trish came at me with the sweeping brush. I couldn't defend myself from her as she beat me over the head and various places around my body. I couldn't walk very well for a couple of days after that while the bruising was coming out. I forgave her though. I know she has had a hard life from her mother who treated her like shit, but she hasn't ever done it again. When she calmed down, she said she was tense and needed a drink. Then following the alcohol came the headaches; the painkillers got rid of them in the short term, but I was convinced she needed to see a doctor. I wanted her to speak to someone professional.

If she were to have hit me like that unprovoked again, I would have suggested another attempt at getting some psychiatric help. I didn't like it when she screamed that she was evil because it was an outburst from the mental abuse caused by her mother. That woman not only damaged her daughter's state of mind in childhood, but in adulthood as well, and it impacted upon our marriage. I do think if she'd spoken to the right people and got professional help for her past abuse, then she could have worked through her demons. If I'd ever walked out of her life, I dread to imagine what it would have done to her.

For the first time in a few weeks, I had decided to finish my taxi shift early and came home to spend some time with my family. I admit it was something I should have done more often, but what with the mortgage and bills, every hour I was home I could have been making money in my taxi instead.

Andrew was in his bedroom; since failing a couple of the modules in his business diploma, I knew he wasn't keen on the idea of returning in September to complete the course. I couldn't understand how a teenage boy could go through life with very few or no friends at all. My life at his age was the complete opposite. I tried to get him into sports, and to do all those father–son things away from the home, but he was never interested. I couldn't force him and I knew that Trish spoiled him too much. She allowed him to do what he wanted, even if it meant isolating himself on his computer games. Looking back now, I see the rift it caused between us.

Andrew had taken the breakup with Katrina very hard; I had said to Trish it was likely his first love, and from my understanding, he had not had any contact with her since then. I was different from Andrew with women in my day: I had a string of them on the go in my youth. My body was in better shape because my father had me working hard on the farm, and through that, I became tanned and toned almost all year. I settled down when Trish became pregnant; I always said that was the day I became a man. The realisation of my responsibilities hit me hard during her pregnancy, and I owned them. All I had ever wanted to do from that day onwards was to make sure my family knew I could provide for them. We had our arguments, Trish and I, even during her pregnancy. I struggled for months with a lack of intimacy. She never wanted me near her, but I watched her suffer with sickness and mood swings almost every other night. I felt guilty in the end but assured her I would back off. Her mood swings were again reminding me of those times in her pregnancy.

Andrew was becoming more distant too. It can't be healthy sitting in your bedroom day in and day out on a games console. I was sure he was using it as a means of distraction from his studies, and I took him aside to remind him of the importance of getting a good career. I didn't want him to end up being a taxi driver like me – not that I am ashamed, because I made that choice off my own back. I knew that if I hadn't fallen in love with Trish when she was pregnant, my life would have been so different. I wanted better for my son than him sitting in a room all day long. I wanted him to grow up into a man with a good career, so he didn't have to work twelve- to fourteen-hour days to feed his family. We were the last of the Mullner line – I wanted Andrew to take our family name and do it proud. It was important to my heritage.

Andrew didn't seem to listen to me or his mother. It was like he wanted no part of our family.

Andrew tiptoed down the stairs dressed in jogging bottoms and a T-shirt that looked creased. I often wondered why he chose not to iron his clothes, but Trish told me it was fashionable and how the kids all wear it nowadays. She never complained about not having to iron any of it, but my own mother wouldn't have let me leave the house with so much as a crease or hair out of place. How the times have changed.

'Dad, can I talk to you for a minute?' he whispered to me, so he didn't wake his mother. 'I need your help. I've been thinking about something for a while now. What with college coming to an end soon.'

'Sure,' I replied. I looked confused as this was already the longest conversation he had had with me in days, but I felt a sense of pride that he could come to me and ask for advice. 'Shall we go upstairs and leave your mother to sleep it off?'

'Perfect,' he responded as he turned around to walk back where he'd come from. 'I have something I want to show you on the computer. If I show you, then I can explain it better after that.'

We walked into his room, but the first thing that hit me was the stale smell of dirty clothes on the bedroom floor. His room hadn't been cleaned in weeks, possibly even months. I didn't know how anyone could live in that room with a smell like that.

'You need to open a window in here, son,' I said. 'Your room looks like a bomb's hit it. Don't you think you need to get some air in here?'

Andrew opened the window, and I had by that time already noticed the website on his computer. The London Eye was centre of the screen and the game development company had the job listed on their website. I had assumed he was going to ask me for a sightseeing trip away. But I didn't think we could afford it. The London skyline filled with skyscrapers appeared a million miles away from Plymouth. I'd have loved to have taken him, but I was thinking that maybe we could take a day trip instead another time.

'Dad, can you close the door?'

I looked at him; I could see that he was nervous. Something was on his mind. I wondered what Trish had done to upset him now.

I hoped she hadn't hurt him.

Trish promised me that she had never hit our son and wouldn't dream of doing so because she loved him too much. The anger issues at times could be too strong for her, but since Andrew spent most of his time in his room, I believed her.

'Dad, I've been thinking about this for some time, and I think I just need to blurt it out. It is a lot to ask, but can you just hear me out?'

'Sure, son,' I replied. 'I will just listen. Whatever it is, just let me know, and I'll give you my opinion, and we'll take it from there.'

For the next few minutes, Andrew explained to me that he had been thinking long and hard about the advice I had given him over the last year. With his college studies a write-off, and nothing else really going on in his life, he asked for my help with a job internship he wanted to apply for in London. It would have meant him moving away for a few weeks, but the experience and opportunity to learn business skills would add value for his development. He was really enthusiastic about it; for the first time I saw my son being driven about his future. I was excited too.

'Plymouth has nothing to offer me,' Andrew said, still shaking a little as he tried to convince me this was a great plan. 'I have tried mentioning it to Mum, but she was having none of it. She didn't even listen to anything I had to say. It's her way or no way at all. This is a great opportunity for me.'

I smiled at him as I admired the moment. My son, asking me for advice.

'This internship would really help me with my studies. It could lead to something big. Dad, can you help me?'

'How am I expected to do that?' I asked, not wanting to disappoint him, but I wasn't convinced he had really thought it through. 'You're seventeen in a couple of weeks, and it is your choice, but I am sure you could work something out in Plymouth. We could visit a few businesses, government buildings or maybe even banks in our own city?'

The only part that had annoyed me was that he wanted to desperately spend those few weeks away from Plymouth. I knew gaming had been his strongest interest throughout most of his childhood and it did sound like a great opportunity. I knew that his mother would be livid, but I felt he had reached an age where he finally wanted experiences. I could finally get him to do something outside of his bedroom.

How would he support himself?

'Andrew, I want to help,' I replied, 'but don't you think we should talk this through with your mother first? It's a massive decision. How are you meant to get there and support yourself? You've never lived anywhere other than here before.'

I could see the disappointment in his face. This was the only time he seemed so serious about something other than playing the latest war game on his console. He looked tearful, which started to make me feel guilty for expressing my concerns.

'You've never really done anything like this on your own before. This is quite a big thing to do, Andrew. Also, the furthest you've been is Wales, and you pretty much hated that too. Why don't you wait until after college?'

He sat on the bed with his head down. I was still feeling a little guilty. I didn't know what else to say.

'Dad, Mum hit me in Wales.'

It was as though he had put a knife right through my stomach. The expression on his face looked terrified.

She promised me she had never touched him.

'What did she do?' I asked, trying to remain calm; otherwise, he might not open up to me. I wasn't used to these conversations with my son. 'Where did she hit you?'

'Face. She hit my face in the caravan just after you went to get some shopping.'

I felt nervous. I had a flashback of the afternoon where I walked into the caravan to see my wife wrapping her arms around my son because he'd hurt himself.

'The marks on your neck?' I asked. 'Was that your mother?'

Andrew started to cry and sob.

'Please, Dad, don't tell her I said anything. I'm begging you not to mention it because you're never here much, and I don't know if she'll do it again.'

In a short space of less than five minutes as a father, I felt like a complete failure to my own son. I sat down on the bed next to him. I too was emotional because I didn't understand why he hadn't told me sooner. I was disappointed that as a father he didn't have me to confide in.

'Andrew,' I said, 'I'm sorry for not being around more, but you know your mother has problems. I have to earn enough to pay for the house, all our bills and the food. It has meant me working long hours. I'm sorry, son.'

Andrew was still crying; he wiped his tears with his hands and then stood up to look out of the bedroom window.

'I have already applied, and they have accepted my application,' Andrew announced. 'I took a chance, but expected a no. All I need is enough money for accommodation for a few weeks. The course is part of the company's training plan and once you've been through it, they might offer you something full time. I don't know what else to do. I don't want to stay here.'

I didn't reply, but I stared at him while listening.

'Dad, this is a real opportunity, and you know how much I love gaming. I can combine my business studies with something that I enjoy. It's perfect for me. It's just a shame I live in Plymouth. Nothing like this would ever happen here. I just need some money for the accommodation and food and stuff.'

'Why didn't you tell me about your mother sooner?' I asked, avoiding the question. I was desperate to know why he was telling me this now. 'Has she done it since?'

'Because I'm afraid of her,' Andrew replied. 'She suffocates me. I only feel safe in my room. I don't think she would let me make my own choices. I always have to do what she wants or tells me. I really want this, Dad. I'm sorry for not saying anything before. I know Mum has her issues, but I can't keep living this way.'

This was the first time he had ever really asked me for anything since he was born. All the decisions in his life had been made by Trish. I could see he really wanted to do it and I couldn't deny how right he was. Trish did always want him close; she did always make decisions for him. I could see that he was growing into a man now; I had to help him make his own decisions.

'I will help you,' I replied, 'but we need to keep this from your mother. It will trigger her issues, and I know she will be furious with us both. If I help you leave, you need to promise me that you will make this work. This is a massive decision to make and a huge lie to your mother. Do you understand me?'

Andrew smiled at me; this was a beautiful father and son moment between us. I felt like a father, it was empowering. I should have made better decisions for him when he was a child. I knew I struggled to bond with him in the past, but he needed me, and for once I could support him.

While Trish continued to sleep off the alcohol downstairs, I agreed to lend Andrew some money from our joint savings account. He promised to organise the internship accommodation from his computer and keep me updated. I was too busy with my own work to organise it myself, all I had to do was part with the cash. We also agreed that he would pretend he lost his mobile phone to explain the lack of contact with us in the meantime. But he would return home in a couple of weeks and, by that time, Trish would see the difference the internship had made to his life. He would have a new-found independence and some real work experience that could open up new doors in his life. That boy needed a future.

'She's going to report you missing, you know that, don't you?' I said as the thought crossed my mind that two or three weeks without him around would send her insane. 'I have to just go with the flow initially and support her. I'll probably have to walk the streets looking for you and knock on doors, but promise me that you will come back safe and sound after two weeks. You have one chance, son.'

'I promise,' Andrew replied. 'It will be an adventure, and I need this opportunity. We both know that if Mum knew anything, then she would come to London and drag me back home. Please don't say anything to Mum?'

Going behind my wife's back was the hardest decision I had ever made, but she had lied to me about not hitting him, and those marks on his neck were prominent enough for me to think about his safety. She shouldn't have been taking her issues out on him like that. It wasn't right and it wasn't healthy for any of us.

I had to help my son; we needed to make changes in our family.

I was nervous about the consequences of my actions, but Andrew had sold it to me. The company on the website looked legit, the accommodation from what Andrew described seemed adequate, and he had promised to put all his efforts into making it work. The poor boy deserved it after the abuse he had suffered in the hands of his mother. We needed to start letting him grow up and make his own decisions. I thought I was helping him. I was trying to be a good father. I know that my father would have done anything for me.

I had decided to hand over to Andrew the two thousand pounds in our savings account in cash. Trish never paid any money into that account and was often too forgetful to even look there or remember we had it. She wouldn't even notice it was missing. Andrew deserved this chance. He made it sound like an opportunity not to be missed.

I owed my son the opportunity, if only for his forgiveness. As a father, I had failed him.

Twenty-Seven

Thursday, 13 September 2018

Sitting on the wooden bench opposite the hospital entrance, I have been waiting for an hour, but it feels like a whole afternoon. A chilly breeze is blowing against my face while I contemplate my next move. I know that time is running out fast while that manipulative, malicious bitch sits in there close to her last breath. I have to act fast, and soon.

I have to kill her.

This hatred is all I can think about, and I need to release my anger in her direction. The pressure has been building for days now. Killing Patricia while I watch and stare her in the face as she pays for what she did to me, now that is justice – that woman ruined my fucking life. This will satisfy my need for revenge, but I really don't have much time now. It will only be a matter of time before someone realises that I am not her sister.

As the tension builds within me, I can feel myself starting to twitch again, curling my hair and talking to myself. I cannot stop it. Those around me are backing away to give me some distance. I recognise those worrying stares as I struggle to hide the long-term effects of my historic drug abuse. I try to keep my tics under control, but as the tension builds mentally my body releases these actions for relief. I'm used to them now, but for those around me it can be distressing.

Thomas has parked his taxi in the car park, and my eyes follow him as he enters the main doors. For that brief minute or so as he walks down, I am fixated on his face. I can see the tiredness in his eyes as walks into the hospital entrance. He looks lost.

Unaware of my presence at the hospital, Thomas has no idea that for months I have been watching their every move. I've even managed to sit in his taxi in a disguise while putting on some ditzy voice. I played dumb, yet all the time I was extracting more and more useful bits of information. I needed to build a picture of their lives. I know his routines, I know what day he goes shopping, I watched as he went to bed alone while that piece of shit drowned in her own sorrows in front of the news. Some days I have watched her down one bottle of booze, and other days I've seen her rush through three. I don't know how she could ever forgive herself for denying my boy a right to see me as his mother.

She owes me an explanation.

I wanted to follow Thomas inside, but I am not ready to expose myself to him as Andrew's real mother just yet. I have assumed that, by now, the doctors have called him about Patricia's heart attack, and they're probably briefing him on her condition. I don't even feel any sadness for him. They both deserve this.

He will be better off without her too. I bet she has held him back for years. Their whole marriage is built on nothing but lies.

He will have the same chat I was given about her body rejecting the treatments and a care team in place ready for her imminent death. I faked an outburst of tears in the waiting room, yet deep down, my anticipation was hard to contain. Thankfully I kept the twitches and tics my body has developed down to a minimum. It is difficult to keep my mind from talking out loud. My mind has a collection of words it needs to release; I plan events out in my head, and I have to keep talking to remind myself. Patricia created an empty void that has disturbed me for years.

'I need to get some air,' I'd informed the nurses. 'I'll return soon, I just need some time alone to gather my thoughts.'

All those times when I watched her with my binoculars, I wish I could have stormed in and demanded answers, but instead, I satisfy myself by fuelling the hatred. In some weird twisted way, I felt like a small part of their family as I watched them both in their own surroundings. Their house was the home my son lived in, the only family he knew – by observing their functions, routines and flaws I have a connection with Andrew. Watching them gives me a sense of closeness, I also felt like I knew them, and if I knew them, then I would know my son.

Every evening I sat in the bushes as the sun went down, obscured from the sight of everyone. Some nights I cried as I watched Patricia cry from a distance, other nights I told myself I would knock on their door. I had never built up the courage to confront her on her own doorstep. I also enjoyed knowing they couldn't see me because it was my secret over them. I felt I had the upper hand and that I could be ready to confront them at any minute I chose. I am not sure if Thomas doesn't really know the truth after all these years. I watched him go to work and back on many occasions, enough to witness that he is a simple man who enjoys simple tasks.

I doubt he would have stayed with her if he had known Andrew wasn't his son.

It felt powerful watching them while I remained distant in the trees. Elmton is a small, quiet village where at night there are hardly any street lights, so you can walk through it without being noticed. I considered moving closer, but it's too expensive. The income from my part-time job and benefit support wouldn't stretch that far. I have no choice but to live in more urban surroundings where you have to double lock your doors at night, and check that all your windows are shut.

Patricia stole my son, and I want her to hurry up and die so this suffering is over. Today, this must end. She is so close to death; I could almost smell it on her.

Why did she destroy my life? What drove my son away from that family?

Thomas must be aware of her heart attack by now. Patricia could have even died in the hour I have been out here for all I know.

Unable to move forward with my life, there are questions I need answering. Simple questions a mother would instinctively know.

Andrew's favourite colour? His favourite meal? What were his interests? Did he have a girlfriend? Has he made any kind of fucking contact to come home?

I have been denied all of this knowledge about his growing up by that one individual, Patricia Mullner. The damage one human can cause to another is life-changing; for myself, this has been both mentally and physically. Only the hope of finding my son is giving me a purpose; not only has Patricia denied me being part of his life – she has forced him so far away from me. I may never see or find him. Andrew has no knowledge that I am his real mother, so why would he even think about me if he doesn't know I exist? The more I think about her, the more I am raging on the inside.

You will pay for this, Patricia!

All those years, I had no purpose, hope or support from anyone. Friends around me dying in squats as their last hit was to be their final breath. I have witnessed poverty, suffering, distress and violence in the drug-infested world I once surrendered my dignity to. Clinging on to the hope that I had a son out in the world waiting for his mother to contact him kept me alive. I still have hope that one day he will return even if I am exposed as Patricia's murderer, it will be worth it for him to know who I really am.

Maybe the death of Patricia would bring him home if the news spread?

I know I can do this, because almost every day this week I have come so close to murdering that beast. I feel my excitement brewing at confronting her. Not even death itself really feels like justice for my loss.

Despite my tiredness from the excitement of last night's event, I still have no regrets about calling the ambulance to rescue her as I watched her overdose. I have watched her have a heart attack today, but I am yet to see her die.

The end is approaching, and the removal of such scum from this earth is best for us all.

I am ready to kill her.

I walk in through the hospital entrance, blending in with a family crowd. I keep my head down so as not to look suspicious as people walk at me in different directions. The sensation that my view is spinning starts to happen as more and more people walk in front of me – at least it seems busy.

The hospital is so large that I had to carefully remember the route back, so I do not have to engage in any form of conversation with hospital staff. I see the cleaners on the left side of me wheeling around their trollies, while visitors are starting to form queues in the food outlets scattered by the entrance. I head straight for the stairs while large gatherings begin to form around the elevators. Everyone seems to need to keep moving forward. No one is looking at me, not yet.

My calves tighten due to the number of stairs I have to endure on the way upwards, but I make it. As I creep back onto the Intensive Care Unit, I see Patricia's room straight ahead. She'd better be ready with some answers.

This is it!

'Can I help you?' a young nurse in a blue uniform asks as I slowly manoeuvre my way to Patricia's room. 'Is everything all right, madam?'

I must remember not to look so defensive and make sure I am still pulling off the act of looking like Patricia's traumatised sister. With my fingers crawling through my hair, I realise she's seen one of my tics.

Keep it under control.

'I'm fine, thank you.'

I lower my head slightly, remove my hands from my hair and try not to start talking out loud to myself. Hopefully, she will move on fairly quickly. All the while she is standing there, I am thinking of an alternate plan should I be questioned.

I'm lost – I'll just pretend I am on the wrong ward. If all else fails, just keep running. Maybe I should run anyway?

The nurse turns away and heads back into a room, leaving me looking at Patricia's door. It is closed, but I can see movement in there. It must be Thomas. I fixate on them again, reminding myself of all the times I stood outside in the cold with a perfect view of their living room. Something soothes me when I witness their lives while they aren't aware of my presence. I have a split-second flashback of the crows and their squawks. I can virtually hear the birds again, along with the whistling of the wind. A memory stops me in my tracks; it is a vision of them arguing. I remember seeing her swaying with a bottle in her hand while Thomas stormed out of the room. I used to wish so badly I could listen in on their conversations. I had even planned to get a listening device into the house but failed.

I place a hand on the door handle, its coldness snaps me back out of the flashback, and I am standing there with the door open. I have revealed myself to Thomas. He is an emotional wreck, shaking and distracted. Thankfully he hasn't recognised me without my Rachael disguise. I knew this day would come, and here I am.

The continuous heartbeat sound from the monitor reassures me that the bitch is still alive. I still have that pang of hatred when I look at that despicable face. At least it's breathing. It can answer my demands.

Thomas is looking at me, his eyes moving upwards and downwards while I contemplate what I will say. I didn't prepare enough for this, I know, but I am running out of time.

'Thomas?' I ask. 'How is Patricia holding up?'

The confused look on his face is revealing, I can see he has no idea who the hell I am, but I've given it away that I know who they both are. I am ready to finish this bitch off.

'This isn't good timing,' he responds, wiping tears away from his eyes with the sleeve of his top. 'You can see that my wife is seriously ill. Who are you, have we met before?'

'Melanie,' I reply. 'I'm your wife's sister – well, half-sister. The police got in touch with me about the overdose yesterday, and I came to the hospital straight away. I know we've not spoken in years, but I needed to be with her.'

The expression on his face changes dramatically.

'Come inside and shut the door behind you. I know that Trish doesn't have a sister, so who are you and why are you here?'

I step inside while remaining calm, and I close the door behind me. The catch snaps shut, and for the first time, we are all together in the same room.

'We need to talk.'

I tighten my lips and raise my eyebrows. My confidence is building, but I can feel my hands wanting to twitch and play with my hair. All the thoughts in my mind are racing at once. I have no choice but to admit the truth. I have to say it.

'Andrew is my son, and she stole him from me. Patricia took my baby boy. He was mine. *Mine* and she fucking destroyed my life in the process. She has ruined my whole fucking life.'

I gasp for air, throw my hands to my face as the tears gush in an emotional release. Thomas's eyes widen in the moment of surprise. I can see the confusion on his face.

There, I have finally said it. The secret is out.

Twenty-Eight

The Watcher, Patricia and Thomas Mullner – Now

Thursday, 13 September 2018

'I don't understand how all of this can be happening?'

Thomas shakes his head in disbelief. I stand by the door as he starts to walk around the room. Nervous and feeling uneasy, I try to remain calm. I hadn't planned to confront them together in this hospital room. There were so many other ideas I had considered in revealing myself to her.

Patricia even had to go and ruin this. I wanted to drop further clues, I needed to drop enough hints that she would remember who I am. The plan was to drive her crazy until one day she would beg me to kill her, just to end her suffering. She fucking had to take an overdose too soon.

How many people have suffered at her hands?

'My name is Melanie, and I'm not her sister. You're right, I know she doesn't have one,' I reply. 'But you need to know the truth about your wife. She's been hiding a secret from you.'

Thomas glares at me with hatred. He's shaking his head and he looks angry.

'I don't understand. How did you end up here at the hospital?' he asks. 'Why, after all this time, have you managed to appear here? Why now?'

'I trusted her with my son about twenty years ago. I believed that she would look after him. I handed him over to her, and you were both meant to look after him. Then, I saw on the news a few years ago that he had vanished, which led me to find you both in Elmton. She promised me that I was going to be part of his life.'

I watch him shaking. He appears to be panicked. I recognise the shock. I turn to look at that helpless creature, and it repulses me. The woman that was the root cause of all this trauma and stress is trapped in that bed – dying in front of us both. I am trembling as the impulsive urge to strangle her embraces me again. My mouth is twitching as I want to have an outburst, but I hold it back. The more I glance in the direction of her bed, the more I can feel myself struggling to keep my urges under control while the beeping of her heart monitor is annoying me.

I fucking hate her. Drop down fucking dead you disgusting bitch.

'She told me,' Thomas replies, his voice softening as he sighs. 'I can't handle this right now, it's all too much, all at once. I'm struggling to take it all in. To be honest with you, Andrew is still our son, regardless. He will always be our son. I am the only father that boy has ever known and Trish is his mother. I don't think for one minute that he has any idea what he has put us through.'

How fucking dare he call that manipulating bastard Andrew's mother.

'I am his mother,' I reply, biting my lip in annoyance. 'Patricia is not his fucking mother.'

'My wife, for god's sake, is dying. This whole fucking week has been nothing but trauma. Trish is seriously ill; can't you fucking see that? Look at her. Take a look.'

Patricia is starting to mumble in the background. I watch as she tries to move her head. He doesn't know that I've seen the pillow on the floor beside the bed. If I was to make a run for it and smother her face, he is too close and would be able to hold me back. His raised voice has started to waken her.

It's not the right time. A few more minutes, maybe?

'If you don't leave now, I will shout for the doctor, or even the police. I just want to be with my wife – alone. Give us both some privacy before I press the call button.'

'How long have you known about Andrew?' I ask, ignoring his request because I still need an explanation. I didn't come this far to walk away. For years I have thought about this very moment. 'Patricia made me swear to never, ever tell you that Andrew was not your son, so when did you find out?'

'I'm going to call the police.' Thomas raises his voice, grabbing his phone from his pocket. 'My wife is dying, and our son has disappeared. Let us both have some peace. My wife is dying. I can't forgive myself for what I have done.'

'I'm not leaving,' I blurt out. I am trying to display a positive, confident impression, but inside I am a wreck. My mental state is hanging on by a thread, and I can feel my body craving the drugs. The cravings never leave you. 'Why don't you call them and we can discuss what you stole from me. Let's tell the police you aren't his fucking parents. Go on,' I yell at him. 'Call the police. Do it. Let's get this over with and they can charge her. This two-faced lying cunt isn't his fucking mother.'

I have my hands grabbing at my hair as the twitches start in sync with my anxiety. My mouth is dry as the nerves are getting to me. I am going to say it. I keep thinking it over in these fast few seconds that tick by. I have to say it out loud. He needs to know.

'You had a daughter.'

Thomas put the mobile phone back into his pocket. He still stares in the direction of Patricia, who appears to be semi-conscious in the bed. With the effects of her overdose beyond repair and her body filling up with fluids, he should take one last look at the vindictive animal and move on with his life. I still don't feel an ounce of remorse. I don't even look at her as being human.

Someone needs to put that cunt down.

'You had a little girl, but she thought you would be disappointed.'

Thomas doesn't look surprised. He closes his eyes tightly and then opens them again before taking a breath of air.

'She told me before you got here,' Thomas replies. 'It hasn't even really sunk in yet. I know she wasn't his mother; I know I am not his biological father. I haven't even the time to come to terms with it all. She has never mentioned your name to me before. Not in the whole time we have been married. Not once.'

For the next few seconds, we both stand and look each other in the eye. Emotionless, broken and connected in this twisted circumstance.

'She told me she had an accident and it was quite a forceful fall to inflict a miscarriage. She didn't want it.

That baby girl would have ruined everything. She manipulated you to get her out of the hole she was living in. Her pregnancy was real, her baby was not. I believe that she threw herself down the steps because she wanted that miscarriage. She wanted my son instead.'

I watch as this man's world crumbles beneath his feet, yet I can't stop myself from stabbing the knife in some more. He appears to have been caught up in her game-playing.

'She manipulated you too. I remember her telling me that you wanted a son so much that she was convinced you would walk out on her. She manipulated me to hand over my baby because I was vulnerable. Everything is her fault. She manipulated all of this. Andrew was my son, and I had a right to see him.'

'I don't know if I can deal with this,' Thomas replies, stopping my flow of confession. 'It's all too much right now. I can't think straight.'

'I was a suicidal drug addict who couldn't look after myself, let alone bring a baby into this world. Patricia convinced me that you could both provide him a better life, but I would be in the background watching him grow up. She used to give me drugs; she befriended me and then left me out in the dark. I had no idea where you lived until you were all over the papers when Andrew went missing.'

Thomas stands there trembling, I can see the emotion building, but I continue. I don't think he realises I am as much a victim of this bitch as he is.

'She told me about the abuse she received at the hands of her mother. I could relate to her because no one gave me any direction in life either – that's how we connected.

I was just a kid with no hope, and she manipulated me. It's not a lie.'

I can see him listening to me. I know too much about her past for it to be a lie. I have his full attention.

'I almost overdosed on many kinds of drugs over the years, but the one hope I couldn't let go of was that my son was out there waiting for me to make contact. I tried to find Patricia for years. I had almost given up hope.'

'Why didn't you contact us sooner?' Thomas asks. 'Why haven't we seen you before now?'

'Nothing more than fear. Coming face to face with her after all this time – I didn't know what might happen. I wanted to watch you both; I needed to understand how you lived, what might have caused Andrew to run away. I liked to stay hidden in the background.'

I feel anger brewing. I am going to unleash it unless I keep breathing to control it. Patricia still appears unconscious in her bed. It will only be a matter of time before a nurse or doctor walks in on us.

'This isn't making any sense,' Thomas says, raising his trembling hands to his face. I can see he is trying to stop the tears. 'What the fuck is going on? How long have you been watching us?'

Patricia is stirring again. I can see her eyes twitching. She is trying to speak. I slowly walk closer because I am trying to contain Thomas as he deals with the revelations of his wife's past. I ignore his question and edge closer to the beast.

'Patricia, it's Melanie. Can you hear me?'

Fucking evil bitch.

Thomas walks backwards to stand close to the wall. He is in floods of tears as the turmoil sinks in. He looks broken and distressed, but I take this opportunity to strike.

'It's me, Andrew's real mother. Do you remember me?'

I watch her eyes widen and the break in her breathing at the realisation that her past has come back to haunt her. I breathe in some air to control my temper as I am faced with the monster who denied me a relationship with my son. I can never forgive her. I try to hide my temper while I watch her look at every part of my face. I see that she knows exactly who I am.

'Why did you do this to me?' I ask, not raising my voice. I am calm, and intent on explanations. 'Why did you cut me out of his life, and what drove my son to disappear? He could be dead for all I know. Did you kill him?'

My breathing is heavy and hard. Patricia looks at me, her eyes appear glazed, and her chest sounds dreadful. The gargling noise from her lungs is persisting.

'You were not fit to be a mother,' Patricia struggles to whisper in my direction. 'What life could you have given that boy?'

I put my face into hers. I grit my teeth. I whisper back.

'I should have fucking left you to die in that chair, you evil piece of shit.'

My heart palpitations return as the rage is building inside of me to an uncontrollable level. I twitch my hair while I try to remain calm yet again.

I still need answers. She's not fucking answering me.

'What did you do to my son after you stole him from me?'

From the corner of my eye I can see Thomas is still sobbing against the wall. Patricia is at death's door, but I have spent so many years of my life dealing with the regret, the upset and fear. Most of all, it is the guilt that surfaces over my rollercoaster of emotions. I owe it to myself to watch her die if only to witness that she can no longer haunt me. Tormented by this anguish and hate I can't live with these feelings much longer.

'I need to know why you never came back to find me. Why didn't you bother?'

'We had to move away and hide,' Patricia whispers. She takes a cough to clear her throat. 'I lived in fear that someone would find out he was never ours.'

I start to move backwards and stand up straighter but I maintain eye contact. The sound of the heart machine is nothing more than an echo in the background as I concentrate on her quiet voice.

'Andrew hated me. The child you gave me was damaged, just as you are. You are nothing to him.'

My fast-beating heart is alight with anger.

'How fucking dare you,' I snap at her. 'You aren't even fucking sorry, are you. Your own mother didn't want you. You've manipulated everyone around you, and you are not even fucking sorry for what you have done. You didn't deserve him.'

'It was your face at the window, wasn't it? You should have left me.' I hear her groan. 'You should have let me die.'

'I need answers,' I shout at her. I am holding on to the bed rails so hard I could snap them in half. 'I need to know why my son vanished. I have been watching your every move.'

My chest is pounding. I have a sense of nervousness and frustration that is making my legs feel weak. I stare at her as she cannot move her body, not knowing what to do or reply as I look into her eyes, I just want to rip her apart. I look at her throat and imagine grabbing it hard. I am aware I am trembling head to toe. I take one quick glance behind me to see Thomas sitting on the floor, back against the wall with his head in his hands. This moment is all mine.

I have to act fast. This is for you, Andrew. This is all for you.

Twenty-Nine

The Watcher – Now

Thursday, 13 September 2018

I turn my head to take another look over my shoulder at Thomas. I can see that he is still seated with his back against the wall, unaware of my intentions. Driven by my urges, combined with the tension from my suffering, I gather my energy to deliver my promise. An overwhelming sense of calm overpowers my emotions. I am ready.

'Die,' I mouth at Patricia, who is staring me in the eyes. Our gazes lock with my burning desire to end her life firing through my soul. 'You evil bitch.'

I bend down to grab the pillow that has been on the floor since I entered the room, and I place it on her chest. Thomas shouldn't notice since he is behind me with his head in his hands. I take one last look at the face of the manipulating, evil, sadistic woman who stole my motherhood from me and nothing else in this world matters to me more than ending her life. She is nodding at me as she continues her gaze; I interpret her glances as a pleading need for this to be completed as quickly as possible.

We both want this to happen.

I have a brief flashback of when she took her overdose. Restricted then by the window that was between us, I felt helpless without the answers I needed for closure. Now, nothing can stop me. I am totally in control. Patricia is not going to need a cocktail of painkillers and alcohol to cut her life short today – this is my reward for waiting and watching her all that time. I am ready.

She isn't even sorry for what she has done.

Patricia nods her head as her eyes bulge. I gather the saliva flooding my mouth and in one spit it is plastered over her cheeks. I bend down to give her my final words before I get to seize my closure. She looks petrified, and I am glad because even death itself still doesn't feel enough punishment for everything I have been through. I want to get my hands and rip apart the layers of skin on her face.

'You don't deserve to live,' I whisper into her ear. 'I've waited a long time to do this to you, and I'm going to fucking enjoy every last minute of it.'

I place the pillow over her head. With one arm forced down in the centre, over her nose and mouth, I force the other arm over her chest with all my weight. I am shaking with fear, but the excitement and adrenaline hit me all at the same time. The feeling of euphoria is a blast in my mind.

Everything is happening so quickly, but I refuse to let go – forcing my arms down hard on the pillow and her chest. I hope that in these final few minutes of her life she feels some remorse. I think of nothing but a moment of glory as I watch her inability to free herself from my force. Within this beautiful moment, I am oblivious to my surroundings as my eyes fixate on her bitter end.

Fucking die, evil bitch.

'Fucking die,' I scream at the top of my voice, growling with rage and hatred. 'I hope you fucking go to hell. Evil, evil, evil.'

I hear the heart monitor beeping away like crazy and a crowd gathering in the room. Thomas is pulling at my waist while I refuse to move. I am amazed at the strength I never knew I had. I see the nurses and doctors screaming by the opening of their mouths, yet I am unable to hear them. I am unaffected by the movement of people around me in this whirlwind moment. The bed has been dragged across the room as I refuse to let go. Then, I see the lack of movement and the stillness of her arms.

Not a single tear is shed while I keep pushing down so very hard on her face. The flatline is like music to my ears. I kept my word.

As I let go of the pillow, I am pushed to the ground with a violent force that bangs my head. The pain shifts through my temples as my hands are held tightly behind my back. I have been restrained, and all I wish for is that it is too late to revive her. My ears are listening as the flatline continues to echo its noise around these walls. My own heart is pounding; I know I have succeeded. As Patricia lies there at the mercy of death, I know I have beaten her. I know I won't suffer any longer watching her living a regular life while she destroyed mine.

The release of tension has resulted in my joyous laughter. I cannot stop myself. It is as though all my problems have died with Patricia inside this very hospital room. I am overjoyed with a sense of achievement.

I have my reasons; I know justice has been served.

As I am restrained on the floor by force, I do not even attempt to find my freedom. I already feel free and relieved that she knew in her last breath how much I hated her for what she did to me. Thomas will hate me for what I have done, but I hope he will understand why I had no choice but to kill her.

Patricia Mullner was nothing shy of a monster. A source of evil who should have been drowned at birth. The mental torment that raged through my mind day in and day out should now calm itself. My obsession with her has come to a natural end.

She was helpless in my hands, and I know I will feel no guilt.

You fucking deserved it.

The pillow I suffocated her with is visible on the floor opposite me as it too was thrown to the ground. I smile, I laugh, I feel like the old me again. I could have kept my baby boy, I could have had more support, I only needed a reason to live. She took away my opportunities, and the mental suffering has created the person I am today.

I hate you for what you did. Hate you with all my being.

'Chest compressions have failed. Supplemental oxygen has failed. Stand clear.'

I heard the electrical buzz of the defibrillator as a hand forces my head to the ground. This is the only detail left between life and death, a force of electricity to restart her dying heart. I turn my head slightly to watch as Thomas is screeching out sobs of misery. He looks in my direction and I can see that he's horrified that he failed to stop me from killing his wife, although she hasn't officially been declared dead. I am holding out hope that the announcement will shortly be given. As I listen to the end of her life, I will embrace my new beginnings. I accept the consequences of my actions; I am by no means guilty.

She fucking deserved it.

'Pupillary reflexes checked. The pupils are fixed. The central pulse has been absent for more than one and a half minutes now. Respiratory sounds are absent, and no response to pain. Death has been verified, and the time of death is seventeen-hundred hours.'

Silence sweeps across the room as the team leave with a few nurses gathered around Thomas. The hand behind my head is revealed to belong to a member of the hospital security staff. I look at Patricia's lifeless body while I still smile in her direction.

'I did that,' I tell myself. 'You can't hurt me no more.'

'I am sorry for your loss, Mr Mullner.' I hear the nurses as he wails in their arms. 'The police are on their way.'

Unable to speak because the shock is settling in, I glance in Thomas's direction while I am dragged out of the room. He lifts his head and looks at me with an expression of deep disappointment. His attempts to drag me off Patricia had failed.

'She asked me to kill her,' he says. 'My wife begged me to do it. She begged me. I couldn't, I just couldn't do it.'

I am restrained and forced out of the room.

'She begged me to do it too,' I announce, the only words I will speak until the police arrive to arrest me. 'That evil bitch stole my son and begged me to do it. She wanted this death. She wanted our help.'

Patricia's body is covered with a white sheet, and the curtains around her pulled closed. The situation is surreal; I can't believe I have fulfilled that wish, and I know the events that follow will be difficult. I had my reasons, I had my motives, but when the news of her death reaches the media, my son will surely realise that I exist. I have a story to tell, and it needs to be heard.

I need you to know I am your mother, Andrew. I did this for both of us.

All I can hope for now is that Andrew can forgive me.

Thomas remains in the other room with Patricia's body. I still can't believe I had the strength and courage to end her life, but I have the closure I was seeking. Revenge has been served, but the relief I feel is glorious.

I did this for you, Andrew.

Thirty

Thomas Mullner – Now

Friday, 14 September 2018

I look around the four grey walls while I wait for the detective constable to return. She is a woman not to be reckoned with and due to her interrogation, I am starting to doubt my own innocence. Detective Constable Mason has tried to put words into my mouth because I admitted to Trish begging me to smother her. I know the police have a job to do, but my wife has barely been cold for twenty-four hours. I am an honest man who did not plot to murder my wife. Mason has not shown me an ounce of compassion.

How dare she think that I could murder my wife.

The constant questioning has been draining, combined with the grief I am experiencing over Trish's death; I am grateful to have this short break. I only agreed to have this voluntary interview to prove that Melanie and I had not concocted a plan to kill her together. I feel astounded that I have to show my innocence in this twisted situation. This is too much for me to handle, and I cannot cope. I need some air.

How could they think I had any involvement in her death? I didn't even know Melanie existed until yesterday; surely Mason believes me?

In trying to come to terms with the loss of my wife, who was murdered in front of my eyes. I am also trying to forgive her for the declaration on her death bed that Andrew is not our son. The sharp shock as I relive the memories of yesterday has me in a state of distress. I burst into tears at random intervals, yet other times, I feel strong enough to hold them back. My guilt attacks me regularly. I tried to tackle Melanie to the floor, but her strength during those few minutes made her impossible to move. It all happened so fast – in a flash, my wife faded away.

Was there more I could have done for her? Did I let her down in any way?

Random questions rush around my head, and Trish is not here to answer them. In the space of an hour, I thought my wife was dying after having a heart attack. I was informed I had had a daughter who she forcibly miscarried, and a son I brought up for seventeen years until he vanished who wasn't even mine. Some crazy woman arrives out of nowhere and pretends to be her sister, and then smothers her to death with a pillow – the very pillow I threw to the floor because I couldn't bring myself to kill her myself.

This just does not happen to ordinary people like us.

In that short moment of weakness, I looked at my wife with the pain and suffering she must have felt. I loved her enough to consider supporting her wish to die, but I knew that if I ended her life, my own would be wrecked. I have never been a criminal.

When I think about yesterday, it was as though I never knew her at all. The Trish I married would never have begged me to suffocate her. She would have been strong-minded and determined to live. Her body was deteriorating fast, yet her mental state had died long before her last breath.

Without Andrew, the last three years have been nothing but a constant misery. The depression took its toll on her, and there was no coming back. If Andrew had returned, she might have felt more purpose, and now I know why she could never forgive herself when he walked out the door: he was never her son. I've been going around in circles with this insane thought that I am to blame for all this trauma. If I hadn't provided Andrew with the money, he would not have had the funds to disappear. He convinced me to hand over enough money for him to fund an internship in London. Andrew said he would disappear and get in touch in a couple of weeks to confirm his location. I believed the lies he told me. I trusted him. I believed him when he said he needed that opportunity; he took our money and ran away.

When we first reported Andrew missing, no one took it very seriously because of his age, but as the weeks went on we discovered he had not left the country. If I had come clean about handing over the money, Trish would have disowned me. If I had so much as hinted that I contributed to his disappearance, our whole marriage would have been compromised.

While Trish was drowning her sorrows in the living room some nights, I tried to remember the website that Andrew showed me. I used to sneak in his room to look at his computer. I remember the London skyline background, but the internet has a million sites for business apprentices and internships. I was lost until I found it searching for information on London colleges and universities to see if he had enrolled. I realised Andrew had tricked me because it wasn't an internship at all. It was a website advertising a university placement. Andrew was barely scraping through college; there's no way he could have been accepted into a university. I guess the money he took from me was collateral damage.

Andrew had tricked me out of our savings and when I called some colleges and universities in London, they had never heard of him. I suspected he took the money and ran away somewhere else. I convinced myself after time that he would return home when he was ready. If we moved, then I was sure he would find us somehow, if he really wanted.

No one could have made me believe that Trish would end up so depressed that she would live off a constant cocktail of drugs and vodka – I would have said not a chance. For years she had been slowly killing herself from the inside out. Destroying this family with every sip she took.

I can't forgive myself either for being the consistent provider of her vodka over the recent months. I knew it kept her sweet, and keeping her happy meant I had less stress at home. My ignorance and arrogance have contributed to killing her. I never kept a bottle count, and I am sure she never disclosed her exact consumption. I caught her that one time filling the bottle with water, but it just went to the back of my mind. I had forgotten as the years went by how many times she promised to drink less. I accepted that it was part of her life.

With my need to be out working all hours to pay the bills, the mortgage and keep our finances in shape, I couldn't keep my eye on the ball with everything. I never expected her to commit suicide. My Trish was stronger minded than that, but it goes to show that suicidal thoughts are not about mental strength. It has made me realise that it was a symptom of her poor mental health. None of this seems real to me. I can't believe it.

I am so sorry, Trish. I love you so much. I don't know how to even begin to come to terms with this.

I didn't disclose assisting Andrew to leave in any of the early police interviews because I convinced myself he would come home. It was only meant to be for a few weeks. He made me promise not to tell his mother. I had to keep my promise. I owed him that at least for the damage Trish had caused him – almost choking him to death in the caravan.

I never expected Andrew to just vanish off the face of the earth, but I hope he is out there – alive. He is all I have left now. The only son I ever knew. I don't know how I'd ever tell him that we are not his parents. I couldn't imagine being in his shoes. All this pain and hurt, and he never belonged to us in the first place. He has been robbed of so much by Trish. She took away all his choices, denied him his real family.

I feared Andrew might have started a new life abroad with the money I gave him, but in discovering he never left the country, and with no body ever found, I feel like I know he is out there somewhere. I am sorry for all the times I was never there for him, but he must have hated us to have planned his escape from our home. Trish only ever had good intentions, and I will always live with the guilt that I wasn't around to support my son.

With this time of reflection, some of our history is starting to make sense to me. The reason Trish never took Andrew to the hospital when he was ill as a child, keeping the police at arm's length when she thought the necklace appeared on the doorstep. All of the time during the first few months when he was missing, she said she was shy about having interviews and talking to reporters. The truth was that she was hiding a terrible secret and tried for years to keep it buried. Trish only ever wanted to be the mother she never had herself. She was a good, loving mother, and I know Andrew found her strict at times, but she did the best she could with her own issues – we both did.

The door opens as Detective Constable Mason returns to the room. Her blonde hair, not a strand out of place and her harsh tone of voice that tells me she suspects all kinds of wrongdoing. The evidence is clear: I tried to save my wife from being smothered to death, not assist her murderer. I just want to be left alone to return to my home and grieve. My whole life has disintegrated in a week.

Please don't keep me here much longer.

'Mr Mullner, there has been some development with our investigations,' Detective Constable Mason confirms. 'Melanie has pleaded guilty to the murder of your wife, Patricia Mullner. In confirming that she willingly intended to kill your wife by using deceptive means to get as close to her as she could in the hospital and that she acted entirely alone – we do not need to ask you any further questions. She has now been formally charged.'

'What happens next?' I ask. 'How did you get her to confess. After the hospital, she just remained silent and staring into space. No one could get any response from her.'

Detective Constable Mason returns to her seat. In her hands is a file; I can see some photographs starting to slip out from the edges.

'I'm going to show you some photographs that were taken from Melanie's property after we gained entry.'

Mason displays the images in a neat, orderly fashion with what appears to be a perfect five-centimetre gap between them, not a picture out of line. I lower my eyes, look at the images and gasp for air.

'She has been taking photographs of you both for years,' Mason says, still pushing the images of myself and Trish into a neat line for me to see.

I hold a hand to my chest as the severity of the circumstances makes me realise that I too could have been in great danger.

'That's not everything,' Mason confirms. 'We found plenty of old newspaper cuttings from when Andrew, your son, first went missing. She has been collecting these, I would say for about two to three years.'

'What about the photographs of us?' I ask, shaking and confused. 'Where was she able to take them from, without being seen?'

'Judging by the photographs,' Mason continues, 'she has been watching you both from an area behind your property. A woodland area with a view into your kitchen and lounge window. She watched your wife's suicide attempt and called the ambulance. Melanie appears to have wanted Mrs Mullner to survive so that she could have the opportunity to murder her herself.'

I can feel the tears starting to build up in my eyes as another emotional outburst is brewing. This is the stuff that you only see on television or in movies. You never expect this to be *your* life.

This woman is fucking crazy!

Detective Constable Mason hands me a tissue to wipe my eyes. I take the tissue and use it to blow my nose.

'The motive is there, Mr Mullner.' Mason continues to speak while I dry my eyes. 'She has plotted and planned revenge attacks on both of you. We have located notes, drawings and other evidence to support the fact that she has been stalking the both of you for a considerable amount of time. She is still claiming to be Andrew's biological mother, and with the admission that you described from your wife about taking him, we have no reason to doubt her. This is a revenge attack on Mrs Mullner.'

'Am I safe, Detective?' I ask, concerned for my welfare at this moment. 'I guess that she will be locked up for some time and now that she has admitted everything, she will go to prison. Is there anyone else involved?'

'It might get complicated before sentencing,' Mason replies; I watch her take a look at my shocked expression. 'Her lawyer could go down the route of a mental disorder defence. It means that he will go for leniency while claiming she is not responsible for her actions due to her mental health conditions.'

I stand up from my seat because I can't believe what I am hearing. Mason looks me in the eye and lowers her hand and I take it as a signal to sit back down.

'With her drug abuse past, and clear evidence of history there between your wife and Melanie over Andrew, a mental disorder defence may be likely in this case. There does not appear to be any other known individual supporting her motives. It's all been about revenge.'

'So, she's going to get away with it?' I respond, knowing Mason detects the anger in my raised voice. 'She just walks into a hospital and kills my wife, and fucking gets away with it. Where's the justice in that?'

'There are other factors to consider, Mr Mullner,' Mason replies. 'Your wife also begged to be killed; you stated that she requested this from you, and Melanie is claiming this too. It could be a manslaughter charge instead of murder. I'm making you aware upfront of the different situations that we will face as we build a case. Unfortunately, law and fairness are two different things. We have to take into account the whole picture.'

I stand up, ready to leave the interview. My head is aching from the constant thinking, and my body is tired from the lack of sleep. I don't know if I will ever be able to have a decent night's sleep again. Every time I close my eyes, I can still see her face, especially that stillness after she had died. A look of emptiness while she was at peace. This aching void in my life without my family is going to destroy me, but after my son walked out, and with my wife murdered, I need to make changes. I can't think of myself living in that house alone. Far too many memories will haunt me.

'You know who I feel sorry for the most in all of this,' I say out loud. 'I feel sorry for Andrew, because he is unaware of the truth. Neither of us were his parents, and his mother is a psychopath. That poor lad has no idea. Maybe he is better off wherever he is out there.'

'I am sorry for your loss, Mr Mullner.' Mason ends the conversation with her final line. 'We will be in touch shortly before sentencing to look over your witness statement again. I understand that this is a very difficult time for you, but I would suggest you speak to our counselling team. The number is on the back of this card, they will offer you support when you need it.'

I take the card and place it in my back pocket. I couldn't be any more ready to leave. I wish I could go to sleep and wake up to discover it's all been an evil nightmare.

I might consider calling the number.

'Thank you, Detective. I'm ready to go home.'

I walk out of the station, and the blinding flash of cameras blurs my vision. Journalists swarm at me with their questioning. I realise my wife's murder has attracted national news attention; I have a story to tell.

I hope this news will reach you, Andrew.

My life will never be the same again.

Thirty-One

Andrew Mullner – Then

Wednesday, 9 September 2015

Dad played right into my hands by giving me the money. I knew that by showing him a few fake emails, a job advert and images that I created on my computer, he'd buy into the idea of me having an internship in London. When I mentioned that Mum had hit me, I was relying on the guilt to bias his decision. It worked better than I had anticipated, and when my seventeenth birthday came around, I didn't intend to stick around.

I was practically an adult: I could live without them.

For a couple of years prior to my birthday, Dad had pressured me to think about doing something with my life that was more meaningful than sitting in my room all day and night. If they wanted me to be honest, I hated the sight and sound of them both. I resented them for not giving me a better upbringing. I might not have been bullied at school for my weight, I might have had more friends, I might have even been allowed a girlfriend.

When I think back over all of the birthdays I can remember, Dad hadn't taken a day off work for any one of them. Mum was very odd; every time there was a mention of travelling anywhere or going out when I was a child, I got the impression she wanted to hide me away and have no one else ever see or speak to me. I felt trapped.

This wasn't normal.

I grew up thinking it was normal to have a mother that was forgetful, clumsy and always talking about how evil my grandmother was. She never mentioned my grandfather or talked in the same way about him. I was given the impression he was just as much a victim of my grandmother's behaviours as my mother was. I'm glad I never got to meet my grandparents on my mother's side, from everything that she had described. I can't help but wonder either if I even really knew my own mother. I didn't trust her.

It was during my school years and listening to other kids talk about what they did during the school holidays, or other random conversations about parents, that I realised no one else I knew lived a life like I did. That made me feel very alone. I was just the fat kid at school with no friends and with a freak for a mother.

'Does your mum fall down the stairs drunk,' I used to say. 'I heard my mum shouting *evil, evil, evil* at herself in the bathroom mirror.'

I was never allowed to talk to anyone either. If I ever mentioned anyone talking to me at school, I was always questioned about it.

What did they say? What did they want? What did you say?

Rather than anyone listening to me or taking notice, I was made to feel isolated and often bullied at school. Not only was I the fat kid at school that everyone laughed at, but I was the fat kid at college with weird parents that nobody bothered with. I had to change. I had to escape this life.

Playing on my computer most days gave me escapism, but now I was getting older; I thought that if I didn't leave home, life would stay the same forever – that decision to walk away from my parents gave me a sense of hope. I hoped that I was making the best decision I could for myself.

I had grown up to hate them both because I had a mother that spent the last seventeen years drinking until it knocked her out unconscious, while my father was out working all the hours under the sun to pay for it all. He didn't stand up to her either, and I knew full well that she had started to argue with him in drunken rages. I'm sure they thought I couldn't hear what was going on between them when he came home from work. I had learnt to ignore the banging of the pots and pans, the screaming, and the thudding up the stairs.

It was just her vile tongue again like it always was.

When she grabbed hold of my neck to strangle me with the gold chain on our break away, that was the deciding moment that I couldn't trust her. I knew I needed to escape. I had planned so many different means of leaving the house, but without money I knew I wouldn't get very far. I thought about going to the police when she tried to strangle me too. They would have sent me back home. To ensure I would never return I eventually thought of a fool-proof way to get some money from Dad. It worked.

It is hard to have a mother as evil as mine because, in my head, I sometimes forgive her for it. I can see the mental health issues, but I remind myself that she was the parent and should take responsibility for her actions.

I never understood why I could never visit anyone, never speak to anyone. She wanted to watch me all the time, and in the end I gave up on asking to do stuff. The answer to the question was always *No*.

'No, you can't go here. No, you can't go there. No, you can't see this. No, you can't visit...'

Who would be so restrictive to their own son?

For a whole year, I had planned it out. I wanted to vanish and never be found. I knew that Dad would think that in two weeks I would return home with better job prospects, but two weeks was enough time for me to travel to a remote location where no one knew me, change my name and find a job doing anything I could for some money.

I had to start my life from scratch and invent a whole new past. My biggest fear soon became the fear of having to return home if I couldn't support myself.

That was the last thing I wanted.

I knew that the money Dad had given me would be enough to last a few months if it was spent wisely. When I walked out of that door, I didn't ever want to return.

There was no looking back.

I had everything carefully planned. I knew they might have looked at my browsing history on the computer; I knew they could have checked travel sites, hospitals, anything that could lead them to my location. More importantly, I had to make sure that the police couldn't find me if they were involved.

I had packed scissors and razors in my college bag because I intended to cut my hair and shave the rest of it off, and to change my clothes into something they couldn't recognise. My mother would have seen me wearing my regular bottoms and hoodie, but I planned to remove my clothes in the public toilets in town.

I couldn't believe that I had resorted to doing this, but it felt right. Our house wasn't a home anymore. All my mother talked about was the horrible life her own mother put her through, but I never saw her act any differently herself.

She is evil, and I fucking hate her.

Weirdly, I missed them both because it was the only way of life I had ever known. But I knew that this was not the life for me anymore. Dad always talked about growing up and making my own decisions, well – this was it, I did exactly that. He took the bait, and I had gone past the point of caring what anyone thought. I just had to make sure I had the money to leave. I remembered the money in his savings account. I'm not sure how I would have left without it.

I made my decision, and nothing could change it.

As much as my mother denied it, I should have known she was evil when Max died. She tried to blame me for leaving the skipping rope outside, and when I think about my childhood, there were so many other little things that she blamed on me.

It was her fault Katrina dumped me; I know that she scared her off with that sharp aggressive tongue of hers. It wasn't worth Katrina's time to argue back. Katrina was also bullied at school, it's how we ended up becoming friends. Being chased by the same people, hiding in the same corners at school – until my mother got involved. After my mother met her, Katrina never looked at me nor spoke to me again. It was hurtful.

I remember bringing school friends around the house when I was really young too, some begged never to come back. One girl cried as she clung on to her mother's leg when she came to pick her up. We were only about six at the time.

Maybe that girl could sense something.

Never once had I heard my mother really say she was sorry for anything she had done. The control she had over our family was unbearable. This was my time to take that step and walk away with no looking back.

I'd got dressed, packed my bag, and was ready to start my new life. I spoke to Dad the night before because he would be out on his taxi shift and I knew I'd never see him again. Mum, I knew, would think it was just another day of going back to college to finish my business diploma. I was scared, but I had to keep things normal in case she suspected something. I looked at my room knowing I would never see it again. It had been my safe place for so many years, but I had grown to hate it. It became my prison.

I walked down the stairs, turned into the kitchen off the hallway, and I could see my mother sitting at the table. I realised I hadn't even shaved that morning as I had packed the razors away in my bag the night before. I feared she would notice the stubble on my chin because I didn't generally leave any. Hoping that it didn't give her any clue whatsoever, I made my way through the kitchen.

All I could think about was looking straight ahead. I was masking my fears with a smile and trying to remain calm within myself. She might have sensed that something was not right, but she would never have guessed in a million years that she would never see me again. All I had to do was make it out of the back door.

I had to do this; I had to leave home. I had to remain strong-minded.

I smiled at her as I walked to the door. I saw the birthday card on the table – she had been waiting for me.

'Happy birthday, son,' she said. 'Here's your card, and I am waiting on your father to come home later with your birthday present. I'll make a cake later too.'

'I'll open it tonight,' I replied, smiling at her. 'Thank you, Mum. I'll open it when I'm back from college, with my present when you're both here. I'm going to be late for the bus if I don't hurry.'

I remained smiling but distracted while looking at the back door, which was closer than ever now. I opened it slowly before I simply left.

I was proud of myself and my dad for pulling it off. The money was in cash in my bag, because I didn't even have a bank account, and I clutched on to it tightly as I made my way to the bus stop.

Thank you, Dad.

I was terrified, and I felt very alone, but there was a whole world out there, and everything I had so carefully plotted and planned had to take shape. I couldn't live as a victim of Mum's past life. I kept my head down in a remote village up north. If Dad did any investigating, he would find out that I never applied for any internship after all – it was just a decoy.

Hopefully, nobody would recognise me. I prayed that nobody would find me.

Thirty-Two

Thomas Mullner

Two Weeks Later

Trish and I had never spoken about our funeral arrangements in the whole of our history together. We're both barely middle-aged, so there was no urgency, and when you're younger, death feels like something that only happens to old people or the very unfortunate. How was I to know that I'd eventually fall into the latter category.

Not only did my wife die recently, but my son had decided to leave his family for a new life, and I can't shift the constant guilt. It's like I have inherited everything my wife was feeling. I am strong enough to resist the urge to drink alcohol. That wouldn't be enough to solve my problems.

I knew Trish had always wanted to be cremated, at least. I remember that cropping up in conversation when she talked about her parents' death. I knew they had been killed in a car accident, but the bodies weren't whole, and this haunted her for years. I, on the other hand, wanted to be buried, because I quite like the idea of having somewhere people can visit me, sit and reflect on how I impacted their lives. I hope Andrew will one day visit my grave if he ever finds out after I have passed away.

What became of you, Andrew?

Both Trish and I assumed that we would die in our old age from cancer, heart failure or maybe a quick stroke. But I am coming to terms with her murder. I have no choice other than to accept that this was a twisted game that she created for herself the day she took Andrew from the hospital. I am the one left here to face the reality of it all. I have to keep going on with daily routines, with people in the street stopping and staring at me – again. Sometimes the smallest thing can be a struggle, but it is all the little steps that lead to more significant progress. Unlike Trish, I recognise my mistakes, my worries, and I am doing the right thing in going to discussion group therapy.

Well, that's what the counselling team are telling me anyway.

The cremation service for her was beautiful. I sat through the whole of it still thinking this cannot be real. My Trish in that small box with a lid on it. She hated to be boxed in in small spaces. Never did I expect to be at my wife's funeral service surrounded by the local villagers who barely even spoke to us or made eye contact. I am sure they only turned up for a day out, something to talk about at the next village hall meeting over the weekend.

We never made many friends in Elmton. I just couldn't handle the small talk and simple-mindedness of the village community. I appreciated their support when Andrew first went missing, but I soon learnt that some people only got close to us for the gossip. Friends became more distant, and after a few years, we just stopped bothering with anyone. I didn't even want to live here. We should have made a fresh start in Somerset when we had the chance, when we had the money.

Patricia had an oak veneer coffin, nothing too fancy because we aren't made of money, but I know she would have liked lighter wood colours instead of dark oak. I placed a bouquet of red roses on top of it because I always bought her some for Valentine's Day; it has been a tradition of mine since we first met. She always knew I bought them for her, it was no surprise, but she loved them all the same. They never lived very long, and she wasn't keen on chocolates.

I miss her terribly. I still cannot get the images of her dying moments out of my mind. I'll never stop thinking of her.

Those final minutes where I watched my wife smothered with a pillow keep me awake at night. I close my eyes, and I try to force myself to sleep with great difficulty, but eventually, it is like I blackout. After a few hours of a deep sleep, I awake, and for that split second, I open my eyes, and it is as though I am unaware of the trauma that has embraced me. Then, shortly after, I realise. I lie here in bed, alone. She is gone.

The neighbours have been great these past two weeks, albeit probably for the gossip again, but I haven't had to make many meals since Joe next door has done his best to make sure I eat well. Every other day he checks in on me to make sure I am all right in myself. I sometimes forget to wash when I get up in the morning, but all in all, I am managing myself adequately. I know that if I need someone to talk to, he is there for me. I tell him it's just to make sure I haven't killed myself either. He doesn't see the funny side, but I know that he cares. At least someone cares.

I'm trying to maintain my income by going to work, but my motivation is lacking. With very little sleep, I am struggling to drive my taxi, and for my own safety it is better that I stay indoors. I have some savings left over after the funeral, which will get me by for a few weeks, but as upsetting as it is – I have decided that I will put our house on the market. I can't live here anymore because I have to make life-changing choices. Choices I should have taken control over before now.

Maybe Trish would still be alive if we had moved.

I can be a taxi driver anywhere, or I might even try something new, something less intensive on the hours. Maybe even part-time if I get the full asking price on the house. Unlike Trish, I don't have the same attachment because I have convinced myself that Andrew will never return or make contact.

My story made the national newspapers. When the news broke that Trish had been killed by Andrew's biological mother I was in the spotlight for a few days. It was so intense that I couldn't walk out of my front door without being mobbed. The truth is out now, and Melanie's psychopathic revenge attack should see her get sent to prison for a very long time. She has been assessed, and I have been assured that she is well enough to stand trial.

I can never forgive Melanie for what she has done to this family, but I struggle every day to come to terms with the fact that we share the same loss in Andrew.

Trish joked a few years ago about the brakes on her parents' car. I am starting to wonder if she played a hand in her mother's death. I begin to question the depths of her deception.

I never knew my wife at all.

I remember the day when I found the dog dead in the garden with the skipping rope round around his neck; I knew that dog got on her nerves at times, but Andrew loved him. I wonder if she killed him. If the dog had bitten Andrew to the point of needing to go to hospital for stitches, it could have exposed some truths.

In a different world, if all of our past could be rewritten, I would be standing here now with my wife beside me, and our grown-up daughter might just be leaving home. Trish and I could be thinking about downsizing the house and using the extra money for a decent holiday, or as a little nest egg for our old age.

If Trish hadn't gotten pregnant twenty years ago, then the likelihood of us remaining together would have been very slim. I never loved her at the beginning of our relationship, and it was the sudden pregnancy that encouraged me to commit to her and start a family life. She was a completely different woman in the beginning. I was drawn in by feeling sorry for her. I could see the abuse from her mother, and all I wanted to do was grow to love her and support her. I wanted to provide for my family the best I could. I gave Trish a whole new start, and she cheated me. She played on my giving nature and manipulated my whole life.

I feel cheated, with mixed emotions of loss, grief, denial and a whole flurry of questions that can now never be answered because she is no longer here. I was scared to live with her, but more fearful of losing her. I didn't want to admit my family was breaking apart.

I do forgive you though, Trish. I have to move on with my life.

I've had to make some difficult decisions these past two weeks, but the encouragement and support from the counselling team have gotten me through some dark emotional times. I am strong enough to pull through this, and all I can do now is rebuild my life one small step at a time. Small steps will lead to big changes.

I accept that Andrew may never return home. I accept that Trish had her reasons for trying to contain her secrets, and I accept that we are all victims.

Wherever Andrew is right now, if he is capable of listening to the news or reading it – I hope he will learn the truth. I will always miss him, and the family life we had, but because of Trish none of it even feels real anymore. The message I made very clear in all of my press interviews is that I hope he can forgive, accept and someday try to find me.

He will always be my son.

I never knew that Trish's abuse as a child could destroy the lives and happiness of others in her adulthood. Her mother called her evil, destructive and unwanted for most of her life; I can only assume that the worthlessness she felt made her live up to everything she had been accused of and called. I too am a victim of this behaviour and have to accept my wife, the woman I loved for all of those years – committed an act that cheated someone from having a life with their son. Unfortunately for Trish, this woman was Melanie, a psychotic drug user. It all makes sense to me now.

My biggest regret is that Andrew didn't feel he could come to me and tell me the truth. I could have confronted

Trish and tried to fix my broken family. By giving Andrew the money from our savings account that he needed to walk out on us, I've only contributed to making him keep his distance. I believed that he was going to use it to support getting himself an internship. I thought he would find that drive to better his life, to build on his college studies. I can only assume that he took the money and travelled somewhere far, far away from Plymouth to start a whole new life for himself. Without those funds to support him, he may have stayed at home, but then we all would have continued living our lives under the lies that Trish had set up for us all.

I recognise now that as Andrew was growing older Trish had needed to keep him trapped in the house. The worry of keeping her secrets contributed to the drinking, which in turn brought on the aggression and memories of her distressing life as a child.

We couldn't continue to live in fear of her actions.

I struggle to come to terms with the fact that I love a boy who was never really mine, and Trish terminated a little girl who was my own flesh and blood. The more I think it over, the more I can't believe this has happened to me. I don't know anymore if I am grieving for my wife or grieving for the life I once had. I believed I lived with my very ordinary family. I couldn't have been more wrong.

The murder trial is expected in a couple of weeks because Melanie is not pleading guilty and her lawyers are pursuing a mental disorder defence. I shall give evidence to support that my wife was murdered in the most vindictive of circumstances. I don't know what to think anymore or who to trust, but I have thrown away all of the vodka bottles, all of the tablets in the house, and given most of Trish's belongings to the charity shop. I can't let everything that has happened to me destroy me. Only time can heal my broken state of mind, and only I can change my destiny. I am unable to rewrite history, but I can change my future.

I have to stay strong-minded.

Behind closed doors, do we *really* know anyone? Or do we only see what people want us to see and believe. Sometimes I wonder whether knowing the truth destroyed me; was the lie better than the reality?

Epilogue

Andrew Mullner – Now

Monday, 9 September 2019

It's my twenty-first birthday. I'm drinking my tea and thinking that I really should go out to celebrate tonight with my mates. They've been pestering me for days about doing something, just to get out of the village for one night. I don't like to get drunk; I'm afraid of what I might say, or what I might expose. I don't really want people to know who I am. I'm happy to sit here in my caravan on the campsite where I work and just have a few drinks in the clubhouse.

I saw the damage alcohol did to my mother.

Every birthday since I was seventeen, I remember waking up that morning and having to leave home. I will never forget how nervous I was, but it was also the best decision I ever made. I've grown a lot since then, though. I've changed how I think, too. I've lost a lot of weight thanks to the gym, and I don't resemble the boy that lived at home with his mother. Disguised now by my full beard, I have remained in a rural Yorkshire village – no one knows me as Andrew Mullner.

Happy Birthday, Darren. Have a fantastic day.
Lots of love, Mum and Dad. Xxx

I write my own birthday cards and pretend they're from my family. It would look strange if I never received any cards. I could have pretended that they'd both died in a car crash, but that memory haunts me of my mother and my grandparents. I don't hate my mother anymore. In fact, she was so drunk that I don't even know if she would remember what she told me. Once I was able to take it all in, I knew I had to get away from her.

She was evil.

'I helped kill my own mother and father,' she revealed in a drunken rage when I tried to confront her about Katrina. 'If you love that girl, stay away from her. I can do damage, believe me.'

I knew exactly what she was implying. I cried in front of her and saw no emotion towards me. No regret, nothing to be sorry about, but instead I was looking into the eyes of a sinister, twisted woman who had turned into an alcoholic like her own father.

'Leave Katrina alone?' I asked, shouting at her, but afraid she would attack me. 'Why did you kill them?'

While my mother swigged more vodka straight from the bottle, my father was working another night shift on the cabs. She explained that the brake pipe was under the wheel arch and she had managed to cut it in the middle of the night. She knew my grandfather was a heavy drinker and had laced his booze with some sleeping tablets he'd been prescribed. They were in his system anyway. I don't think she expected them both to die, but they caused a horrific accident on the motorway.

At least they died very quickly.

My mother told me about the abuse she suffered. I could have gone to the police with what I knew, but she would have denied it. I know she would have twisted it all round to get her own way like she always used to do.

I found a job on a campsite that came with accommodation and have been here ever since. I started out cleaning caravans, but now I'm on the maintenance side of things and often get called out in the night for gas bottle changes or broken televisions. The pay isn't all that great, but I don't have many bills. Just food and my mobile phone. It's quite a busy job, and the only friends I've made are the guys who work here too. Some come from all over the world, work seasonally and then go back home. I live on-site, full time. It's my home.

This is where I met my girlfriend, Emma, who works in reception. We both started working together on-site when I moved up here. We both share the same caravan now and it's the first time I've lived with someone other than my parents. I don't like lying to Emma. I love her. She's only ever known me as Darren James: a guy who has never been bullied, never feared his own parents, always had friends growing up. I told her that my parents live in London, to hide the truth.

I don't want to turn out like my mother.

I need to be honest with Emma and tell her who I really am. I'm more secure in my life now, and I know my mother could never hurt me. Thankfully she's never found me and I'm confident it will stay that way. I know Emma loves me too. I would like to think she would understand why I have lied. It was all before we met, and if I explain my childhood and where I've come from – she'll understand.

The biggest fear I have is that Emma will leave me. I know that telling her I am Andrew Mullner, that teenager who ran away from Plymouth, will be a shock at first, but I'm still the same guy she met and fell in love with. I'm still the same kind guy that wants to take care of her. I have a past that I've never spoken about, but to make this work, and for our future together – all I want now is to be honest.

Emma is carrying my baby. We're having a baby boy.

A Letter From JA Andrews

Hello Reader,

Thank you for taking the time to read my novel. This is my debut psychological thriller which I hope you enjoyed the suspense, the drama and the twists. I can't deny there were challenges in writing about some of the content, but I wanted the characters point of views to be as descriptive as possible.

Although *Mummy's Boy*, is set in Elmton, Plymouth, it is a completely fictional place. I have lived in many parts of Plymouth, from St Budeaux, to Ivybridge, Brixton and Yealmpton. I tried to be as realistic as possible with a small village that may sit on the outskirts of the locality, but it isn't based on any one area in particular.

Now that this novel is complete, I am sat here wondering who is reading this and hopefully that you enjoyed it? That's the unfortunate thing about books; that you don't know who has read them until someone leaves a review or shares their thoughts on social media.

There have been many times myself where I have read a great book, talked about it in work and even recommended it to friends. I never considered how important feedback was to an author until now. Now I am in that moment of sharing with others the story I have written, but I have no idea if you enjoyed reading *Mummy's Boy*, as much as I enjoyed writing it?

If you could be kind enough to rate and review this book, I will find it. I might even share it too. In fact, I'll also promise to leave more reviews for the books that I read. Does that sound like a deal?

Oh, before I go and leave you in peace. I want you to know that I have another book coming out soon. It's also quite sinister and full of secrets waiting to be explored. If you enjoyed *Mummy's Boy*, you shouldn't be disappointed...

Have a great day,

Thank you.

J A Andrews

Acknowledgments

I really need to thank a few people that have supported me and helped in many ways through this novels journey from a small idea to a whopping great story full of twists and surprises. I'll start with Matthew Chetwynd, who was my flat mate in 2018 when I first told him about a plot line centred around a mother who was grieving for the loss of her son. He listened to my long list of evil ideas and helped me ditch off the far-fetched and the unrealistic thoughts in the story's beginning.

I first put pen to paper on September 9th 2018, and wrote my first line that evening. I was sat alone in dimmed light in my bedroom. I settled on that date as the first day of grief in the opening chapter and used it for Andrew's birthday. That also is coincidentally the day at which I was first made aware of publishers, Keshini Naidoo and Lindsey Mooney, who formed Hera. I often follow many authors and publishers on social media and spotted a tweet of their new venture. I am a strong believer in fate – so I wanted Hera to be the first pitch for my novel, and here we are, they published it!

I can't thank Keshini Naidoo and Lindsey Mooney from Hera enough for their support and bringing *Mummy's Boy* to readers and fans of psychological suspense. I have to sincerely thank Keshini too for her critique in the editing process that has really helped shape it, along with copy editor, Eleanor Leese.

Thank you too to Vicki Vrint for proofreading every page to ensure *Mummy's Boy* is as error free as humanly possible, and to Lisa Brewster for designing a cover that captures everything about this twisted story in one single image. The two faces, the bars, the dark sinister tones that reflect the on-going suspense throughout the story. It's hard to believe what started out as blank pages with me staring into space, wondering what to write next, is now a complete finished novel.

I also have to thank Enda Hannigan, who listened to me every single day at work during breaks discussing this poor mother's missing boy. For months I couldn't shake off Patricia's traits that I then knew her true character and I rewrote many parts again. Enda endured her suffering as I discussed daily the alcoholism and mental health of the character. In addition, I would also like to thank Rebecca Wignell and Sally Lord for their continued enthusiasm towards my writing because it has helped to keep me motivated.

I would also like to thank my family for their on-going support and finally, to my boyfriend, Gary Mullen who has put up with me endlessly sat at a laptop at any given opportunity to finish each chapter. For months on end he has cooked all my meals, gone shopping alone, walked the dog alone, and has given me the space and time I needed to perfect and polish this novel.

Thank you so much to everyone xx